About the Author

Caitlin Davies is a novelist, non-fiction writer, journalist and teacher – and likes nothing better than outdoor swimming. Many of her books are inspired by the stories of forgotten women from the past, and several have a watery theme. Her ground-breaking history of Thames swimming, *Downstream,* was described by the *Independent* as 'a fascinating cultural history of swimming', and resulted in the Museum of London's first ever Wild Swimming Display.

Caitlin was born in London in 1964, and after training as an English teacher she moved to Botswana where she became a journalist for the country's first tabloid newspaper, the *Voice.* While working as editor of the *Okavango Observer* she was arrested for 'causing fear and alarm', and also received a Journalist of the Year award. Four of her books are set in the Okavango Delta, where she lived for 12 years, including the critically acclaimed memoir *Place of Reeds.*

Caitlin is currently a Royal Literary Fund Fellow at the University of Westminster, Harrow, in the School of Media, Arts & Design.

Caitlindavies.co.uk

@CaitlinDavies2

Also by Caitlin Davies

Fiction

Family Likeness
The Ghost of Lily Painter
Friends Like Us
Black Mulberries
Jamestown Blues

Non-fiction

Bad Girls: A History of Rebels and Renegades
Downstream: A History and Celebration of Swimming the River
Thames
Camden Lock and the Market
Taking the Waters: A Swim Around Hampstead Heath
Place of Reeds
The Return of El Negro: Africa's Unknown Soldier

DAISY BELLE

DAISY BELLE

SWIMMING CHAMPION OF THE WORLD

CAITLIN DAVIES

This edition first published in 2018

Unbound

6th Floor Mutual House, 70 Conduit Street, London W1S 2GF

www.unbound.com

ISBN (eBook): 978-1-911586-49-4

ISBN (Paperback): 978-1-911586-48-7

Design by Mecob

Printed in Great Britain by Clays Ltd, Elcograf S.p.A

In memory of Glyn Roberts, a champion lifeguard on Hampstead Heath.

Dear Reader,

The book you are holding came about in a rather different way to most others. It was funded directly by readers through a new website: Unbound.

Unbound is the creation of three writers. We started the company because we believed there had to be a better deal for both writers and readers. On the Unbound website, authors share the ideas for the books they want to write directly with readers. If enough of you support the book by pledging for it in advance, we produce a beautifully bound special subscribers' edition and distribute a regular edition and e-book wherever books are sold, in shops and online.

This new way of publishing is actually a very old idea (Samuel Johnson funded his dictionary this way). We're just using the internet to build each writer a network of patrons. Here, at the back of this book, you'll find the names of all the people who made it happen.

Publishing in this way means readers are no longer just passive consumers of the books they buy, and authors are free to write the books they really want. They get a much fairer return too – half the profits their books generate, rather than a tiny percentage of the cover price.

If you're not yet a subscriber, we hope that you'll want to join our publishing revolution and have your name listed in one of our books in the future. To get you started, here is a £5 discount on your first pledge. Just visit unbound.com, make your pledge and type DAISY18 in the promo code box when you check out.

Thank you for your support,

Dan, Justin and John
Founders, Unbound

Super Patrons

Carleen Anderson
Theo Antoni
Debbie Bamberger
Jackie Benson
Melvyn Bragg
Sarah Brown
Karen Brown
David Browne
Hilary Browning
Ailsa Butler-Robinson
BWW
Julie Cameron
Stephen A. Cameron
Marie-Clare Castree
Joanna Chadwick
Frank Chalmers
Christine Clinton
David Cooke
Shirley Cooke
Anthony & Gill Cooke
Amanda Craig
Zoe Davies
Jake Davies
Hunter Davies
Helen De Meyer
Chris Demetriou
Simon Dixon
Sally Doganis
Bernadette Driscoll
Lucinda Duckett
Ella Foote
Pauline Forster

Shirley Forster
Mark Forsyth
Kirsty Foster
Bill Fulford
Brian Gautier
Bruce Gill
Nicole Gordon
Jill Gregory
Valerie Grove
Judy Hallgarten
Katherine Hallgarten
The Mixed Pond Association, Hampstead Heath
Julia Hobsbawm
Johanna Hogan
Simon Inglis
Christine Jackson
Sue John
Beatty Jones
Iain Keenan
Dan Kieran
Sue King
Amarisse Kingue Kouta
Sarah Kingue Kouta
Sienna Kingue Kouta
Robert Kirby
Jenny Landreth
Margaret Legg
Sophie Levey
Andreas Loizou
Claire Lowman
Sean Macaulay
Margaret Maddern
Nadine Majaro
Anna Mansi
The Margate Bookie
Paul Maskell

Jackie McGlone
Patrick McLennan
Audrey Meade
Innes Meek
John Mitchinson
Fiona Mullane
Leeroy Murray
Andy Nation
Caroline Neary
Amy Norman
Prue Norton
Theodora Ooms
Yvonne Osborne
Bridgit Owen
Wendy Pajak
Michael Palin
Cathy Palmer
Matthew Parris
Anne Parsons
Pat Pearn
Gemma Pettman
Piers Plowright
Justin Pollard
Ross Priestley
Peter Rae
Nigel Ramdial
Gillian Rees-Mogg
Chris Romer-Lee, Thames Baths CIC
Jacey Salles
Daisy Solomons
Justine Solomons
Anthea Stewart
Claire Thornton
John Tierney
Katia Vastiau
Joan Warren

Corinne Westacott
Marie Weston
Jane Withers

Prologue

I watched you that day at the pond, you know, peering secretly through the foliage, seeing you swim before you saw me. It was one of those strange early autumn mornings when the sky is so surprisingly blue that a person would think summer was on its way. But instead it was the last burst of colour before the days darkened and the season ended. We'd come late that morning; it was a difficult journey for me. I didn't know if you'd already arrived with the other girls. I could not even be certain that you would come again, for what if your father had found out? What if he knew where we were?

We were in a rush, Billy and I. But when we reached the point where the path split, one way leading east up an incline to a patch of woodland and the other straight ahead to the gate of the pond, I told my brother to stop. Let us wait awhile right here, I said, for I had noticed to my left an oval of light and a sliver of water through the trees. Billy handed me my stick and I raised myself up, leaning one hand on the fence. It was as if I were looking through a tunnel, between the branches of the maple trees and in through the bushes to the water. Only a fraction of the pond was visible, the shape of a crooked triangle, but it was enough to see a swan pass by, as majestic as a silent steamship.

Then came the sound of splashing and there you were, your hair as black and wet as a seal. 'She's here,' I whispered to Billy. I could see your mouth just above the water, breathing as I had told you to, and the sheer joy on your face as you swam. The water was smooth that day and the reflections of the clouds made it seem as if you were swimming in the sky.

Still I watched. You were passing out of sight now, heading towards another girl. I could hear her calling your name, see you speed up your stroke. And I stayed there, grasping the wooden post, because I had decided that today was the day I would tell you. You must know who you were and how you had come to be here. It had to be done; right here and right now as Father used to say, and the

1

very thought of him took me back to my childhood when I too first learned to swim.

Then Billy coughed. The silence on the path was interrupted by footsteps, the sound of boots crunching on the stones behind us. Men were coming on their way for a swim; we didn't have long, ladies' hours would be over soon. On we went, down the path and through the gate past the boatman's hut. Its door was open. I smelled pipe smoke on the wind, heard the insistent tapping of a woodpecker high up in the poplar tree, hidden amongst its heart-shaped leaves. And there on the left was the pond, its surface as flat as a plate.

We stopped by the jetty that reached across the water like a wooden tongue. On the opposite bank the branches of the weeping willows sank low, as if dipping down to drink. I knew what they would look like from water level, I could almost feel their fluttery leaves, and I so longed to join you in the pond and to feel the power of my body again.

Billy settled me on a patch of grass and sat down beside me. Together we watched the girls in the pond, and especially we watched you. Miss Hope was on the jetty, shouting out instructions, while the white-haired boatman stood next to her, leaning on his hook. At the southern end of the pond boys were fishing by the cause-way, and even though they shouldn't have been there during ladies' hours, they were watching too. How fast you were in the water, how determined your stroke as you raced ahead of the other girl. You reminded me so much of myself as a child, when no one but my family knew my name, and I wondered how I would ever find the right words to tell you a story like mine.

Then you caught sight of us and put up one hand, and it broke my heart to see you wave and not know who I really was. I felt the grip of fear in my stomach, for what if I did tell you everything and I lost you again? What if this time it was forever? But this is the tale I wanted to tell you, when the time was right. Bear with me while I try to explain, for this is a story of another little girl who loved the water more than anything else in the world.

CHAPTER ONE

I was born in 1862 in Margate, a seaside town that lived for holiday people and where the air was as pure and fresh as any in England. You will never see as many blues as you will in Margate, from a turquoise sea to an inky sky and every shade in between. It was there that I first discovered my love for the sea, which was little wonder seeing as my father spent half his life in it. They called me 'tadpole' and that is what I was, little Daisy Belle the tadpole, sleek and wet and stout. But I don't believe anyone, not even Father, thought that one day I would become a champion lady swimmer of the world.

It was my brother Billy who introduced me to the water; Father would not have considered it otherwise. I was the youngest and the only girl and he hadn't thought of me as a swimmer. But then one morning Billy carried me down to the Margate sands where the milky sea washed up against the jetty and little boys dabbled with their buckets. It was here that Father came to take his daily swim, one mile to the head of the jetty and back, before he went off to work at the brewery. He came from a seafaring family and water was in his blood.

We were early that morning, Billy and I, the tide was in and the beach was small as we walked along the shore towards the row of ladies' bathing machines. These were like Wild West wagons and they put the ladies' ones right at the far end of the beach away from prying men's eyes. There had been a storm the night before and some of the bathing machine awnings had been blown away, the wheels as well. One year, before I was born, an enormous wave had carried the machines right into the sea, with the people still inside, and the bathers had been forced to run out half-naked and scramble to shore. Father didn't think much of the machines: the way they jerked and jolted and lurched, the sloppy, gritty floors, the shrieks of the terrified children as the dippers put them in the sea and told them to swim. Where, he asked, was the pleasure in that? It took away the whole poetry of the thing; it was not how swimming should be.

Father's sister, my Auntie Jessie, was a dipper. She was an enormous mountain of a woman and she put the children in head first and then scooped them up again. This caused all manner of disagreements between her and my father. He said it was a way to drown, not to swim, and they argued about it constantly as they did most things. But I was very fond of Auntie Jessie. I liked to visit her home on Love Lane, where she rented out rooms after her husband died, and she was the only one who called me by my given name, Daisy Mae.

Billy and I stopped to undress, piling our clothes under a well-chosen stone, then he picked me up and walked towards the sea. He stopped every now and again to point out something of interest: a tiny shell that a mermaid had left, the feet marks of a bird that had been dancing. Billy liked to tell me stories; he was a great lover of make-believe and although he'd had little schooling he had already taught himself to read.

We reached the edge of the ocean, with lapping waves like the hem of a dress, and Billy pointed to a boat, out where the sea was as still as a tabletop. I wondered how it stayed like that above the water. I had so many questions inside me: why didn't the boat sink? What made the water blue? Would it move up and down like that with me? I could see that every wave was different from the next, and I wanted to know what it would be like to feel the white on the crest.

Billy waded slowly in, holding me in his arms, and I clung to him, my fingers nudging at the little dimple he had below the bone of his right shoulder. The sea was cold; I could feel it seeping up my legs and I let out a cry. 'Don't be afraid,' said my brother, 'don't you want to catch some fish for dinner?' But I wasn't afraid at all; I knew we were about to do something naughty and that I would like it when we did. I was far from a docile child; instead I would do anything to go on an adventure.

I loved my brother the way the youngest in a family can love the oldest. I was far closer to him than to my other brothers, Charlie and Tom-tom, and from the moment I was born Billy saw it as his task to look after me. He was already a fast swimmer; despite his awkwardness on land, water was his element. But he'd been very delicate as a child: he'd shown no sign of walking and as a two-year-old he could not even sit up, his bones were so painful and soft. The doctor said it was rickets, but that exercise would be good for his legs and that Margate was the ideal place to be. And indeed it was. Five minutes on the jetty or the promenade was enough to give anyone a healthy appetite and even ladies who didn't like sea bathing were happy to get a pretty glow afterwards. Father encouraged Billy to exercise and taught him to swim and soon my brother grew stronger, although it pained him to walk sometimes and his right leg was permanently turned in at the knee.

Billy looked a lot like our father, with unruly eyebrows and a slight gap between his front teeth, and in profile they were exactly the same, always with their jaw jutted out. My brother swam most days in the ocean. He soon developed a powerful overarm stroke and Father thought he had the makings of a champion. When he was younger Father had been the fastest swimmer on the Kentish coast, and now he wanted someone to follow his example.

Billy stopped at the point where the water reached the top of his chest. He blew, once, twice, quickly on my face and when my eyes closed in surprise, he took me under. Down we went, into the sea. I tasted salt in my mouth and I couldn't hear a thing. Then I opened my eyes and for a moment we looked at each other, my brother and me. His lips were closed, his cheeks puffed with breath, his hair waving like a black anemone. A string of seaweed floated across his forehead and as he tried to brush it away I let go of him and for a moment or two I paddled on my own. It was a confidence born of intuition, I don't know how I did it but I did, and I kicked away with my fat little legs until up I popped back into the air. Then so did Billy and he laughed and said I was a little tadpole.

We stayed there a little longer, splashing together and enjoying the gentle swell. From the shore it had seemed as if the sea were made of individual waves, but now I could feel it was the same water rising and falling, rolling sleepily forward and then tumbling back again. There we were, part of this vast changing motion, each wave perishing only to be succeeded by the next.

Then Billy said it was time to get out, and we came back onto the sand and he rubbed me dry with his shirt. We put on our clothes and hand in hand we set off to the jetty to watch the herring boats. The jetty was crowded with people that day, waiting for a steamboat from

London, and while we had come to meet Father, Mother had been at the harbour and she was there as well.

'What on earth?' she cried, looking me up and down. 'Why is your hair wet?'

Billy told our parents what I had done, the way I had paddled in the sea on my own.

'Did she really?' asked Father. 'Then I've half a mind to train her too,' and he looked at me then as if seeing me for the first time.

'Don't be ridiculous!' Mother picked me up and clutched me in her arms. 'She's my little doll. How can you even think of such a thing?' Then she cuffed Billy round the head and asked him what he thought he was playing at. Did he want to kill me? Couldn't he *see* there was a storm coming?

I was very close to Mother, she liked it like that and so did I. As a small child I thought she was the most beautiful woman in the world, with her soft round cheeks and her dreamy, serene way of smiling. But her softness was all on the outside; inside she wasn't serene at all. Mother was always anxious about the sea, as she was about so many things, forever seeing danger in the most ordinary situations. If she heard a dog howl, an owl hoot or a bird flutter in the chimney then something bad was certain to happen. She came from Wiltshire; she was a farmer's daughter and had never even seen the sea until she was eighteen. She was terrified of water and nothing could persuade her to bathe in the ocean. In that, and in many other ways, she was the wrong type of woman for my father.

But she was right about the storm. When we had come down to the beach the sea and the sky were both calm. Everything had looked so clean and new that it had been impossible to believe anything dreadful in the world could ever happen. Yet now the air was beginning to darken and the sand on the beach was turning from yellow to brown. Then came the wind, whistling around the jetty, pulling seagulls up into the sky. Out on the horizon we could see the storm heading our way, coming into Margate, and when that happens there is nothing a person can do.

We heard the hoot of a steamer and the boat came into view, piled high with holidaymakers from London. How lucky they were to be there on top of the water, how envious I was as I watched the steamer speed ever nearer. Soon I could see the people's faces, and the bright red hat of a little girl being held aloft by a man.

'They are standing too close to the rail,' muttered Father, as the passengers laughed and waved to those on shore.

Above us thunder rumbled in the air and I felt the first fat drops of rain on my head. The sea was turning rougher now and the steamer began to lurch from side to side as lightning flashed from behind the clouds. Then a wave as big as a house came crashing against the jetty and the rain started to pour from the sky. The boat had almost reached us, it had nearly made dry land, when all of a sudden it gave a terrible lurch, the gentleman at the rail stumbled and the little girl in the red hat dashed headlong into the water.

A gasp came up from the people on the jetty and ladies began to scream, but as for Father, he did not hesitate. With one rapid movement he lifted his arms, off flew his hat, and he dived fully clothed into the sea.

'Jeffery!' called Mother, her face turned as white as a sheet. 'No!' But it was too late; Father was in the ocean. At once the waves began buffeting him around the head, as he swam towards the girl who had fallen in. 'Hurry up!' cried the people on the jetty, pointing to where the sea had swallowed her up. 'Look, there she is!' 'No, she's over there!' 'Oh goodness, they'll both drown themselves!'

'The hat, the hat!' shouted a man as a flash of red appeared on the water. But Father had seen something else, the flaxen head of a little girl just two yards away, and he was battling through the water to reach her. A second later a huge cheer went up; he had caught her by the hair. She was saved.

I don't remember walking back to the beach, but there we were on the shore when Father staggered out from the ocean. People were running from every direction to come and take a look: men throwing down their nets, girls rushing from out of the oyster shop, children dropping their buckets of crabs. For against all the odds Father had snatched a girl from the jaws of death and here he was, holding her in his arms, bringing her safely to land.

I remember she looked strangely relaxed as he laid her down on the sand, curled on her side with her head tilted forward. She was sleeping, I thought, she must be very tired. Gently Father rolled the girl onto her back, and that was when I saw her face. Her skin had turned a dull blue and there was a fine white foam around her mouth. One eye was open but the other was covered with a rock. What had happened to her eye? Then legs appeared on either side of the rock and the ladies screamed as it turned into a crab and scuttled across the girl's face. Still she didn't move.

There was an awful hush then as the terrible truth dawned. She wasn't saved at all. Father had pulled a dead girl from the ocean.

The crowd on the beach drew back. They were a superstitious lot and no one would touch a drowned person, it was the work of the Devil and would bring bad luck. But Father kneeled down and opened the girl's mouth, pulling out her tongue. He pinched her nose, slapped her face with the back of his hand. But still she didn't move. He grasped her arms and began to lift them up and down as if working a stubborn water pump. Up and down, up and down, he went, grunting with the effort. Then he stopped and listened to the girl's heart, hoping for the spark of life.

'It's no good,' said a fisherman. 'It is too late.'

But Father refused to listen; his jaw was clenched, his face shone with sweat, as up and down he worked her arms. The people told him to stop; they shouted that his efforts were useless. Yet on he went, stubbornly believing that he alone could bring a dead girl back to life. I was not even four years old and I had just learned the power of the sea.

The girl had not known how to swim of course, and nor had anyone on the boat. It was no wonder so many people died in the sea at Margate. Some drowned in the harbour, others fell from boats or were crushed in a collision. Even fishermen filled their pockets with stones so if they fell overboard they would have a quicker death than trying to reach the shore.

That evening at home there was a terrible row. 'What if you had died?' I heard Mother sob. 'Then what would *we* have done? What would have become of us, Jeffery?'

I didn't know why she wasn't more proud of him; I couldn't understand her reaction. Father didn't stop to think when there was something to be done; he wasn't troubled by self-doubt. He was a doer, not a dreamer.

At the inquest the coroner praised my father, and the jury did as well, but his failure troubled him badly. He railed against the inability of people to swim, and the lack of life buoy or anything else with which to rescue people. 'We are a nation of sailors,' he cried, 'and by the honour of God, we don't know how to swim!'

That very summer we left Margate. Father had applied for a job as a swimming instructor at the Lambeth Baths in London. He saw a chance to pursue a swimming career and to teach others too, so that never again would a poor innocent child drown in the raging sea. 'The ability to save a life,' he said, 'is the glorious privilege of a swimmer.' Those were words that I would never forget.

CHAPTER TWO

We arrived in Lambeth on a Saturday night. I'd fallen asleep on the train and bus and when I woke up in Mother's arms my first sight of our new home was a light so bright I thought the street was on fire. The gutters were crowded with hundreds of stalls and each had a light, whether candles in turnips or white globes that hung like full moons. Everything was bright on the New-cut market, everything sparkled, and you couldn't move a few yards without a seller calling out, 'Buy, buy, buy bu-u-uy!' 'Over here!' 'Walk inside!' Father stopped to buy a baked chestnut and I held it steaming in my hand, marvelling at the confusion and uproar. I was a Margate child and now I was in London, where the pavements were made of gold and any moment I would see a lion. I could not believe there was anything in the country *beyond* London; to me, it was the entire centre of life.

Father elbowed his way through the crowds, not at all alarmed, only looking for the correct address, while Mother kept her shawl tightly bound around the two of us. We had rented lodgings above a chemist shop belonging to a Mr Hallway: there were just the two small rooms and they smelled of boiled whelks.

The next morning Father took my brothers and me out exploring, past the public houses with their frosted windows, down lanes that curved into darkness as if a river had worn down the cobbles and turned the alley from one direction to the next. Happily for Father there were plenty of public houses in the neighbourhood and many a street where sporting men gathered to wager on every race or fight imaginable, whether it was between men, dogs, cockerels or rats. Our father loved to bet; it was the thrill of the thing that appealed to him, the split-second chance of a fortune made or lost. He liked nothing better than to arrange a wager, but when he did win he very often spent the money all at once.

Billy nudged me and pointed down a passageway where a group

of boys were gathered in a ring. I saw one toss a coin in the air and heard shouts, then from round the corner came a man with a dog, its legs trembling and its head covered with a bloody handkerchief.

'What has happened to the dog?' I asked.

'It hurt itself,' said Billy, giving me a sweet. My brother always had something nice to eat in his pockets and often produced a little lump of peppermint rock to keep me quiet.

As we continued down the road with Father there didn't seem to be many other people about, just a woman at a doorway and two men leaning on the handle of a barrow, watching. The houses here had broken windows and dirty curtains, the doors were all open and mattresses lay in the muddy road. But when we reached Westminster Bridge Road the homes were grander, and as we passed along an alleyway between two rows of houses we came to the Lambeth Baths. It was a vast building, a little like a railway station, built of sand-coloured stone, with a row of black doors flanked with marble pillars and at the top a chimney as tall as a spire. I heard my boots tapping as we climbed up the steps. It was early, the baths were not yet open and Father was going to show us around. He had been appointed swimming instructor and soon he would become coach and organiser of entertainments. For it was here at Lambeth that we would make a new life for ourselves.

We came in through one of the doors and I was cowed for a moment, the building was so big and I so small. The walls were glazed green and there seemed to be corridors leading in all directions. I sniffed at the air; it smelled of newly scrubbed wood and damp towels and the unfamiliar scent of bleaching powder.

We passed through a turnstile, I slid myself easily underneath, and then we stopped at a little room that was the pay office. Father waited by a glass window and I stood on tiptoe next to him, barely tall enough to see in.

'Can I have one of those?' I asked, pointing at a pile of cakes on the counter.

He laughed. 'You want to eat some soap, Daisy?' Then he knocked on the glass and a man sleeping in an armchair got up and stretched himself.

'Ticket?' he growled as he lifted the window.

'Sorry to have disturbed you in your sleep,' said Father, introducing himself. The man waved that he could go where he pleased, shut the window and returned to his armchair.

Then my brothers and I set off down a passageway with iron doors on either side, each with a shiny brass knob. I stopped, putting my hand out, but Billy slapped it away.

'Don't you dare,' said Father. 'Those are the hot water taps for the slipper baths and you are never to touch them.' He didn't think much of slipper baths: why soak yourself for half an hour like a vegetable in your own mucky water? But he was overjoyed with the baths, marvelling at the cost it had required to build them. 'These,' he told us as we carried on with our tour, 'are the largest in Europe. In fact,' he said, for Father was never one for understatement, 'they are the largest in the world.'

We went into the first-class waiting room, with panelled walls and handsome armchairs for the gentlemen, and along another corridor where Father pulled open a heavy wooden door. And there it was; never had I seen anything so beautiful as the first-class pool. It was hard not to gasp at the sight; I felt as if I had entered a cathedral. The walls were smooth with white porcelain tiles and a lattice-like roof rose high above our heads. In the middle of the pool was a terracotta fountain, while at one end was a lofty springboard that I couldn't wait to climb. At the far end, the morning sun flooded in through three arched windows set with coloured glass, sending rippling waves of light across the water. The sense of peace was overwhelming; I almost expected to hear a choir sing. I was a worshipper at my very own church.

'I want to get in,' I said, struggling with my coat, unable to contain my excitement.

'Daisy!' my father reprimanded. 'Behave.'

'But I want to —' I protested.

'Well, you can't. You're a girl.'

'So where can I swim?'

'You can't. It's men and boys only.'

'That's not fair!'

'Life,' said Father, 'is not fair. And anyway, you don't know how to swim.'

'I do, I do!'

'No you don't,' said Charlie and he stuck out his tongue. For although I had bobbed on my own in the sea that day with Billy, Father had not begun to teach me the way he had with my brothers, and somehow I knew that this was my opportunity to show him what I could do.

I was still protesting as Billy popped a sweet in my mouth and took me by the hand. 'Let's go up there,' he said, pointing to two elegant staircases that led up to the private slipper baths and a gallery where spectators could sit on wooden pews. I didn't want to be up there, I wanted to be in the water, but I followed him up the steps, watched as he opened a grey slate door to see a bath coloured a pretty pink inside.

'Come on!' called Father, just as I was about to reach for the handsome chain and bell hanging on the wall. 'Get back down, we haven't got all day.'

He led us into a room with mirrors on the wall and brushes and clean combs all laid out ready for use on the sideboard. Father said it was the ladies' waiting room.

'What do they wait for?' I asked. 'A swim?'

He laughed. 'For their slipper baths, silly.'

Next we entered the room where the stoker men worked, shovelling coal into the boilers to keep the water hot, and then into the steam-filled washhouses where women cleaned their families' clothes. Then at last we came to another set of wooden doors and the second-class bath. It was smaller and darker than the first pool, with a stage at one end on which sat a glass tank. There were spittoons along the poolside here, the smell of bleaching powder stung my nose and the water didn't look as clean, but still I would have liked to get in.

Then we heard a cough and turned to see a man in a peaked cap and a coat with brass buttons all the way down the front. 'Ah, Mr Belle,' he said in a rumbling voice, as if he had hot potatoes in his mouth.

Father gave a bow, and the two men shook hands. 'Children,' he said, 'this is Mr Peach, the baths' superintendent. From now on, you will do as he says. There is to be no horseplay. Remember that this is a swimming bath, not a romping playground.'

Mr Peach laughed and the two of them strolled off to talk at the side of the pool. It was then that I sensed my chance. Quickly, before anyone could notice, I left the second-class bath and I ran along hallways and past waiting rooms, instinct telling me the right way to go, until I was back at the first-class pool. Luckily for me the door stood open, for I never would have managed it myself. It was empty and silent inside, but for the gentle sound of water cascading from the fountain and my footsteps echoing off the porcelain walls. I knew I didn't have much time, that soon I would be caught, and so I tore at my coat and threw it on the floor, wrestled with the buttons on my boots and removed my clothes. I felt my heart racing, I knew for certain I would get in trouble, but I just couldn't help myself. Then I stood there for a second before walking to the side and jumping straight in. Down I went and then *whoosh!* I was up again.

The water was warm and that surprised me; I had expected it to be as cold as the sea. The bath didn't move like the ocean, there were no crested waves, no seaweed or sand or rocks, just little Daisy Belle, a half-naked little girl bobbing in the men's first-class bath. I don't know how I knew what do to, I just did, and it must have been a funny sight for I had my feet hopping up and down and my hands in the air, making my way along the pool like a seahorse.

The next thing I knew Billy had me by the shoulders and was dragging me backwards. I hadn't even made it to the fountain; I had only just begun to swim. Stubbornly I tried to resist, but he pulled me to the steps and right out of the pool.

'Well I never,' said Mr Peach, who had come hurrying in after my father. 'She's a young one to take to the water like that!'

'That's enough,' said Father. 'Billy, get her dressed. Just wait,' he warned with a shake of his finger, "til I get you home.' But then, when Mr Peach wasn't looking, I was certain he gave me a wink and instead of being angry he had been rather impressed. Because it was at that moment in the pool at the Lambeth Baths that Father realised what I already knew. There was no doubt about it: I was a natural-born swimmer.

CHAPTER THREE

When we returned from the baths Mother was waiting, standing by the window above Mr Hallway's chemist shop, worriedly watching the world outside. London was too big a city for her; she didn't like us being out and about, even if we were with Father.

'I want you to knit Daisy a costume,' he said, as he took off his coat and began emptying out his pockets, looking for his tobacco.

But Mother hadn't heard him; instead she was looking at me. 'Why is your face so flushed?'

'She jumped in the bath,' said Charlie, who never could keep his mouth shut when there was something that didn't need to be told.

'What?' Mother held up her hands in alarm. 'Why on earth would you do a thing like that, don't you know you'll drown yourself?' She turned to Father. 'Why weren't you watching her?'

'I was.' He smiled and began to fill his pipe. 'That's why I want you to knit her a costume.'

'Pardon?'

'A costume.'

'What does *she* need a costume for?'

'For swimming,' said Father. 'We've come to Lambeth to work, my dear. I'm going to teach her and she'll need it by next week.'

'I'll do no such thing,' said Mother. 'She's a girl not a boy, why do you want her to do what boys do?'

'It's precisely because she is a girl,' said Father, 'that's the novelty of the thing, don't you see? So now you will make her a costume.'

The following week Father asked if the costume was ready. I had seen Mother knitting, I knew she had made me an outfit and I couldn't wait to try it on. I was so delighted at the idea; I had never worn something made especially for me. All my clothes were hand-me-downs from Auntie Jessie's daughters and this was the first time I would have something of my own. But oh! the disappointment when Mother brought the costume out. It was nothing like the suit Billy wore: this would cover every part of my body, with blue woollen sleeves to the wrists and legs down to the ankles.

'Put it on,' said Father, lighting his pipe and looking amused.

So I did, struggling to get my feet into the legs of the costume, to pull the scratchy wool up over my chest and thrust my arms into the sleeves. How ever would I swim in this?

Charlie burst out laughing. 'You look like a teddy bear!'

'No she doesn't,' said Billy loyally.

'I can't move,' I said. The wool was beginning to prickle me and my skin was growing uncomfortably hot. 'I don't like it.'

'Don't be so ungrateful,' said Father, although I could see he was trying not to smile.

But I was nearly in tears now as I fought to get the costume off, pulling at the sleeves, tugging it down to my stomach. 'I want one like Billy has.'

'Well, you can't,' said Mother, 'you're a girl.'

This was beginning to sound like the story of my life and I'd had enough. I sat down on the floor and sobbed. Father took no notice: he smoked his pipe, drank a cup of tea and ate his breakfast. Then he began gathering his things together and put on his coat.

'Right,' he said, 'let's be off to the baths.'

'Daisy can stay here,' said Mother and she crossed the room to stand in front of me.

'No!' I wailed, 'I want to go to the baths!'

'If you don't want her to swim,' said Father, pushing Mother out of the way and hauling me up from the floor, 'then why make her a costume?'

'You know full well why!' she snapped. 'What wife doesn't do what she's told?' She knew, as we all knew, that Father's word was law and however much she might oppose him, in the end she would always say, 'I suppose you know best, Jeffery.' My mother was a martyr, she would make it clear she was under duress, but if Father wanted something doing then she would do it. Perhaps she thought that if she appeased him for now then we would both tire of the idea of me swimming, and in that of course she could not have been more wrong.

'So,' said Father mildly, 'let's go. There's no use having a swimming costume if a girl hasn't yet learned how to swim.'

It was still early in the morning when we arrived at the baths, well before the men began jostling at the pay office and the washerwomen started queuing with their loads. Soon it would get crowded, for Father had put an advert in the local newspapers announcing swimming lessons during the summer drowning season and already he'd had quite a response. When we reached the second-class pool he handed me my costume and pointed to one of the dressing boxes. 'Change in there,' he said. 'Today is the day you learn to swim.'

So I took off my clothes, put on the costume and although I didn't like the feel of it, I couldn't wait to get in the bath. I pulled the sleeves up to my armpits, rolled up the legs until they came to my knees, then pushed open the half-door like a racing horse coming out of a stable.

My first skill was to learn to float and Father took a hands-on approach; I was to lie in the pool where it was shallow with his arm held firmly under my back. The best place to learn was the ocean, he explained, for seawater gives more support than dead water, but a bath would serve the purpose nearly as well. 'Here,' he said, standing next to me in his bathing drawers and patting my chest, 'this is where the floating power is, here in your lungs. Trust the water, Daisy. Before you learn to swim, you learn to float. It may seem simple but not everyone can do it well. If you can float you can do all sorts of things. You must appreciate the supporting power of the water and learn to confide in that power. Buoyancy, remember that.' Buoyancy: it was such a wonderful word, so full of promise and bounce, and I laid myself out on the water, balancing on Father's hand, knowing that he was there to carry me. I trusted my father, I had no reason not to, and more than anything in the world I wanted him to be proud of me. He had taken me here against Mother's wishes, no other girls were allowed in the bath, and I had to make him want to bring me again. After a while I cast my eyes to the right and there he was, standing with both arms by his side. I couldn't think what was so remarkable about this, until I realised that he was no longer holding me. I was floating by myself. Look at me! I wanted to cry. Will you just look at me!

Then Charlie appeared, running into the bath to spoil my moment. 'She can only float because she is fat!' he cried and I lost my concentration, rolled to one side and began to splutter.

'Indeed she is fat,' said Father, 'but even a thin person like you could float if only your legs wouldn't sink. Now off you go, we're busy.'

When he was satisfied with my floating, Father taught me to tread water, walking my feet up and down as if I were climbing a flight of stairs. Then he brought a small tank from the far end of the bath, placed it on the poolside and told me to get out. 'Come and look,' he said, as a big green frog popped up out of the murky water and blinked its eyes. 'Watch carefully, experience is better than theory. See how they kick their legs? They are the model for human swimmers.' But while frogs could swim because they had the gift of nature, a person could do what no fish or frog could do: we could swim with our face up or down, we could swim on our right side or left. We could stand in the water, sit in it, lie on it and even, if we chose, walk on the bottom.

'Now remember,' said Father, 'it's easier to push the body *through* the water than to pull it. So when you get back in the bath, use your hands to *open* a way for the rest of you.'

Soon, under his repeated instruction, I could manage several strokes one after the other and in no time at all I was propelling myself successfully across the width of the pool, just like a frog. I felt as wonderful as I had that morning in the sea at Margate with Billy, because this was where I belonged. I was myself in the water, only more so. When I swam, my body became me.

'There you have it!' cried Father when I had crossed the pool for the second time. 'That's the ABC of swimming!' and he laughed and pulled me out of the bath with one strong swoop of his arms.

Billy took me home that morning and all the way I prattled on, about how good a swimmer I was, how I could float and do my strokes. I was so proud of myself that the moment we came indoors I went rushing up to Mother, shouting, 'I can swim!'

'Can you really?' Mother didn't look at me; she was busy threading a needle, and I so wanted her to put down her sewing and open her arms, to share in my success. But as she stabbed the needle into the pincushion on her lap I knew she was angry. She didn't like it that Father was teaching me to do what boys did. She would not praise my efforts; instead she wouldn't pay me any attention at all.

As the weeks went by I never wanted to leave the baths. The only topic we spoke about at home was swimming and a day not spent in water might as well have been a blank in my existence. I complained bitterly every morning when I was told to get out and the pool was filled with naked boys and men, splashing and shouting with no notion at all about how to swim. I wanted to spend my life in that water, safely contained within the stone walls; I couldn't wait to race Charlie and Tom-tom, to see who was the fastest and to know that one day it would be me. But for now I had to get out.

Then one morning Father announced he would put on a fete; it was a novel idea and something that hadn't been done before, and it would require a great deal of preparation. He visited other baths to see what London swimming clubs were up to, and then he began to devise a routine. He wanted to teach men to swim, but first he had to show them how. The important thing, he always said, was to bring oneself to the notice of the public.

All of us would help with the fete; no one was allowed to be idle. If we wanted to eat, then we must work. Billy would race against the other boys, Father would perform, but what would I do? That's what I wanted to know. 'Practise floating as I've told you to,' he said, 'and learn all you can, Daisy, the poorest trick may come in useful some day. Swimming is a skill that must be properly learned. If you can manage a whole length without stopping, then you will be in the show.' I was overjoyed and at once I started practicing. Within a week I could swim a length and I had earned my place in the show.

Each morning Father drilled me, along with Charlie and Tom-tom, and we went through our routines under his watchful eye. But he wouldn't allow us to watch while he practised for his performance, and the bath was closed to everyone but for himself and Billy. Some-

21

times we hid in the gallery, me and Charlie and Tom-tom, and we saw him do the oddest of things. One day Father walked into the water wearing a heavy coat, another time a pair of boots. Once we saw him lying on his back with a leg in the air and often, when he got out of the bath, he stood by the side puffing intently on a cigar until it was hot and smoky. Then he removed it from his mouth and stared at it with great concentration as if deciding what to do.

'Jeffery,' Mother demanded when she saw him doing this at home, 'either smoke it or put it out! What are you doing?'

'Practising,' said Father, 'just practising.' For he knew that nothing must go wrong in the upcoming fete; it was his first chance to show the world his Family of Frogs.

CHAPTER FOUR

I could barely sleep the night before the gala. I was so excited that I kept my brothers awake for hours with my chattering, until Charlie pushed me out of bed and Mother came in and cried, 'Enough!' She wasn't happy with the fete; she resented the baths that dominated my father's life. And as for the idea that I would take part, I don't know what upset her most: the thought that I would drown or the idea that people would be watching while I did.

But Father had made up his mind and so instead of spoiling me as she once had, Mother tried her utmost to ensure that I knew my place at home. 'Boys first!' she said whenever there was something to be given out, whether meat or pudding or sweets, and she made me wait until all my brothers had what they needed before finally turning to me.

That night before the fete I woke in the early hours to see a shadowy figure at the doorway and smell the smoke from my father's cigar. 'Don't let me down,' he said quietly, as if speaking to himself, and I was certain he was talking just to me. I closed my eyes and pretended to still be asleep, while in my head I told him I would never, ever let him down. I had practised long and hard and would do everything he had taught me. I heard the old wooden boards of the house creak as a lodger went up the stairs, the slam of the door as Father left, and then I must have fallen asleep because it was light in the room. A woman was crying 'Milk!' outside, and I knew that at last the day of the fete had come.

Mother said she was poorly, a bird had pecked at the window during the night and she would not say goodbye to us when we left for the baths at midday. Billy was excited about the gala just like me, perhaps even more so, for he knew he had to beat the other boys and that Father had wagered ten pounds that he would. He took the lead as we left the house, while Charlie began to lag, complaining he was tired and that swimming made his eyes sore.

'You're going to drown,' he taunted me. 'You're just a baby and you don't know how to swim.'

'I do!' I said. 'I can float better than you. And I'm going to do more in the gala than you!'

'Ignore him,' said Billy, 'let's march.'

So we did, and I felt so full of self-importance as my brother swung the bag with my costume inside that by the time we got to the end of the road I didn't care what Charlie said or that Mother wouldn't come to watch.

When we arrived at the Lambeth Baths the walls outside were covered with posters and people were already jostling to get in, women shrieking as rough men shouldered them out of the way and pushed through the turnstile. Billy led us down the hallway to the second-class pool, where the sides were dense with spectators and the donated prizes – the medals and cufflinks – were arranged for the winners on the stage in front of the band.

'All ready?' Father asked. 'Now go and get changed, then sit on that bench there and wait quietly until it's your turn.' When we came back he had climbed onto the stage with a megaphone in his hand. How proud I was that he was my father! How fine he looked in his best suit, with a clean shirt collar, a white waistcoat and a red cravat. How wonderfully loud his voice was, and when he spoke every single person around that bath stopped to listen.

'Ladies and gentlemen!' he announced, 'I welcome you to the Lambeth Baths. Today for your entertainment, in what is acknowledged to be the *finest* display *ever* brought before the public, I am delighted to present to you… London's very first fete of natation!'

Then the show began and I watched a group of boys line up at the shallow end for the opening race. In they dived to swim 400 yards and at once there was chaos in the bath. I saw one boy not following a straight course at all and when he neared the side he thought it was the end, stopped to turn himself around and was kicked in the head. I was just leaning forward to see what would happen to a boy who had climbed upon another's back and was trying to win that way when my view was swamped by dozens of top hats and frock coats and portly stomachs. Everywhere were shouting men, leaning over the water, pointing hands and shaking fists, urging on the boys.

I didn't even see who won the race, but all around the poolside the gentlemen were dipping into pockets to honour their bets.

Then the boys left the bath and the handicapped race began. Billy stood with half a dozen older boys, all looking awkward in their unfamiliar bathing drawers. I knew he was feeling self-conscious, aware that people were already laughing at the way his leg turned in at the knee and asking, 'What will *that* boy do?' But while Billy was the last to enter the bath he started as if he'd been shot out of a pistol and at this the betting men yelled and stamped their feet, the air growing hot and thick with smoke. Up in the gallery the handful of ladies craned their necks, following the progression of the swimmers in the pool. Still the din increased as the boys made it halfway down the length of the bath, Billy's arms turning like windmills, pushing him ferociously through the water. As he took the lead and was half a yard from the end a great wave of noise filled the room, more deafening even than the New-cut on a Saturday night. I heard a man shouting, 'You fatheaded chunk!' to his son who was floundering in the middle of the pool, while Mr Peach was urging the gentlemen back towards the wall, crying 'Ord-a-ar! Ord-a-ar!' Then the race was over, Billy had won and I was on my feet cheering with the rest.

At last the crowd grew quiet and the pool was empty again. A cornet player began to blow a gentle tune, the lights were dimmed, the ladies settled back in their seats and everyone waited to see what would happen next. It was then that Father appeared, still in his best suit, walking slowly down the steps and into the shallow end of the bath, all the while puffing on a cigar.

'What is he doing?' I heard someone ask, as suddenly Father thrust the lighted end of the cigar into his mouth and dived in. 'Well I never!' they cried. 'How does he do that? He's smoking under the water!' I laughed in delight as curls of smoke began to rise up to the surface of the bath. So that was what all the practising had been about; our father was as clever as a magician and the spectators cheered so loudly that the flowers in the hanging baskets trembled.

Then he came to the surface and tossed the cigar away, turned himself on his back, and with one leg raised in the air he used his hands to scull himself head first down the pool. When he got halfway he raised the other leg and, his jaw tight with the effort, began to rotate his body like a spinning top while the crowd clapped and cheered. But then, just as he was about to get out of the bath, he started to thrash around, to sink below the surface and rise up again, spluttering and crying, 'Help!' There was a bustle of excitement among the spectators, shouts of, 'He's drowning! He's sinking! Get a rope!' I was afraid and clutched at Tom-tom beside me, remembering the day in Margate when Father had pulled the dead girl from the sea. A woman screamed, the drummer raised his sticks and gave a roll of the drums, and at that very moment I turned my head and looked up to the gallery to see Billy. How had he got up there? I hadn't even seen him leave the poolside. But there he was, standing balanced on the edge of the rail. What was he doing, would he fall? But then he gave me a wink and I knew with a sigh of relief that Father's drowning was all part of the show. I saw Billy steady himself, tip forward on his toes – and then flawlessly he dived down amid shouts of 'See the cripple boy!' and swam rapidly to Father's rescue. He grasped him by the shoulders and swam with him to the steps while Father waved to show the crowd that he was fine.

'Ord-a-ar!' cried Mr Peach as everyone began to clap and cheer, to surge forward for a better look, while Father triumphantly got out of the pool and patted Billy on the back.

'There you have it, ladies and gentlemen!' he cried, as Mr Peach handed him the megaphone. '*That* is how to save someone! And all of you here today…' he pointed at the men around the pool, '*all* of you here,' he swept his arm up to the ladies in the gallery, 'can learn to swim if you choose. Yes! Even a child can swim if he is properly taught, as you will see. This evening, in our grand finale, I introduce to you… Professor Belle's Family of Frogs. Behold and marvel!'

The lamps were turned up high then and the audience turned as one to look at us, standing in a row by the edge of the pool, facing the vast expanse of water. I glanced at my brothers: Charlie was squinting his eyes, Tom-tom was biting his nails, but as for me, I was bouncing up and down because I couldn't wait to start.

'Charlie!' Father cried and my brother gave a bow. 'Tom-tom! And not forgetting… little Daisy Belle, just two years old!'

I saw Charlie open his mouth to correct him, to say I wasn't two, I was four, but Father raised his voice even louder. 'Look at her,' he told the audience. 'She has only had four lessons.'

'Four lessons?' a man gasped and beside me Charlie muttered that this wasn't true.

I made a curtsey then, as Father had taught me, and as I straightened up I felt a rush of blood to my head, for now it was me the people were clapping and I hadn't yet done a thing.

Then the whistle blew and we threw ourselves in, and taking great gulps of air I began to thrash my way to the other side of the bath. The crowd could not believe it. A girl! A little girl able to swim like this. How was it possible? How could I manage it? Why didn't I sink and drown? I heard their roars; saw the gallery ahead of me packed with people leaning down over the railings, waving their arms and hats, a vast slanting mass of heads yelling and swaying and cheering for me. I was halfway now and I'd lost any sense of a stroke, I just had to get across that bath any way I could. Then at last I grasped the rail: I had made it.

My brothers got out but I remained in the pool, treading water as Father had taught me. 'If you please!' he shouted, waiting until the audience had quietened down. 'My littlest frog Daisy will now demonstrate how to float.'

'Impossible,' I heard a man cry.

'Does lead not float mercury?' Father demanded. 'Does water not float wood? A buoy floats, a corpse floats...'

'Ooh!' cried a woman.

'You would float too, madam,' said Father, to which the men by the poolside laughed, 'when you fall into the water, but you cannot because your fears prevent you and consequently you sink. But the art of swimming teaches there is no need to feel alarm or despair. The swimmer obeys the laws of gravity. Observe and you will see...'

At this I turned myself on my back and laid my hands on my stomach. I stretched out my legs, closed my eyes, and felt that most wonderful sensation that comes when the water is dense and holds your body as if it is a cork. I sensed it around my face, rippling across my forehead and down my cheeks, heard a gentle sloshing in my ears.

I could have stayed there for hours: it took no effort at all. But I heard the people cry 'Bravo! Bravo!' and when I opened my eyes there they were once again waving and cheering, throwing nut shells and orange peel into the pool. That was when I knew, without any doubt, what I wanted to do with the rest of my life. There were no two ways about it; I must swim and I must perform.

CHAPTER FIVE

By the time I was six I was no longer a frog, I was a duck. But although Father continued to teach me it was Billy he trained even harder. My brother was making a name for himself now; he'd adopted a daredevil air and there were plenty of girls in Lambeth eager to see him perform. Every morning he walked two miles, rising at five o'clock when not a shutter in the street was open and not a bus was about. Walking was good exercise for a side swimmer, and it also strengthened Billy's legs, and when he returned Father was waiting to vigorously rub him down. He was very strict with Billy: 'Don't let him have any fat, and don't let him drink too much,' he warned our mother at dinnertime. 'Where are you off to?' he'd ask if ever my brother appeared to be going out unaccompanied. 'You're supposed to be at the baths.'

Each night he told us stories as we sat round the fire, filling my brother's head with tales of Greeks and Romans, of Leander who nightly crossed the Hellespont to be with his lover Hero, and of Caesar who, in the midst of battle, swam between enemy boats. But it was I, not Billy, who listened most intently to these stories, especially to the tale of Cloelia, the maiden who escaped her capturers by leading a band of girls across the Tiber to Rome, swimming through a hail of spears.

Soon Billy had beaten his nearest rival Harry Parker, a sturdy boy with legs as wide as cricket bats, and my father proclaimed him champion of south London. But then one day on his way back from the baths, Billy stopped at a market stall to buy some sweets and by the time he got home it was clear that something was very wrong. He began to sweat as if he had a fever and soon he was shaking all over and his gums turned blue. Mother was frantic. Was it catching? Was it the baths, had he caught some dreadful disease from the water? But then Father searched Billy's pockets and found the remaining sweets, and when he saw their bright yellow colour he guessed what had happened. My brother had been poisoned by lead.

Father mixed up warm mustard to make Billy sick, but all that seemed to come out of him was bath water. By morning the vomiting had stopped, but when my brother got out of bed he couldn't lift his right foot. Father put him on his back and carried him to the doctor, and there he was told the dreadful news: the limb must come off. But Father was having none of this. He brought Billy home and massaged his foot with oils and lotions, wrapping the leg in strips of plaster. We all watched while Billy whimpered and ground his teeth and Father told him, 'Don't holler, be a man.' Then he told my brother to drink a special potion and go to bed until morning.

For a week or more Billy had to scuff his toes along the ground as he walked, but eventually his foot was back to how it had been. Father never did find the man who had sold him the sweets, though he looked for him long and hard; and while he was sympathetic when my brother was sick, he was also keen for him to get back to the baths. He needed to start training properly again.

'On your legs!' he urged him. 'It's time to swim.' But Billy didn't want to; he said the very smell of the baths made him sick. 'You need to earn your keep just like the rest of us,' said Father, 'or where do you think your next meal's coming from?'

'Why?' cried Mother. 'Where has all the money gone, Jeffery?'

'Expenses!' he bellowed, slamming the door and heading back to the baths.

That afternoon, while I was in the shallow end playing with Charlie and Tom-tom, for we were children still and wanted to have fun and not always be at our lessons, I became aware of an argument. Father was insisting on something and Billy was refusing. 'Get in right now!' Father ordered. 'How will you ever build up your strength if you don't do as you're told?' Then he took the towel he had draped around his neck and he whipped Billy round the head, saying he didn't know why he'd ever bothered to make him a champion.

I'd never seen Father lose his temper like this, and so I thought the best thing to do was to pretend it had never happened. I returned to playing with Tom-tom: he had a wooden ark that Auntie Jessie had sent for Christmas and I wanted it for myself. When he wouldn't give it to me I began to fuss and then to cry, so everyone would know I was being wronged. A moment later Father was in the shallow end beside me, hauling me out by the arm.

'What's going on?' he roared.

'I want the ark...'

'By the honour of God! Cry if you're badly hurt but never, *ever* just to get something you want.' Still he held me by the arm, and the next thing I knew he was slapping me with the towel as well, once, twice, three times round my head. I stopped crying then, even though the towel was wet and its sting was as sharp as a cat's claw, and as I stood there on the poolside, my ears burning, Father's scowling face looming over me, for the first time in my life I saw him as an adversary. He was angry with Mother for asking about money, and he was angry with Billy for refusing to train, but why was he angry with me? I might have been afraid then, but the real reason I stopped crying was because I wouldn't give him the satisfaction of knowing the slaps had hurt.

The moment he let go of my arm I ran, out of the bath and down the corridors, dripping water as I went. I was so intent on getting away that I didn't even notice Mr Peach until I ran straight into him.

'What's going on, Daisy Belle?' he asked. 'Professor on the warpath? You wouldn't be running away, would you now?'

I shook my head, trying not to cry. We were in the hallway where people were waiting for their slipper baths and I was embarrassed because they were looking at me.

'Come along,' said Mr Peach, 'you can wait for the Professor at the pay office.'

When we reached the office a lady was standing by the glass window. She seemed very richly dressed to be at the Lambeth Baths, with shiny ringlet hair and a smart hat on her head. Her dress was a golden colour, she had a parasol to match, and her lips were the reddest I had ever seen. I was surprised when she bade Mr Peach good afternoon and asked where she could find Professor Belle. What did she want with my father? Was she a swimmer – could this lady be a swimmer like me?

Mr Peach gave her a quick look up and down and said, 'The Professor is not here today,' and this was odder still because I knew exactly where my father was, at the second-class bath.

'Is she a swimmer?' I asked after the lady had walked away.

'I wouldn't call her that, no,' said Mr Peach.

I was about to ask more when Billy came rushing up carrying my clothes, and I remembered that Father had hit me and I was running away. 'Here, little tadpole,' he said, 'put them on and let's go.' I didn't know where we were going or why, as we made our way down Westminster Bridge Road, under the railway line and along unfamiliar roads, until we came down an alleyway and I stopped in delight at the river.

I'd never seen the Thames up close before. Mother didn't like us going anywhere near it, she said the very smell of the place would make us sick. But as we came onto the foreshore there it was, rolling heavily through the city as grey as iron. It was a windy, fluttery day and there was a smell of dried fish in the air as I stood at the river's edge, watching it lap at the sand in frothy waves. A man in a rowing boat came past, his oars like an insect's legs dwarfed by the great flat bulks of the barges on the opposite bank.

'Where are we going?' I asked Billy as I followed him, stumbling on the pebbles and stones and broken timber, stopping to look at a group of children in tattered clothes huddled under a boat builder's sign. But my brother wouldn't answer and I had to trot as fast as I could to keep up. The smell grew worse, a dreadful mixture of manure and rotting vegetables, and once I looked down at a patch of mud and saw it swarming with bright red worms. Billy rushed me on, between dirty boats and big brick potteries, past the backs of tenement houses and a boat builder's yard, then at last he stopped. We were at the stairs to Westminster Bridge and there on the other side of the river was the golden tower of Big Ben.

There is a grace about Westminster Bridge when the river was high, as it was that day, and we walked up the stairs, joining a mob of people standing in the middle. Below us the river was alive with tugs and steamers, paddle wheels churning up the water, decks piled high with people going down-river.

'He says he wants me to race Harry Parker in there,' said Billy. 'As soon as I'm better, that's what he wants. I'm to swim the Thames.'

I was astounded; Father wanted my brother to swim in here? The river was a swarm of barges and lighters, ship masts and billowing sails: wherever would someone go amid all the boats? I was also old enough to feel left out. Was this what they had been arguing about, and why hadn't Father told me the plan?

'He says it's the only way to get a bigger crowd. I don't want to do it. I don't feel right.'

I looked at Billy, his face turned away from me as he peered over the bridge. I thought he loved swimming as much as me. I thought he had recovered from the poisoning and soon he was going to be champion of England.

'Do you know what?' he asked. 'All I thought about when Father took me to the doctor was, how would I look with a wooden leg?'

'But you don't have a wooden leg.'

'I know, Daisy,' he sighed, 'but I think I've lost my nerve.'

'I can do it,' I said.

Billy laughed.

'I could!' I stretched up to look over the railings of Westminster Bridge. I thought how exciting it would be to swim in a river as wide as the sea; I wanted to know what it would feel like to pass under this bridge and to have people standing up here looking down on me.

'No you can't.'

'I can.'

'You're only six years old!'

'Then when I'm seven I can.'

'You can't.'

'I can!'

'You can't race a *boy*!'

'Why not? I want to swim in the river.'

'No!' Billy grabbed my hand and I laughed – I wasn't going to do it right there and then.

As we stood there still arguing Big Ben chimed six o'clock, we heard a sudden cry from below and the mob of people rushed to the other side of the bridge. Down on the river two lightermen were standing on the bow of their boat, one with a rope in his hands, watching as a bundle come floating by. I thought it was the body of a dog lying on its back, but then I saw the limbs were too long for a dog's and there wasn't a tail. As the lightermen threw the rope I glimpsed an upturned neck and the glint of a button on the chest and I knew, with a tightening of my stomach, that it was a person and they were dead.

'Is it a man?' asked a gentleman on the bridge as the lightermen hauled the lifeless body, limbs flopping, onto the boat. 'Or a woman?'

'It's a child,' a lady replied, 'the poor little mite.'

I looked down at the water and I wondered how the child had come to be in the Thames. Had they fallen from a boat or paddled out from shore? Had they been running by the river and tumbled in? Could it have been one of the children we had seen near the foreshore huddled under the boat builder's sign? Was it a girl like me or a boy like Billy and had they known how to swim?

'Let's go,' said my brother, still holding onto my hand.

But I was rooted to the spot; I could sense the water rippling beneath me and I felt such a mix of emotions, fear of seeing the body and excitement at the possibility of swimming the Thames. Then as I looked up a great curtain of fog came sweeping up the river, the air grew dark and people began hurrying off the bridge. The buildings on the opposite bank seemed to sway as if I had dreamed them, the boat masts turning as indistinct as the lines of a spider's web. A minute later all the solid landmarks, the chimneys and Big Ben, the barges and boats, were lost to sight.

'Keep your mouth closed,' said Billy, as we started to walk slowly back across the bridge. We could see nothing ahead of us in the orange-coloured air; our future was blank until we reached it, and then when we looked back the way we had come the world had closed around us and everything had disappeared. The sounds were muffled at first, behind us the soft whistle of a boat, ahead the murmur of pedestrians, a polite cough answered by another. Then there was a smash, the sound of breaking glass and running footsteps, a cry of 'What's happened?' and another one of 'Help!'

'Quickly!' said Billy. 'This way.'

Still we stumbled along, more afraid with every step, not knowing what we were treading in, whether we would hit a lamp post or fall down a cellar hole.

We felt our way along grimy walls and shuttered doors, stopping at the sound of wheels on the cobbles, waiting until the wagon had passed. Then at last my brother said he knew where we were; he'd found the lamp-lit window of Mr Hallway's chemist shop.

Mother was on us at once, the moment we came in, slapping us and grabbing us by the shoulders. 'What's wrong with you both? Where have you been in a fog like this?'

'We saw a body,' I ventured.

'Where?' She stopped. 'Where did you see a body?'

I knew then I had made a terrible mistake.

'Have you been to the river?' She looked at my brother. 'What have I told you? You are never to go there, it's a filthy stinking deathtrap!'

We heard a door bang then and Father walked into the room, his clothes damp and dishevelled.

'Look at your children!' cried Mother.

But he didn't say a word, he just gathered me up in his arms and I was happy because I knew that this was his way of telling me he was sorry for what he had done and the way he had hit me at the baths.

Later that night Father came to our bedroom and tiptoed over to the bed.

'I want to do it,' I murmured, quietly so as to not wake my brothers.

'You want to do what, Daisy?' He sounded weary.

'I want to swim the Thames.'

'Do you really?' he asked and I sensed, in the darkness of the room, that he was smiling. But then, as he bent down and patted my head, I realised he didn't believe me. Yet the draw of the Thames was as strong as the pull of the sea and I would never forget that afternoon standing on Westminster Bridge with my brother and thinking I could swim the river. The sight of the child was a terrible thing, but nothing could turn me away from the water. And after all, I was a swimmer.

Old Father Thames, Father called it, as if the river were a friend of his. But the Thames, like the sea, has an unpredictable character, as I would come to know. There was nothing more destructive than the river at flood, when it left a trail of misery, breaking down walls and filling rooms with mud. But there was nothing as peaceful as the river at dawn when the sun rose into the sky and turned the water to quicksilver, when the cargoes in the barges were covered in cloth as if the boats were sleeping and the great river enjoyed a moment of silence as it flowed through the city and out to the sea.

That night I dreamed a dream as vivid as one of Mother's premonitions and I woke with the knowledge that if Billy didn't want to race in the river, then it would be me. I would be the first girl to swim the Thames.

CHAPTER SIX

In the spring of 1869, the year that I turned seven, Father decided to turn his attention to the art of diving. It was to him almost a mystical pursuit and he spoke of those who dived in exotic seas for fish and coral and turtles. But neither Billy nor my other brothers were interested, and so Father started with me. Because if diving did prove attractive to the masses, then think how more daring it would be if the diver were a girl.

'Sit on the side,' said Father on the morning of my first lesson, 'and watch me.' Then he bent his knees, tucked his head between his arms and flipped forward into the bath. 'Now you try,' he called, after he'd come to the surface. 'Stay sitting there, hold your nostrils with your hand, bend your head and go!'

I wasn't sure how to 'go', but I closed my eyes and tumbled head first into the water with an enormous splash.

'Hmm,' said Father, 'what a fiasco.' Then, without a word of explanation, he swam towards me, grabbed both my hands and opened them out until my palms were flat. 'What are you laughing at?'

'I can dive!'

'Not yet you can't.' Then he lifted my hands and smacked them down on the water with such force that tears pricked the back of my eyes.

'If you fall wrongly, it will hurt,' he said, still holding my hands. 'Do you understand? This is serious and you weren't concentrating. Now get out and try again.'

So out I got and stood on the side, clutching my hands together, my palms stinging. I could hear rain beginning to fall on the roof and I looked at the water and shivered a little at the thought of what I was going to do.

'Are you afraid?' asked Father.

'No!' I said, although I was. It had never occurred to me that I could hurt myself, but Father knew that it was the possibility of danger that sharpens a diver's awareness and clears the mind of trivial things. So this time I focused properly; I bent my knees, tucked my head and tumbled forward more easily. Oh the joy of the thing! To fall into water head first, to feel my body thrust completely under by the force of the dive and then released back into the air.

'Better,' said Father. 'Now do it again. Practice equals perfection.'

Then he placed a small stool by the side of the bath and told me to climb on top. It wobbled a little as I got on, and as I tried to adjust my balance he became impatient. 'Don't waver! Indecision is the enemy of a diver! Breathe long and hard, empty your lungs of air. Then go!'

So I did, and the feel of the dive was even more powerful from the height of the stool. I could sense myself accelerating as I fell towards the bath and then slowing when I hit the water and it thrust me out.

The next day Father asked again if I was afraid to dive and I said no, I loved to dive, the higher the better. 'Is that so?' he laughed. 'Then let's see you try.' It was a Sunday morning and we had more time than usual before the men and boys arrived. Father called two of the bath attendants and told them to rig up a board at the deep end of the pool. I watched as they set up a ladder and attached a plank of wood. It didn't look too sturdy to me and by the time they had finished I wasn't so sure of myself.

'Up you get,' said Father, holding the ladder as I stepped up one foot at a time. 'Move onto the plank!' But I began to feel giddy; I was four feet above the pool yet it felt like twenty to me. 'Move further forward,' he said. 'Get to the edge, you can't dive from there.'

'I can't!' I cried, my legs starting to tremble. 'I want to come down.'

'Then you will never, ever be a diver.'

'I will!' I cried, 'I will!' and as I pushed myself off from the plank and flew down towards the bath I felt a freedom so brief and intoxicating it was as if I had left my heart behind on the poolside. I hit the water as straight as an arrow and knew I had found the way to dive.

Father laughed as I rushed back to the ladder to try again; the bathing attendants clapped and blew their whistles, and he began to sing, '*Oh she floats thro' the air with the greatest of ease, you'd think her a man on the flying trapeze.*'

Now that I could dive from a height, I was to see how long I could stay under without coming up to breathe. If a foreigner could do it for two minutes, said Father, then so could I. I got in the bath and obediently ducked my head halfway into the water so it just covered my mouth.

'Don't shirk it!' he cried. 'Go right under!'

So I did: I held my nose and submerged myself fully in the pool, closed my mouth and eyes and held my breath. I would stay under two minutes or more, I was sure. But soon I felt a pressure building in my nose, spreading to my ears and around my head. I counted up to twenty but it was no good, I would burst if I couldn't get air, and so I kicked my legs against the bottom of the bath to surface. It was then that I felt something pressing down on me and I thought I had come up under the bath rail. Again I kicked away with my legs, but it was no use; I was being held under, trapped like a jack that couldn't get out of the box. I put up my arms to work my way free and instead of touching cold metal I felt something warm and alive. It was my father's hands. My body began to thrash around in panic: I couldn't stay under any longer. Why wouldn't he let me go? And then, just as I could bear it no more, he released me. I came to the surface choking and gasping and there was Father standing next to me looking at his watch.

'Only seventy seconds,' he said. 'Take a breath and try again. If you give up the first time you'll never improve.'

I didn't want to try again; I was sick from lack of air, but his hands came down once more and pushed me under. I held my breath, counted in my head: I had to show him I could do it or he wouldn't let me up. This time I managed eighty seconds and when I was done I shot right out of the water like a rocket on Bonfire Night.

It was then that I saw a lady at the poolside: Mrs Peach, the wife of the baths' superintendent. She had recently joined her husband at the Lambeth Baths and was rather a fearsome woman who always carried a cane under one arm. 'Oh my word!' she said. 'That girl's as white as a sheet.'

'Daisy is doing fine,' replied Father. But Mrs Peach was an obstinate lady and she didn't turn to go but stood there, watching.

'All right, that's enough of that,' Father told me. 'Get on my back'. He bent himself forward and, still breathless, I climbed on top. Then I laughed as we sped along, all my fears forgotten now. My father was a porpoise romping in the sea and I was his baby, and I knew that this would be excellent entertainment for a show. So I waved to Mrs Peach and blew kisses too, to show her I was fine and she had no need to worry about me.

When the session had finished, Father sent me off with the instruction to sing all the way home as loud as I could to exercise my lungs. I only stopped singing when I reached Mr Hallway's chemist shop. Mother was ill and I wasn't to make a noise and disturb her, so I lit the fire and made the tea and tried to stay as quiet as a mouse. Billy had told me she had lost a baby and I didn't understand how, for I had not seen a baby, but my brother wouldn't explain.

'Where is he?' Mother always asked when I came home. 'Where is your father?' Although she knew where he was.

I so hated coming back to face her questions. Why couldn't she ever come and see what I could do? She hadn't seen my debut or any of the other galas; she had no idea of my skill. As a child in Margate I had been her doll, we had been as close as mother and daughter could be. But now that I had chosen the life of a swimmer there was a distance between us that grew wider every day. I was a success at the baths; I had proved myself to Father and everyone else; why couldn't she ever be proud of me?

'Is he at the baths?' asked Mother.

'Yes.'

'Alone?'

I didn't know what she meant; of course he wasn't alone, the baths were full of people. 'I can hold my breath for eighty seconds,' I told her.

'Why would you want to do that? You'll faint.'

'No I won't. I'm going to be a pearl diver.'

'Don't be ridiculous. Think what it will do to your insides.'

My insides? But I loved the feeling in my insides when I dived.

'Yes,' said Mother, 'that and making a spectacle of yourself. You're growing up fast, it's about time you learned some proper skills.'

I sat down dejectedly on the floor. Mother had said this several times in recent weeks and she had begun setting me domestic tasks that I was unable to do. I wasn't handy with a knife or a pot or a nee-dle, I only wanted to be in the pool.

'Your brothers' handkerchiefs need hemming,' she said. 'Sit there until these are done.' Then she licked a piece of thread, worked it through the needle and handed it to me. 'Diving! Whoever heard of such a thing?'

I pushed the needle clumsily into the handkerchief and attempted to pull it out the other side.

'Why do you always want to be at the baths?' asked Mother.

I didn't answer. I had pricked myself and was sucking the blood from my thumb.

'Why do you want to parade yourself like a savage?'

I looked up. Her face was flushed and she was shaking her finger in a menacing fashion. 'You will never have children if you carry on like this, Daisy. Do you hear me? You will *never* have children!' She stood up then, her voice so shrill that I cowered a little on the floor. 'What sort of man will want to marry you? You with your big muscles. Have you thought about that? While you paint your face and parade your-self.'

I had no idea what she was talking about. I didn't paint my face, I was a child. I couldn't understand it: why was she forcing me to do something I clearly could not do?

When Father came home there I was, still on the floor, attempting to hem my brothers' handkerchiefs. 'What's going on here?' he asked, aware of the ominous silence in the room.

'Daisy is sewing,' said Mother, mildly.

I sucked at my bleeding fingers, looked up at Father to await his reply.

'Well,' he said, 'I need her at the baths tomorrow. I'm planning a new show. People love to see the girl and they will pay good money, remember that.'

CHAPTER SEVEN

Our father had by now established himself as a swimming professor of some repute. He had formed a club at the baths, and when he set his pupils to race against other clubs they nearly always came first. He invited champions from outside London to perform as well, and one day he introduced a new friend, Robert Winkle, the renowned sporting journalist. He was a well-educated, well-dressed man who Billy and I privately called Mr Kettle, for he had a large stomach and a nose as long and shiny as a spout. He had recently formed his own swimming press, which was how Father had met him, and as a man of letters he always had a stub of pencil and a notebook in his hands.

I was instructed to show him my diving routine and Mr Winkle was impressed, giving a slow clap as I got out of the bath. 'Jeff, my man, how long can she stay under?'

'One minute thirty-six seconds,' said Father. 'Longer than any other girl.'

Mr Winkle licked the end of his pencil and made a note.

'And how far can she swim?'

'As far as necessary.'

Eagerly I waited to see what Mr Winkle would say next, sensing he might have a plan for me, but instead they went on to discuss other matters. 'Do you know the fellow Bedford?' he asked Father. 'He says his son will swim twenty miles in open water or in the bath for any sum anyone is willing to wager. His trials so far have been terrible. Who do you have that could match him?'

'Billy,' said Father at once, although he knew full well my brother would not be keen and that he rarely if ever put any energy into his training. But Father was so delighted with his new friend that he invited him back to our home that very afternoon. Such was the success of his swimming enterprises at the Lambeth Baths that we had recently moved lodgings, to a house in Johanna Street where we had both the first and second floors. We had, said my father, gone up in the world, and what did my mother make of that?

'Robert's going to join us as a handicapper at the next gala,' he explained, striding into the room with his new friend.

'They call me the executioner!' said Mr Winkle with a laugh.

Mother frowned, although I didn't know why: I thought him very funny and dandy.

'You must be very proud of your daughter, Mrs Belle. I've been watching her this morning.'

'Have you really?' she asked. Normally by now she would have called the maid and offered a visitor a cup of tea or some other refreshment, but in this case she had not.

'Yes indeed I have, she's quite a performer!'

My mother sniffed.

'And all the lucky ladies your clever husband has been teaching!' Mr Winkle beamed. 'You must be looking forward to seeing Miss Mane.'

Mother picked up her needle. 'Miss who?'

'Miss Mane, from Brighton. I told Jeff to put her in a show, wait 'til you see what she can do…'

Billy came home then, which was just as well, for Mother's face was growing flushed and I feared what she might say next.

'Ah,' said Robert Winkle, 'the champion swimmer! I might have a proposition for you young man.'

Later, after Mr Winkle had left, I heard my father saying what a gentleman he was and my mother replied, 'A *gentleman* is he? I know his sort.'

On the day of the special gala there was a considerable crowd at the Lambeth Baths, all eager to see a lady swim. Father had learned several lessons since the show in which I'd first performed; he'd switched venue to the first-class pool and removed the fountain so it could properly be used for races. He'd introduced a scoring board at the shallow end, instead of a brass band he had a piano and a pianist, and this time he'd printed hundreds of programmes, with a special one for members of the press.

I took my usual place on the bench by the shallow end to watch the younger boys race, and so desperate were they to break a record that three had to be lifted out nearly unconscious. Then it was time for the older boys' cup and the first race Billy had agreed to enter for a long time. He'd had little choice; Father had put his name on the posters and wagered fifteen pounds on him. As I watched my brother take his place at the side of the pool I saw how worried he looked: he had none of the focus needed for the start of a race, instead he was glancing around the crowds with a distracted air. Then the gun fired and in the boys leaped. But while Billy kept abreast with the fastest two the whole way, in the final yard he suddenly stopped and clutched his leg.

'What is it?' yelled Father from the poolside. 'Is it cramp? Turn on your back! Kick the bad leg in the air!'

But Billy did no such thing.

'Ignore the pain!' shouted Father. 'Just paddle with the hands!'

But my brother had given up and swum to the side.

Father was furious. There was no cramp, aside from cramp of the stomach, that could possibly be so bad that a boy could lose a race. 'If one limb seizes up,' he hissed as my brother got out of the bath, 'you just use the other three!'

Billy ignored him, looking away with a sullen expression.

'What did you eat?' Father demanded. 'Did you eat or drink before the race? Don't tell me you ate sweets?'

But my brother had not eaten a single sweet since that day he'd been poisoned, and I thought his loss was deliberate. He didn't want to compete any more and failure was the only way he knew of standing up to Father. To defy Professor Belle he had to lose, and he had to do it in public.

Suddenly there was a commotion by the poolside; I heard gasps and whistles as a cubicle door opened and out came Miss Mane. She stood there in her white tights and sleeveless tunic, waiting for Father to introduce her.

'Ladies, take note,' he cried, his good humour restored as he leaped onto the stage with the megaphone, 'and be prepared to be inspired by Miss Mane and her clever doings!'

I couldn't take my eyes off her, she was so pretty and plump, with arms as well developed as a boxer's. I had never in my life seen a woman so strong, aside from Auntie Jessie. Where, I heard the people ask, was her corset? What sort of lady was she? But Miss Mane appeared not to hear the comments, watching instead while a bath attendant slid a hoop across the pool, and then she entered the water. Up in the gallery the audience leaned forward, intrigued as to what she would do, as she sank down, came up under the hoop and grasped the sides with her hands. She lifted one leg and then the other and for a second Miss Mane straddled the hoop, while the men whistled and called out, 'She's enjoying that!'; and indeed from her smile it appeared she did. Then, having settled herself within the hoop, her feet resting on its edge, she began to rock.

I held my breath, entranced by her power and grace, as she started turning somersaults in the water, flying through the hoop like a bird on a perch. Over and over she went, the hoop moving as easily as if it were made of string, her eyes wide open and a smile on her face throughout.

'Ord-a-ar!' shouted Mr Peach as the audience clapped and stamped their feet, as animated as rats in a pit, while from up in the gallery there rained down a storm of nutshells.

'Gentlemen!' cried Father. 'Ladies!' and he leaned forward and threw Miss Mane a large bouquet of flowers, which she caught with one hand. 'Does a lady need to know how to swim?'

'Not likely!' laughed a man.

My father swivelled towards the voice. 'On the contrary, sir. A woman has as much need of knowing how to swim as a man. I would say even more! Who is more likely to be with young children at the water's edge? A man or a mother?'

There was a murmur of agreement.

'Now, what has a lady to do in order to swim? What *terrible* sacrifice does she have to make?' He gestured to Miss Mane, now swimming around the bath with the bouquet held aloft. 'Why, none! She simply has to come to this swimming bath for a few weeks and I will teach her!'

When the performance was over and Miss Mane got out of the bath, Mrs Peach wrapped her quickly in a cloak before she strode along the poolside through a horde of onlookers. I saw Robert Winkle push his way to the front, all the while licking on his pencil, and I squeezed myself between the men, getting as close to her as I could. She had fired my imagination and I couldn't wait to speak to her.

'Did you enjoy the show?' she asked, looking down on me with a warm smile.

I nodded that I had.

'You could do that, you know.'

'I know,' I said, and she laughed.

'Not yet she can't,' said Father, and I felt uncomfortable then at the way he joined us; I didn't like how he stood so close to Miss Mane, as if forgetting I was there. And I liked it even less when her cloak slipped to one side and he touched her naked arm, leaving a red mark on her still-damp skin. Father's job was to train me, not joke with Miss Mane and make all the men laugh.

'I want to be like her,' I told him, after she'd entered her dressing box and closed the door.

'Then swim pretty, Daisy,' he said. 'Keep your head above water so people can see you, and put a smile on your face.'

The very next day he bought a hoop. He thought he would include it in the show, that I would glide and float while he explained the principles of swimming. Tom-tom wanted to try it too but Father said no, this was something for a girl. It was not as easy as I'd thought; the metal wouldn't move the way I wanted and I was clumsy in the water. 'Why are you flipping and flapping your hands?' teased Charlie. But this only made me more determined; I knew I could do it if I tried, and with one final effort I hurtled through. My head was down, my feet were up and over I went, right through the hoop, the watery world whirling in my ears. Then I righted myself and came to the surface and saw what I had done. I stood in the bath shivering with excitement, water gushing from my nostrils. I had done a somersault just like Miss Mane.

'Again!' I cried. 'Again!'

Father looked thoughtful and stroked his chin. 'Daisy, do you think you could dive through the hoop from the plank?'

And I told him yes, I could do anything at all because I wanted to make him proud and be a credit to him. But more than that, I wanted the audience to clap for me as they had for Miss Mane. I wanted powerful arms and a pretty tunic, I wanted to turn in the air with a smile and have bouquets thrown at me. My mother's worst fear was absolutely right: I *wanted* to make an exhibition of myself. And now I knew that I wasn't alone, that I was not the only girl who wanted to swim.

CHAPTER EIGHT

As time went by I could have stayed in the baths all day long if only I'd been allowed. I had no interest in helping Mother at home and my schooling, such as it was, had nearly finished now. I knew how to read and to write, I could name all the Kings and Queens, and as far as Father was concerned swimming was all that mattered and he was the best teacher for that. Soon I could even sleep in the water, hooking my heels onto the rail, taking short quick breaths to keep myself afloat, and then closing my eyes and drifting off to sleep. Father of course said he might include this in a show, but I wanted him to organise not just a gala but a competition. I was eleven years old and I thought it was time I competed against someone else.

'Don't be absurd,' he said, 'you're not a racer, and anyway, who would you swim against?'

'Miss Mane?' I suggested.

'She's an ornamental swimmer and she's nearly twice your age, she wouldn't do at all.'

'One of your ladies?'

Father didn't deign to reply. But sometimes his ladies did take part in the galas; one was able to swim the width of the bath with a cup on her forehead, two could swim holding hands, and every week it seemed he introduced something new. We had royalty in the audience now, and the Earl of this and the Lady of that certainly enjoyed the shows. The ladies became very excitable watching the men in the bath, and once as I was standing next to Robert Winkle in the gallery, he laughed and said, 'Such flimsy trunks, such glistening bodies, I do believe the ladies like a bit of rough.' And I laughed as well, although I didn't really know what he was talking about.

It was around this time that I began to feel a little anxious about how I looked, becoming as conscious of my appearance as I was about how I was performing. My shape was changing, I wasn't a little girl any more, and I sensed a shift in the way the audience saw me as I stood on the board, dived down through the hoop and came to the surface with my costume clinging to every curve of my body.

One afternoon at the second-class bath I was intending to join

Father's lesson for ladies. I had entered a dressing box and was just pulling on my costume when a bath attendant called Cabbage Green barged in. I gave a shriek of surprise and he backed out, straight into Mrs Peach. 'What are *you* doing in here?'

Cabbage Green spluttered something about not knowing I was there.

'Do you know what?' said Mrs Peach, 'my patience has just about run out with you. Oh yes, I've seen you lurking around the bath when the ladies are here, and now you're in Daisy's changing box!'

'Oh they're all a lot of trollops,' muttered Cabbage Green.

Mrs Peach was so incensed at this that she lifted up her cane and hit him clean across the head. 'I'm only sorry I haven't a club in my hands,' she told him, and Cabbage Green was thrown out of the baths and told never to come back.

Charlie told Mother that men had begun to whistle as I got out of the pool and she was furious, not at their behaviour but at mine. I thought she was spoiling my fun, I even told myself she was jealous of the attention. She had never come to watch me, she had tried her best to keep me away from the baths and now she resented my growing success. And what else could I wear to swim? I didn't want to hide myself and why should I? I was becoming well-known, people were coming just to see me, and Father said from now on the baths would charge a larger entrance fee to ensure a more respectable crowd.

But my worries about how others saw me were soon made worse. One evening Father decided to begin a show with a new lifesaving routine, but one of the appointed drowning men failed to turn up and so at the very last minute he sent for a man he knew named Sailor Jim. Father promised him a shilling and instructed him to change in a dressing box, but when Sailor Jim came out and saw Billy and me standing at the poolside he whispered, 'I'll give the fellow coming to save me something to do. You'll see, maybe I'll drown him. I'll lead him such a dance that he'll not want to save any more drowning men!'

We hadn't time to object or to warn Father; the poolside was packed with people and it was time for the demonstration to begin. The first drowning man fell into the bath in his clothes and after waiting a moment Father swam to the spot. He dived under the water, came up behind the man and seized him by the ears. Then he put his knees against the drowning man's back, straightened him out and floated him to the side, to loud applause. The demonstration continued: three more men jumped in and began to splash around, while three lifesavers dived in to help. But Sailor Jim was having none of it; he fought and struggled, gripping his rescuer and hissing furious oaths, refusing to let anyone near his ears. Soon the other drowning men had been saved and just this one was left, locked in mortal combat with his would-be lifesaver. The crowd roared their approval at this exciting turn of events as the two men punched and kicked each other in the pool, until Father himself had to get into the bath and, locking Sailor Jim round the neck, pull him out. Billy and I stood on the poolside laughing fit to burst, but I soon stopped laughing when I went to change for my part of the show.

The moment I got into the cubicle I knew something was wrong. I had had an odd feeling in the pit of my stomach ever since I'd woken up that morning and when I removed my clothes to put on my costume I was shocked to see a patch of blood on the back of my skirts. Where had it come from? I had injured myself a few times while practising in the bath, although never while performing. I had been bruised from the hoop, hit my head once or twice during careless dives or scraped my legs along the bottom of the bath. But I hadn't practised at all that day, so how had I got blood on my clothes when I could neither see nor feel a wound? Had I sat on something unawares? Where had the blood come from and why was it such a dark brown?

I stayed there in my dressing box, listening to the noise outside, Father's voice through the megaphone and people calling my name. Then Mrs Peach came looking for me. She gave a little knock and a 'You all right, Daisy love?', and when I didn't answer she opened the door and found me sitting dejectedly on the bench, my stained skirt in my hands.

'Has your mother told you —?'

I shook my head; I had no idea what Mother was supposed to have told me.

'It's your monthlies,' said Mrs Peach. 'Do you know what to do?'

Again I shook my head.

Mrs Peach went away and came back with a carefully folded rag, told me to use that until another was needed, and showed me how to secure it in place. I did as she said, aware of the increasing din outside and worried that someone would burst in.

'It will happen every month,' said Mrs Peach. 'You're a woman now. It means your seed has come down, Daisy, and one day you can be a mother.'

I didn't understand where this seed had come from, but I felt a little better now. 'Does every woman have this?'

'Every woman,' she nodded. 'Oh, some might take to their bed for a week —'

'A week?' I was aghast.

'But most of us just keep going. You'll get used to it.' Then she laughed. 'A little gin and water usually does the trick.'

I stood up then and an awful thought almost struck me down. How would I ever be able to swim? How could I put on a costume and perform with this rag between my legs? It would fall out, it would be seen; there would be evidence in the pool.

Mrs Peach must have seen the look of panic on my face. 'You're a healthy young girl,' she told me, 'it's no reason to stop you doing anything. Just say you've had a turn or you're out of order, that way you won't need to go into the water. I'll see that your father knows, now off you go home.'

So I did, and although Mother was surprised to see me back so soon she didn't ask me why and I of course didn't tell her. As for Father, he didn't say a word about why I'd been excused from the show, and the following day when I woke up the bleeding had stopped as suddenly as it had begun.

The next time it happened I went straight home from the baths, rushed to the bedroom and shut the door. Then I began upturning boxes and burrowing through bags, looking for the rag I'd used before. I was too young really to look after myself, I didn't know when the bleeding would start and I wasn't prepared when it did. A few moments later Mother came in. 'What's going on?' She had come from the kitchen; an apron was tied round her waist and in her hand was a rolling pin dusted with flour. 'Where's your father?'

I didn't answer; but I watched the way her eyes narrowed as she saw the rag I had just put on the bed.

'Is that what I think it is? You're not even twelve years old! Where have you been today?'

'The baths,' I mumbled, although she already knew this.

'The baths! You've been in the water at a time like this? This is what swimming does to you! Get into bed right now.'

'But I'm not tired,' I said.

'Tired? I'm not talking about tired. Get into bed and let nature do its work.'

'But I feel fine.'

'Well you're *not* fine,' and she stepped towards me, pushing so hard on my chest with the rolling pin that I toppled backwards and onto the mattress. 'You will damage yourself,' she hissed. 'I forbid you to ever swim again. You won't be fit for anything. You will *never* have children and who will marry you?'

I didn't dare to answer. I couldn't say I didn't want to marry, that I knew what I wanted to do and that was to swim. I hoped that when Father came home he would understand. He had trained me as hard as a boy; he had taught ladies to swim; he'd invited Miss Mane to perform. Surely whatever Mother said he would never stop me swimming?

Eventually I heard him come home and I crept to the top of the stairs to listen. 'This has gone far enough,' said Mother. 'She is too old to be making an exhibition of herself.'

'Is that so?' asked Father. 'And do you think I can put on a show without her?'

'Have you no shame?' she shouted. 'It's your *daughter* the men are whistling at.'

'Save your breath,' he snapped, 'and stop your nagging. I need her there. She can stay home for now, but then I want her back. How else do you think we can afford all this?'

That night I was made to move into a small box room in the attic that smelled of mice, and was no longer allowed to sleep with my brothers. I felt so lonely and punished up in that room as I listened to the sounds of my brothers fighting and playing downstairs. I was a woman now, Mrs Peach had said. Was this what it meant to be a woman, that I could no longer do what I wanted? Miserably I stood by the window, looking out over the chimney pots, thinking I would climb out and slide down the roof and run away.

But then the bleeding stopped, and soon I was back at the baths. And if I sometimes had to take a break from swimming Father never asked why. It was a topic we didn't discuss. Only I was to wear a different costume now. The woollen suits that Mother had knitted me every year since I was four were replaced with a tunic and pantaloons. It wasn't so easy to swim like this; the tunic chafed me badly under the arms, the pantaloons filled with water and made it difficult to kick my legs and it took me a while to regain my confidence in the pool. But Father was adamant; I must be properly dressed.

Perhaps it was a result of all the arguing, but he was absent from home even more than usual and Mother was frequently sending one of us to fetch him from the Crown and Cushion on the corner of Westminster Bridge Road. Father spent many an evening in the clubroom there, surrounded by sportsmen and journalists, drinking ale and issuing challenges. 'Billy will swim any man five miles for twenty a side!' he would cry, although he knew my brother would do no such thing. Billy had defied Father: first he had refused to swim against Harry Parker in the Thames, and then he had lost a race because of cramp. So why was Father still wagering that my brother would win? Perhaps he could not face the fact that Billy didn't want to swim, for his talent was far greater than my other brothers', or perhaps Father just could not bear being told 'no'.

One day he bought a greyhound, a sleek creature with weepy eyes, which was said to have good legs and be fit to run with very little training. We named him Hunter and Father wagered he would swim a hundred yards against any other dog. But Hunter had no interest at all in racing; instead he followed Father to the Crown and Cushion and fell asleep on an old pillow behind the bar.

Our father continued to issue challenges; he felt the shows were getting stale. He was growing tired of the rowdy, tepid baths, the ornamental swimming and the lifesaving shows. Professor Belle wanted something new to turn his hand to. But until the day Captain Matthew Webb came to the Lambeth Baths, I don't believe he knew what that would be.

CHAPTER NINE

The first time I met Captain Matthew Webb it was a rainy September morning. I was standing near the pay office at the Lambeth Baths listening to Father's instructions for the following day, when Robert Winkle came hurrying through the turnstile with a man I'd never seen before.

'This is Matt,' he said to Father, introducing the figure behind him, a stocky young man with dull blue eyes and the harsh red skin of a sailor.

Father nodded, not paying too much attention.

'He wants to try swimming the English Channel,' said Robert Winkle, shaking out his umbrella.

'The Channel?' Father smiled incredulously. 'He has it in mind to swim from England to France? Is he as mad as Johnson? How long did he last, an hour?'

'One hour three minutes,' said Robert Winkle, who always had the correct figures to hand.

Father touched his head to indicate he thought his friend was insane as well, but I was intrigued. 'Can I swim the Channel?' I asked.

Father laughed. 'No one has *ever* swum the Channel.'

'That is why Matt will be the first,' said Robert Winkle. 'He has a medal for bravery, you've probably heard. And he recently out-swam a Newfoundland dog —'

'Did he really?' Father looked at the young man with some interest. 'And where was that?'

'The sea. But it was too choppy for a dog's style of swimming and the poor brute nearly drowned.'

But still Father wasn't convinced.

'Look,' said Robert Winkle, 'he actually started bothering me about this last year; he came to my offices saying he wanted to try the longest swim ever. I told him it was of little use either to him or to me, but here he is, back again. Last month he managed thirteen miles off Folkestone. So Jeff my man, I thought you were the right person

to meet. If he *can* conquer the Channel then what a man he will be!
Never been done before, and who will have trained him? Why, it will
have been you.'

'Hmm,' said Father, stroking his chin.

'Give him a trial and see how far he can swim.'

'Where?'

'Where do you think? If he's going to swim some twenty miles
across the Channel then there's only one place, and that's the River
Thames.'

'The Thames?' I whispered, but the men ignored me.

'When?' asked Father.

'Now. Take him at his word and without any preparation.'

'All right,' said Father, 'right here and right now.'

Matt gave him a fine salute and it was agreed that the very next day
they would hire a boatman and take the sailor out onto the Thames.

The following evening Father called for me just before six o'clock;
I had successfully pestered him to take me along and he had agreed
so long as I didn't tell my mother. She was expecting a baby now;
her stomach was big and her legs were swollen and she spent her
time indoors on doctor's orders. Father wanted Billy to come too, he
thought he would be inspired by the adventure, but at the appointed
hour, as I stood waiting outside the Crown and Cushion, my brother
was nowhere to be seen.

We hurried down to Westminster Bridge, Father and Robert Winkle leading the way, Matt and I following behind. The sailor didn't
have much to say for himself; Father had told me that he'd travelled
all over the world but in answer to my questions he would only give
a shrug. He didn't seem particularly excited about what he was about
to do either, and there was a toughness about him that suggested he
didn't give a damn.

We reached the foreshore and walked along the river's edge. It was
the end of a long, warm day. The water was still and the only sounds
were the distant cough-cough of a boat's engine and the muffled cry
of an engine-boy. Eventually we stopped on a small shingle strip of
beach; a boatman was waiting and we clambered into his rowing

boat. I was to sit in the bow and not move around or say anything to distract Matt from his job, and I had to fight to keep myself still, for at last I was going to see someone swim this great river and to travel on it myself. Father settled down behind me, while Robert Winkle sat very upright with his stopwatch, notebook and pencil ready in his hands. I held my breath as the boatman pulled off, the boat swaying a little with our weight, and he rowed upstream between a set of barges and came to a stop. Matt stood up on the stern of the boat just under the arch of the bridge and without further ado he took off his coat. He had a muscular body with fine broad shoulders, and on one arm he had a small blue anchor tattoo. It was a clear evening, there was no sign of fog and very little traffic; conditions were perfect.

'Off you go then,' said Father and Matt dived in. His entry to the water was smooth; a man sitting on a nearby barge, a pipe in his mouth, looked up in surprise, another on a paddle steamer gave a wave, but no one on the bridge had noticed a thing. I crouched up on my knees to watch as Matt cut a neat course between two sailing barges.

'That's the slowest breaststroke I've ever seen,' said Father as we passed under Waterloo Bridge where the slosh of the oars echoed eerily beneath the granite pillars. I watched as still Matt plodded on, mesmerised by the wonderful sweep of his legs. The riverside wharves began to darken and lights appeared on the bridge ahead. A dog barked from somewhere on shore, I heard a ship letting down its anchor, but other than that, the river was quiet.

'Twenty-two strokes to the minute,' said Robert Winkle, scribbling with the stump of his pencil and complaining that his notebook was getting damp.

Still we rowed beside Matt, but he neither looked at nor spoke to us; his broad shoulders just kept pushing through the water. How I wished Billy was with me to see this – and how I longed to join the swim. Father must have sensed this for several times he laid his hand on mine as if to prevent me. Just before London Bridge, Matt began to speed up and the boatman rowed a little faster.

'Twenty-five strokes a minute,' said Robert Winkle.

But Father was growing restless. 'Get him out,' he said, 'I've seen enough, he'll keep us here all night.'

So Robert Winkle signalled to Matt in the water.

'What's the matter?' he asked, his head bobbing up.

'We're satisfied! You can come out.'

'I'm just getting into the thick of it,' said Matt. 'When the tide turns we'll turn with it and swim back.'

Father laughed. 'Then you'll have to turn with it by yourself, we're going home.'

It took quite a while to persuade Matt to stop, and then to hoist him into the boat, for he was a heavy man. But there was no sign that the swim had tired him. Robert Winkle confirmed that his pulse was normal, his body was warm to the touch and his speech was as clear as when he'd begun. Father rubbed Matt down with a rug, covered him up with blankets and offered a glass of port wine, which the sailor drank in one gulp.

'How long?' asked Father.

'One hour, twenty minutes,' said Robert Winkle. 'And a little under six miles.'

'Look at him,' murmured Father, 'he's as fresh as when he started.'

What surprised him, I think, was not so much the distance Captain Webb had swum, for that in itself wasn't too far, but the easy way he had made it. 'He could do three times the distance by the looks of things,' said Father. 'I believe he could be the first man to swim the Channel.' And his face lit up with the realisation that he might well have discovered a financial treasure.

From then on the three men were inseparable, spending every evening together plotting the Channel swim. Matt became a permanent fixture at the Lambeth Baths, arriving early in the morning and spending the entire day swimming up and down in his slow methodical way. Every now and again he would sit on the springboard for a rest, but he didn't seem to need sleep like other people. At the end of the day, when the gas was lit, he drank a glass of ale and then at last he was gone. Mr Peach was quite concerned at first; just what was the man up to? But Father assured him all was as it should be. 'That's

Captain Webb, remember his name because you're going to be hearing a lot about him.'

Some six months later Father made the announcement at the Crown and Cushion, offering twenty to one that a gentleman amateur could swim from England to France. Who that gentleman was, he was not yet prepared to say. But everyone knew about Captain Boyton, the American who had just declared he would cross the Channel in his specially made lifesaving suit. Time was of the essence; the money was raised to hire a boat, pay a pilot, buy provisions and rent lodgings at Dover, and Father, Robert Winkle and Matt set off for the coast.

I was not allowed to come along; I had a baby sister to help look after now and I was needed at home. She was a tiny baby and Mother was still very weak but Father was delighted. 'See how she kicks her legs!' he said as he leaned over the crib.

'No!' Mother cried. 'There are enough swimmers already in this family. This daughter I'm keeping with me.'

I was glad to have a sister and she was such a pretty baby. I had no jealousy of her, not at first. When she was handed to me I thought I would drop her, she was so delicate, but Mother said, 'You should get used to caring for a baby.' They named her Minnie, and Mother was kinder to me now. She didn't care if I spent my time at the baths or what I wore for the shows or even if the men whistled. I no longer interested her; I'd been replaced by another girl.

CHAPTER TEN

Captain Webb's attempt at crossing the Channel was a disaster. Rough sea forced him to give up after less than seven hours and Father returned home in a sombre mood; it seemed the dream was over. But less than two weeks later, while I was keeping him company at the Crown and Cushion, a newspaper boy ran in shouting, 'An Englishman has crossed the Channel!'

'What?' said Father, taking the paper. 'Who is the Englishman?'

I hardly dared to watch as he cast his eyes over the newspaper and realised it was Captain Matthew Webb. A fortune was now at the feet of the Channel hero, he would be the toast of the nation and Father felt sorely betrayed. Instead of being eyewitness to the triumph, he had to read about it in a newspaper report. Why hadn't he known about Matt's second attempt, and who was his trainer and backer now? Why hadn't *he* been there in the escort boat when the sailor landed in France? The journalist who had accompanied Matt was nothing but an Iago, said Robert Winkle, seducing the young man away from his true friends, and he cursed the day he'd ever brought Captain Webb to the Lambeth Baths.

Father slapped the paper down on the counter and it lay there in a puddle of spilled beer. He didn't seem to be listening to Robert Winkle; he was off somewhere else entirely, and that was when I saw my chance.

'I can do it.'

'Do what, Daisy?' he asked as a group of customers came barging into the clubroom singing, 'An Englishman! An Englishman has swum the Channel!' and the barman began filling tankards and lining them up on the counter.

'I could do the Channel.'

'As if I have the money for that now.'

'You could have her race Parker's sister,' said Robert Winkle.

'Who?'

'Professor Parker. His sister is the same age as Daisy and I've heard it said she can swim for hours with no sign of tiredness.'

'Really?' Father sounded disbelieving.

'Jeff my man,' Robert Winkle lowered his voice, 'there are rumours afoot that he's going to place a wager on Emily to swim the Thames.'

Could it be true, I thought: was a girl going to swim the Thames?

Father looked equally amazed. He knew of Professor Parker's son of course, for Harry had been Billy's closest rival for years, but this was the first time he'd heard of Emily. 'Professor Parker has a sister? Where did she come from?'

'He brought her down from Leeds,' said Robert Winkle. 'Just think, a race in the Thames, never been done by a girl.'

'All right,' said Father, 'what else have I got to lose?' For he knew that thanks to Matthew Webb's crossing of the Channel, swimming would now be the mania of the hour. It was the perfect time for my river debut.

I couldn't wait to meet Emily Parker. I wanted to see her right there and then. Father had said there was no one I could swim against, but here was a girl the same age as me. What did she look like, and why didn't I know of her? But it was another two days before Father took me to the Barbican Baths where her brother worked.

It was a glorious afternoon and the streets of the city shimmered in the sunshine as newspaper boys ran past shouting out the latest reports on Captain Webb. He was back in England now and basking in adulation, and Father bit his lip and looked annoyed. We entered the Barbican Baths by a side entrance and it seemed dark and gloomy after the relentless heat outside. We stopped to read a poster on the wall offering free vouchers for those who wanted to learn to swim, and when Father sniffed the air and wondered aloud how often the water was changed I was embarrassed and hoped no one had heard him. He asked a bath attendant the way to the gallery and tipped him sixpence, and up we went, choosing the place where we were least likely to be seen. I looked down on the pool, fascinated by the activity going on along the edge; a teacher with a pole and another with a shepherd's crook, a row of pupils lying on their stomachs on benches waving their arms and kicking their legs like drowning beetles. Father laughed. 'They'll soon lose heart when they fail to learn in one lesson, and that'll be the last anyone sees of them.'

But most puzzling of all was a wire strung a few feet above the bath, with a pulley and wheel at one end. Attached to the wire was a rope with a belt at the bottom in which a man was suspended, his body half submerged in the water.

'Absurd!' cried Father as the man began to travel along the wire and then to flail his arms and shout in alarm as the other swimmers crashed into him. 'Total bunkum. Why would any sane person fasten himself up in that for a sake of a swim?'

I didn't answer for I fancied having a go myself; I thought it would be fun to speed along the water on a wire.

'How is that going to give him any confidence?' asked Father. Then he lowered his voice. 'See Daisy, there she is.'

I moved closer to the balcony rail and looked down. A girl of my age, though of a much slighter build, had appeared at the deep end and was standing with her feet on the edge of the pool. Her hair was wet and neatly parted, her face long and serious with frowning brows and a little double chin, and she wore a tunic just like mine, only hers was green. Nobody seemed to be paying her much attention, not those splashing in the water in clumsy imitation of Captain Webb, or those on the benches kicking their legs. I saw her ready herself and take a deep breath, and it was almost as if I were watching myself as she dived smartly in, barely making a splash. She set off along the bath using a steady breaststroke, although her legs were a little lower in the water than they should have been, and as I saw her reach the end and turn with a strong confident kick I so wanted to dive down and swim with her.

I had never swum with anyone else before, aside from my brothers and Father's ladies who were not nearly as accomplished. I wondered if she loved the water as I did, whether her brother was firm in his training and held her head under and had her dive from heights that made her shake. What did her mother think of her swimming, did she shout at her and call her a savage? How was she even allowed in a pool with men like this? Still, I watched the girl in the bath. I knew she was my competitor and I had to beat her, but I wished she could be my companion.

After Emily Parker had swum a quarter mile or so Father said it was time to go, and all the way home he gave advice. Open water was a very different matter from a bath, he warned. I would have to remember to look up to see where I was and keep my course straight. If I did this properly it wouldn't lessen my speed and would make sure I didn't collide into either my rival or a boat. But he had his doubts too; tidal water wasn't a fair test when it came to a swimming race, for if one competitor got the benefit of the current then they would easily win.

This was not a gala; it didn't matter how much I smiled. I had to improve both my speed and my endurance. I had pluck, but that wasn't enough, I needed proper training. I was to swim a mile in the bath in less than twenty minutes and be able to switch from breaststroke to sidestroke if needed. I nodded at everything he said, delighted that I would be trained to compete and not just to look pretty. But Father was concerned that I appeared older than Emily, being so much stouter, and that as it was both our sex and our youth that would make the swim remarkable it must be made clear we were both fourteen.

Father busied himself consulting old river men; learning the spots where the water was slack and plotting the speediest route, for a straightforward course was not always the best in the long run. He studied the tides and the moon and currents, made a note of high water times at London Bridge, certain that this was where any race would begin, and poured over the daily weather diagrams. Avidly he read *Bell's Life*; for if any announcement were to be made, if someone wished to swim a match, then this was where he would read about it first.

Then finally the day came when Robert Winkle was proved right. Professor Parker had wagered £50 to £30 that his sister Emily could swim five miles in the River Thames from London Bridge. He fixed a date for the swim, the following week on September 3rd, and added that Professor Belle's daughter could join for any sum my Father cared to wager.

This didn't go down too well with Professor Belle. '*Join* the swim?' he asked. 'Who is he to make a challenge like this? I'm not having you join anyone; we'll do it on Wednesday.'

'Wednesday?' I asked, confused. 'But the third is Friday, that's not the date.'

'It is now,' chuckled Father. 'He's obviously been biding his time. If you do it first and alone then that will take away the novelty of her swim. Let's see what her brother makes of that. And I'll more than double the wager.' I wasn't sure about this; I wanted to race Emily Parker. But Father had made up his mind; I would do it alone, and the die was cast.

From then on, he was busy with the necessary arrangements, hiring a boatman and boat, reserving places on a steamer with a band, making sure that the day before my swim the streets of London were covered in posters and boards. Robert Winkle would accompany us and write about it in the press, and even Billy agreed he would come. The excitement over Captain Webb's crossing seemed to have given him a new lease of life: the thrill of his triumph was infectious, and Billy was happy to see his little sister swim and support me on the way.

Father said I couldn't risk a trial in the Thames. Under no circumstances was anyone to find out what I was training for and not even Charlie and Tom-tom were allowed near the pool during practice hours. 'Early to bed, early to rise,' said Father, as he outlined the coming five days. 'Regular meals and not too much to drink. Raw eggs for breakfast, haddock for dinner, prunes in between.'

My preparation would be different from Billy's. My brother had been kept lively when a race drew near because he was the restless type, whereas I was to remain as calm as I could. I was to swim five miles every morning, followed by a long walk in the afternoon, then a few minutes with the skipping rope in the evening. Each morning I woke determined to increase my speed and every day I felt my strength growing. Like Captain Webb before me I lived at the baths, only now no one told me to leave when the boys arrived.

By the end of the second day I could swim a mile in twenty-five minutes but my feet were so blistered from walking the streets of

Lambeth that I had to soak them in salt water. By the third day I had lowered my time in the pool by three minutes and by the fourth I kept this up for the full five miles. But I was so desperate for water to drink as I paced the streets in the afternoon that Father put a pebble in my mouth and told me to suck on that.

Then my training was over and the time for the swim was set. I would begin at five minutes to five o'clock, an hour and a half after high water, when five miles with the tide should take me a little over an hour. This was also the busiest time on London Bridge, the time of day when hundreds of thousands of people would be making their way across the river. And there they would be, just as my dream had predicted, ready to witness the first girl in the world ever to try the Thames.

CHAPTER ELEVEN

On September 1st, 1875, at three o'clock in the afternoon, Father and Robert Winkle took me to Westminster Pier. We travelled by hansom cab for no expense would be spared that day, it was the swiftest way to get through traffic and we had to be on time. I sat with my face pressed against the window, watching as a street singer wove drunkenly along the road and a group of soldiers in crimson jackets standing on the steps of a public house turned to gaze as we went past. It was unusual to see a girl in a hansom; my mother would never have travelled in one, she said no self-respecting lady would.

When we came to Westminster Bridge I thought we would never get across. Its footways were a solid mass of people, it seemed everyone and everything in London had chosen to cross the river. I looked out at them, my mind beginning to whirl with questions. What if something went wrong, what if I had the cramp and was forced to stop, or if I swallowed water and it made me sick? I thought I could do it, so did Father, but we both knew I had never swum in a river before.

I could hear the creak and moan of the heavy wagons, see the frantic gestures of policemen trying to herd the traffic, but then at last we crossed the bridge. Father called up to the driver that we were at our destination, the doors opened and the cabman whipped up the horse again and was gone.

Down at Westminster Pier the air was sharp and clear, the river as calm as if oil had been poured upon the water.

'This is it, Daisy,' said Father, as he drew his arm around me to lead me on. 'Look, there's quite a crowd.'

And he was right, for already onlookers were gathering along the embankment having heard the announcement that a lady would swim the Thames. I felt a rumble in my stomach; I had barely eaten that day and while Father had made me take a pork chop at dinnertime I'd pushed it around my plate, my eyes only on the clock. I had been allowed no exercise at all, told to keep warm and comfortable, even to stay in bed if I liked. But it had not been restful at home. Mother was beside herself, ever since she'd heard the news. She said I would die from the filth in the Thames, to which Father replied, 'Not if she keeps her mouth shut.' 'What good will that do?' she asked, and then she'd refused to say a word for two days.

But as usual Father had his way, and when he'd told her to make me a new costume she had: a beautiful rose pink bathing-dress trimmed with white braid and buttons, which I was to keep covered until my swim began. Mother wouldn't say goodbye to me when the time came. She hugged little Minnie close, saying she could smell roses in the room and that someone would die. I tried to ignore her as I tied up my hair with a ribbon and put on my cloak, not wanting to listen to any of her premonitions.

Shortly before four o'clock the steamboat the *Volunteer* arrived at Westminster Pier, puffing like a locomotive, the sides decked with flags, the band all dressed in smart blazers. 'What is that girl doing?' I heard someone ask as I climbed onboard and saw the captain standing on the bridge, wearing a top hat like an undertaker. He nodded at us and I felt a little stab of fear then, but it was too late to turn back and when I looked behind me the embankment was thronged with people, leaning over the walls and climbing up the street lamps. I had no choice; once the steamer pulled off I would be on my way.

Then the crier sang out, 'Passengers for Greenwich and below!' and at last the steamboat cast off, filled almost to overflowing, slowly heading towards London Bridge so I could show myself to the crowds before I began. I stood on the deck and tried to calm my breathing.

'How old is she?' a man demanded. 'Does she really know how to swim?'

Father didn't reply, only gave a curt nod of his head.

'Will she make it all the way to Greenwich?' asked another passenger. 'Look at her; she's a mere child. She doesn't look strong enough to me.'

And I stood there, not saying a word, only conscious of my wonderful costume beneath my cloak.

Then the call boy shouted down the hatch to the engine room, 'Full speed ahead!' and I saw the crowds on the opposite bank waving hands and hats and handkerchiefs, and for a moment I couldn't believe it, that my dream had come true; they had all come here to see me.

When we reached London Bridge the sides were dense with people, while on the broad stone stairs leading down to the river there was no room to stand. Then we pulled off from Old Swan Pier and steamed slowly through the arch of the bridge, before the engines stopped and I was told to go below deck to ready myself. I was growing more nervous now, worried by all the passengers' questions, and as I went past the refreshment room and into the cabin, again my stomach rumbled.

When I reappeared on deck, Father asked everyone to step back and then slowly he removed my cloak, peeling it from my shoulders and letting it drop to the floor. For a second I felt awkward standing there for everyone to see, but then a great cheer rang out and I felt only pride and eagerness to begin. Father put his arms around my waist, picked me up and passed me over the side of the steamer and down into the referee's small rowing boat.

'Oh good gracious, she's getting into the boat!' said a man leaning over the steamer's rails. The referee put out one hand to help; he was a cool-headed, grey-haired gentleman whom I knew from the Lambeth Baths and he looked me over cautiously and said, 'Are you sure you know what you're doing?'

'She's going to swim,' shouted a woman, 'a girl's going to swim down the Thames, did you ever?'

On and on came the comments as I took my place in the bow, waiting as Father and Robert Winkle got on board and checked we had everything we needed: blankets and rugs, my hoop, a basket with bacon and bread and port wine. Billy took his position in the stern, also in his bathing costume, with a belt around his chest and a lifeline attached, ready to dive in should anything go wrong.

'Half a crown she swims the Thames,' I heard a man cry.

'Sixpence she doesn't,' came the reply.

I stood quite still for a moment, looking ahead at the forest of masts in the distance and the mazy windings of the yellow rippling tide. Any moment now I would be in there myself, I would be at one with the water. Father began to rub me with his hands, his rough palms warming my neck, working their way down each bone in my spine, and my body glowed and came to life.

'Take your time,' he said, as he gave a final rub.

I shifted forward until my feet were on the very edge of the boat.

'Slow and steady,' he cautioned, 'look up to sight and don't be distracted by the noise.'

I felt the boat lurch as the referee stood up, heard him shout 'Go!' and then, to the cheers of the assembled thousands, in I plunged. What a shock the water was – never had I felt anything as cold! It was nothing like the tepid Lambeth Baths; there was no porcelain bottom, no pretty tiled sides, and the temperature quite took my breath away. This was more like the sea than a pool, only saltless and smooth, almost slippery to the touch and with a strong pungent smell. I felt my heart tighten from the cold, told my body to breathe, not to panic. I must be fearless; I could not let anything go wrong. I came to the surface and struck out using breaststroke, careful not to swallow water, travelling in the wake of the referee's boat and giving quick glances up to see where I was heading. I could hear the loose flapping of sails as the wind picked up, the laughter and singing from people on the smaller boats. Oh the freedom of the thing! To swim in the Thames, in the wild openness of a mighty river; never had I been more certain of my success.

But then I felt the water swell as a boat pulled up too close beside me and then another; and within moments I was hemmed in by a crowd of small craft that seemed to be coming from every direction, oars splashing, men, women and children shouting as loud as a flock of wild geese. I felt like a pea in a bowl of soup, bobbing in the water, as still the boats clustered around me until there were fifty or more and I couldn't see a thing. I didn't know which way to go; any moment I would be hit and dragged under. I heard the dashing of paddles, the hoarse cry of a seaman and the shriek of an engine-boy. The air around me darkened and I thought I could hear the great solemn bell of St Paul's.

'Take her out!' someone shouted, followed by snatches of orders for the boats to clear a route, calls for the river police to intervene. But no one paid any attention, such was the deafening noise. I couldn't see where I could take a stroke; I would kick my feet against a boat if I did; and as I stayed there treading water I knew it was over. I was failing before I had even begun; it was impossible for me to swim. I felt my body growing heavy, the belt of my wonderful new costume too tight around my waist, the sodden cloth dragging down on my legs as if I were wrapped in weeds. I was vertical in the water now, gasping for breath, squeezed in on either side.

Again I heard the dreadful words, 'Take her out!'

I opened my mouth to say I would not get out, that if only the boats would move I would swim, as an oar splashed by my head and I took a mouthful of river water and began to cough and then to retch.

'What sort of father would let his daughter do that?' asked the shrill voice of a woman.

'She'll drown herself!' shouted a man. 'Throw a rope!'

In desperation I glanced up to my right; Billy was there in the bow of the boat, one hand resting on the belt around his waist, the other holding up the lifeline. I saw him lean forward; any moment now he would throw the line and dive in.

'Don't!' I wanted to cry. 'Don't rescue me!'

I thought of the day Father had failed to save the girl in Margate and of the afternoon Billy and I had seen the body pulled from the Thames, and now with dreadful certainty I knew that Mother was right, that was going to be me. But as my brother bent down towards me I saw to my surprise that he was smiling. 'Keep going,' he cried, 'don't listen to them, little tadpole, keep going!'

Then miraculously I saw a clear gap of river ahead; the police were clearing a route and some of the boats had moved, a channel of water was opening up before me. The expanse grew wider and I kissed my hand and waved to the people and from every barge and every boat they waved back. Then I put my head down and I swam, my body working like a well-balanced clock, my limbs moving in perfect accord, drawing me effortlessly on. I could hear nothing but the sound of my breathing as my head dipped in and out of the river, a sigh from my mouth each time I rose.

The boats were helping me now, keeping the water smooth ahead, escorting me down the river like a queen. I was Cloelia the Roman maiden making my way across the Tiber and nothing could stop me. Still I swam, past the cranes and the shipyards, the people on the river-side going about their day-to-day life. I saw the criss-cross wooden legs of a jetty and a group of mudlarks on the water's edge, thought I heard the thwack of children playing cricket on the shore. Then I saw nothing but grim walls and a row of portholes, until there before me was the great Tower of London.

I felt a change in the air then, a breeze on my face. In the distance a sail turned orange in the fading rays of the sun, lamps began to gleam along the shore and lights appeared on top of mastheads. When I looked up again it was to see a full pale moon beginning to rise behind the clouds and ahead of me the waters of the Thames growing green and gold like the scales of a fish.

Then Father was waving his arms and I realised he was shouting, 'Switch to the other side! Now!' So I did as I was told, making my way determinedly through the boats, taking full advantage of the strong tide and avoiding a bend in the river. As I did the passengers on a pass-ing saloon steamer roared their applause and the tugboats blew their whistles and I could feel the water carrying me past the docks as if I was flying. I felt the euphoria that comes when the rhythm is right, and I thought I would never stop. I would continue through London, I would swim all the way to the sea on the grandest highway in the world.

Then I heard the boom of a firing cannon, held up my head to see a floating steamboat pier and I knew we had nearly arrived at Green-wich. 'Three cheers!' shouted the people on the riverside and the band onboard the *Volunteer* began to play the opening strains of 'See the Conquering Hero Comes'. I saw Father standing in the bow of the boat, palms upwards to give the prearranged signal, and I stopped swimming for a moment, waiting for Billy to throw me the hoop. I caught it easily, grasped the metal and did a somersault right there in the Thames. Then I set off on the last few yards, still with the hoop in my arms, doing turns and dives along the way, until the salute was fired again. I stopped to catch my breath before making a final som-ersault and as I did I saw a woman by the edge of the pier with a baby on her hip. It was Mother! She had come after all. She had changed her mind and was here to witness my triumph. But when I looked up again I knew I was wrong, for however would she have got to Greenwich before me?

The referee's boat drew close and Father leaned down and with his strong swimmer's arms lifted me out of the water.

'You did it, Daisy,' he whispered in my ear. 'I knew you would.'

'One hour, seven minutes,' said Robert Winkle and he shook my hand as if I were a man.

Then Father's arms were around me again as he lifted me up to the *Volunteer* and I was pulled over the sides of the steamboat, wrapped in blankets and ushered down to the cabin. Inside the silence was shocking as I took off my costume and changed into my ordinary clothes, all the while my ears buzzing and my heart racing because I had done it, I had swum the Thames just like I'd said I would. Then Billy knocked on the door to say I was wanted outside.

'Do you feel tired Miss Belle?' a reporter shouted as we climbed off the steamer and onto the pier, beginning to make our way through the crowds. Father was waiting for me, chaired by dozens of men, carried high on their shoulders like a giant, waving his hat in one hand and a cigar in the other. I thought I recognised a figure amid the people outside the Ship Hotel, a girl with neatly parted hair and frowning brows, but as the crowd jostled forward she was lost to sight.

'Miss Belle,' the reporter cried again, 'are you tired?'

I had never been questioned by a journalist before and, heady with my success, I told him, 'No! I could have swum another five miles.'

'What about the cold?'

'I'm warmer now,' I lied, 'than when I got into the Thames.'

At this there was much laughter.

'Do you not consider it a dangerous feat for a girl?' he asked.

'It depends on the girl,' I replied. 'If you are properly trained then it's no more dangerous than trying to cross Westminster Bridge.'

The reporter smiled and wrote down my words, then a little girl came up and handed me a bouquet of violets.

'Professor Belle,' I heard someone cry, 'you'll be a rich man by the end of today.'

'Nonsense,' said Father; he was standing on his own two feet now and striding towards me. 'She's a credit to my way of teaching. I'm glad I brought her up a lady swimmer.'

'What was the wager again?' asked a man.

'It's not about the money,' said Father, 'it's about the skill.'

At that the people laughed some more.

'I bet your pockets are well lined now, *professor*,' a woman called and I wondered, was it true? But I was also annoyed because what did the money matter? That was not why I had swum the Thames. I had done it to be the first girl and to show the world that I could.

Still Father walked towards me, stopping to shake men's hands and lift his top hat to the ladies. Then one came running up and brazenly linked her arm through his and I heard Robert Winkle roaring with laughter.

'Miss Belle,' called the reporter, 'did you take any refreshment at all?'

'Not a thing,' I replied.

'Nothing was handed to you while in the water?'

'No,' I told him, 'although I'm very hungry now.'

Again the crowd laughed.

'Are you proud, Miss Belle?' the reporter asked.

Robert Winkle was by my side then, saying I should save my comments for later, but I shrugged him off. 'Of course I am,' I told the reporter and I was, not just for myself but because I had restored Father's reputation. Whatever Captain Matthew Webb's achievement in the English Channel, Professor Belle was in the limelight now, and all because of me. I had proved myself and now at last he would let me do whatever I wanted, for nothing succeeds like success.

CHAPTER TWELVE

The summer after my first Thames swim I was back in the river again, only this time I was to cover ten miles. I still regretted that I hadn't raced Emily Parker, and when I heard a few days after my first swim that she had travelled further than me and been awarded a gold medal worth ten guineas I was jealous. Ten guineas! The medal Father had given me after my swim wasn't nearly so valuable. But if Emily Parker could match my five-mile swim and go one better, then I would double it, and I did.

I told Father I could do twenty miles next; I could swim the entire length of the Thames if only he would let me. I was well-known in London now; there was not a swimmer who didn't know the name Daisy Belle. But he said no, I had proved my point in the river, it was time for something new. So I found myself back at the Lambeth Baths performing my dives, my hoop and ornamental swimming, waiting to see what would come next.

We left Johanna Street and moved to a cheerful terrace behind Westminster Bridge Road where Mother had a piano in the parlour. Father took his friends out to watch a match or enjoy dinner and a show, while my two medals joined Billy's above the fireplace, along with congratulatory telegrams from Auntie Jessie. Sometimes I grew bold and asked for something I wanted, like a bicycle. One Saturday I had seen two men tearing down our street on a brand new style, perched up high behind the wheel, and that was what I wanted, to speed along the road and be as fast on land as I was in water. But Father said it was too expensive, he would keep a nest egg for me for when I was older. In the meantime I had to content myself with a new costume, an amber suit trimmed with white lace and a jaunty little straw hat with blue ribbons. Mother didn't like it when I asked for things; she said she'd never heard of a girl having money. She herself had none of her own, she came to Father for every sixpence and that, she said, was married life. And whatever would people say to see a lady sitting on a saddle? If I wanted to pedal, she said, I could make use of her new treadle sewing machine.

But as for my little sister Minnie, she possessed everything a child could want. She had fancy tan boots before she even knew how to walk and a shiny grey rocking horse for when she was old enough to ride. Minnie was generally a happy child and to Mother's delight she had no interest in water at all. She didn't even like a wet flannel on her face and would howl and scream in protest when it was time for a wash. Minnie was Mother's doll now and if my little sister sometimes hit me or bit me when I was looking after her, then the fault was said to be mine. I began to resent her: she was not required to work like the rest of us and her bond with Mother meant she barely left the house.

Shortly before my sixteenth birthday I arrived at the baths early one morning intending to swim a mile before the ladies' lessons began. I was in a bad temper that day; I didn't want to spend my time teaching Father's ladies how to kick their legs, to reassure them that this was indeed the way to swim, and I was looking forward to having the pool to myself. When I walked into the first-class pool I expected to be alone but to my surprise, in the dim light of the bath, I saw someone in the water. I was about to cry out, 'Billy!' amazed that he would choose to be in the pool, when I realised it wasn't my brother at all.

I stepped back against the wall and kept my face in the shadows, watching the man in the bath. He was not fighting the water, he had no desire to conquer it; instead when his face came up his eyes were closed, immersed in a world of his own. You can tell a lot about a man by the way he swims: only watch a man in water and you will know his character on land. But as I stood there in the shadows I began to feel annoyed; I couldn't swim if a man was here. Then I thought that perhaps I could, for who would see me and why should I not? It was my bath and he was the intruder, not I.

So I made my way to a dressing box and put on my training costume, then I sat down on the poolside, the tiles cool under my thighs. I waited until the man reached my end of the bath and then, after he had pushed off with a strong kick, I slipped down into the water and fell into place behind him. I kept my face high, watching his broad back rising and falling, his chest plunging in and out. It was like travelling in the wake of an ocean liner, the way he made a churning passage for me in the water. Never had I swum with someone as strong before and when we reached the far end of the bath and turned together, I couldn't help myself and with a rush of excitement I sped up. We were parallel now and without a doubt he knew I was there, how could he not? I saw a flash of brown eyes, an open mouth, and I so hoped he wouldn't break the spell by speaking or looking at me. And he didn't, instead he increased his speed as well. I began to overtake him and he switched from breaststroke to a strange sort of overarm, reaching forward with his right hand as if to catch something and then drawing himself up and over.

He was faster than me now. I could feel the heat pulsing through my body; the pull of the muscles in my thighs, my very insides stretched tight, as I changed my stroke too. Then, at the exact same time, we touched the rail and turned again and made our way back. We were working together in a rhythm now, neither of us winning; faster and faster we went until blood pounded in my ears. I thought I heard him gasp, felt the slippery sensation of a limb against mine, when suddenly a light was lit and I heard a yelp.

I stopped where I was, panting. Mrs Peach was there on the side of the pool; her trusty cane tucked under one arm. 'Daisy Belle!' she said and I glanced around, looking for the man who I had almost beaten. But he was at the other end of the bath now, hurrying up the steps. I watched the back of him, walking along the poolside. He wore a tight-fitting one-piece costume and he had such a fine figure, with wide shoulders and strong thick thighs. Turn around, I said under my breath, let me properly see your face. But he had gone.

'Well now,' said Mrs Peach as she strode around the bath and lit the other lamps until the room grew bright, 'and what will the Professor make of that?'

I pretended I didn't know what she was talking about, turned on my back and floated for a while, studying the rafters up in the roof.

Still Mrs Peach stood there, her cane under her arm.

At last I could bear it no longer and I turned on my front and swam to the side. 'Who is he?' I asked.

'Who is who?' She gave a smile. 'Why, him? I have no idea.'

I didn't believe her. I knew she was playing a game with me and something told me the man wasn't from here; it was the way he swam. He wasn't from London or even from England, he was a foreigner.

Mrs Peach sighed. 'All I know is…'

'Yes?' I said, still looking up at her.

'His name is Johnnie Heaven.'

I laughed in delight. What a wonderful name for a man who swam like that!

'Mr Peach agreed he could use the bath because he wanted some place where he could train and wouldn't be seen. I told him he could swim before you came and that any funny business and he wouldn't be allowed back in here again. That was the agreement.'

'He didn't know I was here,' I protested. 'It was me who got into the water after him.'

'Was it now?' Mrs Peach asked. 'Well I do know he's from America —'

'America?' I was thrilled. I had heard many stories of America, a land over the ocean where people went to seek their fortune and never came back. 'Does Father know him?'

'Yes,' said Mrs Peach, 'he's come here to try the Channel.'

'Like Matt?' I asked.

'Yes; only he wants to do it the other way round, from France to England. Handsome young man, isn't he?'

And I shrugged and went back to my swim, determined to finish a mile.

That night I dreamed we were racing together in the Thames, Johnnie Heaven and I. On and on we went, with no boats at all, just the two of us in the wide churning river, and I woke with such a feeling of pleasure that I lay there for a long while after, not wanting to open my eyes and lose the dream. I so wanted to grasp and hold it, to stay in it all day long. I might have performed in front of men from a very young age, but aside from my brothers I had never really come into contact with boys. I knew nothing of love or lust. I swam, that was what I did. But now for the first time I began to long to see more of life outside my father's swimming kingdom. I wanted to know about the man in the bath, but who could I ask? Not Father or Robert Winkle, for then they might know I had swum in the water with a man. I had his name, I knew his ambition, and that was all. I wondered if I would see him again, for if he wanted to try the Channel then perhaps Father could train him.

'Right,' said Father at breakfast the very next day. 'I have a plan and you'll need to start practising. Everyone still wants to see Captain Webb, he gets crowds of thousands wherever he goes, so what we'll do is,' he took a sip of his tea, 'an exhibition of how he was fed in the Channel.'

That was all? I was crestfallen; I didn't care how Matt had been fed in the Channel.

'We'll dim the lights to persuade the spectators it's night time,' explained Father, 'and fix a small bottle of brandy at the end of a pole. Charlie can be the sailor. And then we will hold an endurance race at the baths. And you, Daisy, will swim with Matt.'

I thought they were no longer friends, that Father wasn't speaking to the Channel hero any more. 'I'll swim with him?'

'Yes.'

'I'll race against him?'

'No!' Father laughed. 'You can't race a man.'

Yes I can, I thought, and I already have.

Father put down his tea and picked up a sausage from his plate. 'You'll keep Matt going if he flags towards the end. I'll see you at the baths after breakfast.'

CHAPTER THIRTEEN

Johnnie Heaven didn't return to the Lambeth Baths, although I kept my eyes out for him. He must have gone to Dover to train, I thought, but if he did try the Channel then I never heard of it, although I scoured the newspapers for his name. So I tried to forget the man from America and our fleeting, clandestine swim and focus instead on Father's next plan.

In the spring of 1878, he announced a new competition at the Lambeth Baths. If men could walk for six days straight, or cycle the same length of time, then why not have them swim? Placards were put up everywhere offering a hundred pounds' worth of prizes for the man who could cover the longest distance. Father persuaded Billy to enter; I wasn't sure how, but since my Thames swims he seemed to have recovered some of his old enthusiasm and said he felt stronger now. He'd had a long break from swimming and had grown bored with watching from the sidelines. My brother hadn't competed for so long that he barely had a penny to his name and, after all, in his heart he was still a swimmer. And so he returned to the water to train and the tension between my father and Billy appeared to have been put to one side.

Three other professional swimmers entered the race as well, but it was Captain Matthew Webb, of course, who would be the star turn. On every street corner and down every passageway the news was discussed and I could barely make my way home each day without hearing, 'What's the odds on Webb? What's the odds on Billy Belle?' At each stop on the road and outside all the public houses the coming show was the one topic of conversation, and betting on the result was already fast and furious. The competition would start on Monday at nine in the morning, and would continue until the Saturday night. Its aim was straightforward: the men must cover as many miles as possible during fourteen hours of swimming a day. Father assured me it wouldn't be long before one, then two, then three dropped out and once they had then I could take part; his daughter Daisy Belle would swim alongside the great Captain Matthew Webb.

But I was shocked when I saw Matt arrive at the Lambeth Baths. I knew, from hearing Father talk, that since his Channel swim three years earlier, Matt had entered a number of other long races for one reason only: he had frittered away his fortune. Gone were the magnificent trophies and champagne dinners; now he was forced to turn to bath racing and that was why he and Father were friends again.

Of course I was older now and less impressionable – I had swum in the Thames myself – but still I was unprepared for the sight of Matt as he walked into the first-class bath. No longer was he the fine tough sailor I had seen on that rainy September day when Father had laughed at the very idea of anyone crossing the Channel. Instead he had a broken appearance; his eyes were duller, his once stocky body seemed to have shrunk. There might have been great cheers when he began, but few would bet now on Captain Webb to win and it was a cruel race from start to finish.

By Wednesday he'd covered 40 miles with Billy close behind, and by the following day, as Father had anticipated, the other three men had withdrawn. On Friday morning the bath attendants rigged a rope along the pool to form a lane for each swimmer as if they were greyhounds racing along a designated track. Only they were no greyhounds, especially Matt. He was exhausted, everyone could see, and those who had wagered he would fail were rubbing their hands in glee. As it neared lunchtime Father instructed the band to make as much noise as possible with 'See the Conquering Hero Comes' and 'Auld Lang Syne'. When that failed to rouse the weary sailor, Father dipped into his own pocket and told a group of youths to roar themselves hoarse every time Matt completed a length.

My brother was still jolly; I think he enjoyed the fact that only he and Matt remained, but his competitor was fading fast. So Father instructed me to change. New life needed to be brought to the proceedings and so, with a roll of the drums and accompanied by loud cheers, I came out of the dressing box.

'Take it slowly,' said Father.

I nodded; this was his usual advice.

'Daisy,' he said, 'the man is acting half-dead, talk to him, wake him up.'

I looked at him in alarm; if Matt was half-dead then shouldn't he be stopped, why was Father letting this continue? But the audience was waiting for me, clapping and calling my name, and I had no choice. So in I dived and came up by Matt's side, saying a cheerful, 'Afternoon!' I couldn't think what else to say; he was moving so slowly that I was treading water rather than swimming, while Billy flew ahead. Matt ignored me. I don't think he even knew who I was, the girl who had once trailed after him to Westminster Bridge and watched him swim six miles in the Thames.

'Come on, Captain!' I cried. 'Let's show them how!'

This seemed to work for a quarter mile or so, but then he slowed again.

'Do you want to be beaten by a girl?' I teased, although it was quite obvious by now that I could have beaten him with my eyes closed and my legs tied together.

Again this spurred him on, but only for a couple of lengths, and as we plodded pointlessly down the bath I thought of the young American I had seen in the pool. I wondered what had happened to him. He must have given up on his attempt to swim the Channel, I thought, and gone back across the ocean home. How exciting it had been to swim with Johnnie Heaven. This was tragic in comparison and I didn't want to be a part of it. But what could I do but swim on?

At six in the evening Father announced that Billy would hand in the towel, although he looked fresh enough to me. I couldn't understand why he was getting out when he could easily have won, and it was only when I saw Father wink at my brother that I guessed the truth: he had paid him to give up. How embarrassed I was for Billy, that he'd allowed himself to race when there was nothing sporting about the event at all. Did he want money so badly that he would forget his old defiance and agree to anything Father said, even if it meant he had to lose? Father had used both of us, but most of all he had used Matt. Captain Webb might have won the endurance race, but now he was a wreck.

After Billy left the pool the sailor only managed a further quarter mile and as we kicked off together to try another length I turned to see he was no longer with me. Instead the once great Captain

Matthew Webb was clutching the diving board and hanging on to it like grim death.

At once Father was by the poolside, the pistol was fired and Matt declared the winner. He had swum seventy-four miles and won seventy pounds but the cheers, such as they were, sounded half-hearted. Mr Peach and Father fairly carried him to the changing room and I stood outside as they discussed what to do.

Then I heard Father exclaim 'Good God!' and I pushed open the door. There was Captain Webb, collapsed on the bench, coughing fit to burst with a pool of crimson blood on the floor.

There was a dreadful scene then, not just in the changing room but outside on the street. One of the bath attendants ran in to say a group of men had rushed the main door and now they were trying to force it open. They wanted to see Webb; the word had gone out that he was dead, and all along Westminster Bridge Road shopkeepers were hurriedly closing their shutters expecting a riot. Inside the changing room Matt was restless. He said repeatedly that his wife was waiting for him at home and he did not want to worry her.

'How long have we known each other?' asked Father, crouching down by his side and offering a tonic to drink. 'Remember your first time in the Thames? Remember the fried fish dinners we used to have, you, me and Robert, before your Channel swim?'

Matt gave a weak smile.

'So now listen to me, you need to rest.'

'I can't,' said the sailor. 'Next week I sail for America.'

Father sighed. 'Not in this state you won't. Why go there?'

'I have to, I'm to swim Niagara.'

'Matt,' said Father, looking concerned. Perhaps he was regretting the endurance race after all. 'Don't go, you'll never come back alive.'

'I want money,' muttered the sailor, 'and I must have it.'

And that, you see, should have been a lesson for me, as I stood in the doorway watching Father wipe blood from the sailor's mouth. I should have known that performing only for money would never bring anything but grief.

We never saw Captain Matthew Webb again; he died after plunging into the rapids under Niagara. He was sucked into a whirlpool and his bloated body buried far away from the country where he'd reigned supreme. He'd wanted fame and money and he'd paid with his life. Father called it the fickleness of fickle fortune, and he should know, because not long after the six-day swim our own fortunes were on the wane again. Where all the money had gone I did not know; perhaps the event had proved too costly to run; but Mother had to give back her piano, there were no more new toys for little Minnie, and we were to look for a cheaper place to live.

Father absented himself for days at a time at the Crown and Cushion, until finally one evening he came up with a plan. 'Daisy,' he said, 'I've been thinking long and hard and I have an idea. You've done the Thames and so has Emily Parker and God knows who else will try it now. Swimming might be all the rage but diving is more daring still. We've lost the performance element, it's time to bring it back.'

CHAPTER FOURTEEN

Three weeks later we were on our way to the Royal Aquarium. 'When we get inside,' said Father, tightening a shawl around my shoulders and tilting forward my hat, 'keep your eyes down. If anyone speaks to you, I will reply. No one must take any notice of you until the time comes.' Then off we went to join the sightseers entering the Aq. But it was hard to keep my eyes to the ground when we entered the great hall where the air was hot as a summer's day under the vast glass roof. As we walked down the promenade I could hear an orchestra tuning up, water tumbling from a fountain, the shrieks of birds in hanging cages swinging above my head. I wanted to stop, to look at a large blue bird alone in a cage, at the sculpture of a rearing horse and at the exotic trees with fruit the colour of sunshine. But most of all I wanted to gaze at the fish. There they were, in big glass tanks stretching along the sides of the promenade, every creature imaginable. I tugged on Father's sleeve, insisting we take a look, and before he could object I had rushed to a tank and had my face pushed up against the glass. I admired the pretty coral and purple-encrusted rocks, and then suddenly hundreds of tiny fish came floating down like falling snow. They flicked their tails and turned direction, one moment congregating and then just as quickly pulling apart. I saw one chase the other, just as I used to chase my brothers when I was a child, and I wished they were here to see this, the life of the ocean brought indoors.

I moved to the next tank where two starfish were stuck to the side, their fingers outstretched against the glass.

'Have you ever touched a starfish?' asked Father.

I shook my head; he knew I hadn't.

'Why don't you try to now?'

So I reached my hand over the glass, dipped it into the water and gently placed a fingertip on the starfish, surprised at how soft its limbs were and how gritty its skin. 'Why does this one have four legs when that one has five?' I asked, about to touch its friend.

'Ah, they are very clever creatures,' said Father. 'A starfish can lose a leg to a predator and when the predator has gone it can grow it back.'

It could grow back a limb? I stared at the starfish, impressed.

'It will let a predator take a leg,' nodded Father, 'if that's the only way it can escape.'

I went to the next tank where a sheet of sand turned into a ray, its sides flapping like a man in an opera cloak. I saw fish with the skin of a leopard, others that floated backwards and some that seemed to be as thin as paper. I stopped at a tank full of grey and silver fish, swimming and dancing among rocks and corals in their very own city. Did they sense me standing there watching them? At first they seemed to pay me no attention, but then up they came to the glass, mouths open, fins flapping, tails swishing.

'The manatee is dead,' said a gentleman behind me.

'The sea cow?' asked his companion. 'Let's go and see the whale.'

'A whale?' I turned, wide-eyed, to ask Father if there really was a whale but he had left my side and was deep in conversation with a lady who had her back to me. Perhaps she was asking for directions, for he had one hand resting on her shoulder and with the other he was pointing down the promenade. He seemed very keen to show her the way, I thought, as I heard her laugh and saw her twirl a parasol in her hand.

I returned to watching the fish ducking between rockeries, sliding through plants, swimming as far as they could up and down, from one side of the tank to the other. Then another thought occurred to me: perhaps they were not enjoying themselves; perhaps they were looking for a way out. And if they were, if this was why they never stopped moving, I knew they would never find it. I was beginning to feel upset, but then Father was by my side, stroking his chin and looking from me to the tank and back again.

'How do they breathe?' I asked him.

'Oxygen,' he said. 'The plants give out oxygen in the water, so what one breathes in, the other breathes out. The fish can live there forever.'

Was this true? Somehow I didn't think it was and I was about to ask how long a fish could live for when I saw him looking from me to the tank again. I knew exactly what he was thinking; I could read Father's mind as clearly as a picture book. What if it were a human in there? If the tank could be viewed on every side then it would be perfect for a performance. I wondered if I could fit into a tank, crouched up small, and if I could then how people would marvel when they watched me in a mysterious world where humans could breathe underwater.

But this wasn't why we had come to the Aq. There were other amusements that the visitors were far more interested in, and Father had been here several times in recent weeks and reported back on everything he saw. A lady called LaLa with skin as dark as cocoa had a jaw so strong that when she put a rope between her teeth she could lift up and carry three hulking men. There were animals too, performing fleas, packs of fierce wolves, even a bull that could climb a ladder. It was like a circus fairground, he said, with a water show where performers swam, and best of all at five o'clock each day a man dived from a perilously high platform into a shallow tank. And that was why we were here. But he'd never mentioned there being a whale.

'Can we see it?' I asked.

Father consulted his pocket watch. 'Yes, we have half an hour.'

All the way down the promenade and towards the annex I pestered him with questions: where had the whale come from? How did they get it here? There had been another whale, he said, brought from New York, then laid in a box on a bed of seaweed and taken on a steamship to England. Every five minutes, all throughout the day and night, it had been doused with seawater. Then it had been brought to the Aq and put in a tank of fresh water, but it had died so now they had brought another one.

We reached the annex, and went inside where it was very brightly lit, for Father said a whale didn't get on well in the dark. In the middle was an iron tank surrounded by an elevated walkway and I climbed up the steps to take a look. At first there seemed to be nothing in the tank but for a huge stone on the bottom. Then the stone moved and I gasped as slowly it came floating up. It was the oddest-looking creature, like an enormous white seal with a bump-shaped head and two small fins as flat as shovels. Its mouth was closed and it seemed to have a smile on its face as it began to paddle around, using its tail to propel itself forward. Then it sank to the bottom again and rubbed itself vigorously against the sides of the tank.

'What are they?' I asked, pointing at two deep scars on its creamy skin.

'From a harpoon perhaps,' said Father, 'or a spear.'

'It's in good health,' said a gentleman next to me, peering through a monocle. 'It seems perfectly happy and healthy and quite at home. I think this one will live.'

At this the whale rose right up to the surface and let out a giant spurt of water and I laughed so hard I almost fell off the stand. Billy would love this, I thought, for he had often told me childhood stories about whales.

'That's its trap door,' said Father. 'A whale can't keep under for more than about twenty minutes, it must come up and breathe. Look,' he said as two men came into the annex carrying buckets, 'now it's feeding time.'

The men climbed onto the stand and poured hundreds of eels, slithering and slipping, into the water. Having had its meal the monster began to swim again, round and round the tank, giving a slight lurch as it turned to complete the circle. When it rose to the surface I was sure it wanted to speak, to tell me something. Then it submerged and came right up to the side of the tank and gave such a sudden lunge that I jumped in shock. Its mouth was open, its fins held out on either side as if it were waving. It turned its head away for a moment as if playing peek-a-boo, then lunged towards me again like a ghoul. Was it teasing, or did it want to eat me? I stared transfixed at its tiny eyes, like pinpricks in a field of snow, wondering how well it could see. Was it threatening or playful? I wasn't sure.

'Come on Daisy,' said Father, 'we've seen enough, it's nearly time.'

But I couldn't tear myself away from the whale, as it began to roll and lurch, swimming round and round under the water. And all the time it shook its head in a slow, mournful manner as if it were searching for something and knew it would never find it. After a while it came back to my side of the tank, pressing its forehead against the glass. What was it trying to tell me, was it asking me to join it or to leave it alone? How did it feel being locked in this tank when it was used to the vastness of the ocean? It must, I thought, be like locking a person in a cupboard.

'Daisy…' Father warned. 'Come on, the show is starting, we can't be late.'

He hurried me out of the annex and down the promenade until we reached the hall where the diving show was held. At one end was a glass tank, sunk below floor level. Behind this was a stage, while above were a series of ropes and ladders and platforms. We took our place in the front row of seats just as a wiry man came bursting through a set of curtains and onto the stage, wearing bright red tights and yellow trunks.

'Ladies and gentlemen!' shouted Mr Sinclair, the diving manager, a puffy-faced man in a velvet waistcoat. 'This evening for your enter-tainment, Professor Poisson! All the way from Paris!'

'Paris?' muttered Father. 'More like Preston. I recognise him.'

Professor Poisson gave a bow, climbed a few steps up a ladder to the first wooden platform, placed his feet in a loop of rope and with a quick tug from below he was hauled legs first towards the summit of the dome. The spectators held their breath as he travelled up to the second platform, a good sixty feet above the ground. Then he took hold of the ledge, flipped himself around so his feet were on the plank and released the rope. A lady cried that she was feeling giddy, another asked how the man could dive into something so shallow, surely he would kill himself? But a moment later Professor Poisson gave a shout, flung himself off the platform and landed with his arms outstretched, belly first in the water.

The audience stood up, clapping and cheering, as he scrambled out of the tank and ran back to the stage. Then Mr Sinclair called for quiet. 'Ladies and gentlemen! Today we lay a challenge before the world. Is there *any* man who can match what you have seen here this afternoon?' He laughed and looked around. 'We have had no fewer than *seventy* applicants this past six months… and not *one* of them could even do half the height.'

At this Father rose from his seat and waved his hat to get attention. 'I think these diving men are getting a little stale,' he said.

A couple of gentlemen laughed.

'I wonder, sir —' Father looked around, ensuring that everyone was listening. 'Is a lady volunteer eligible?'

'A *lady* volunteer?' asked Mr Sinclair.

Behind me I heard men whistle in disbelief. 'Never!' one cried.

'Yes,' said Father, 'would you accept the challenge from a girl? If so,' he continued, raising his voice, 'I will back her from a hundred to five hundred pounds... or for an engagement similar to Professor Poisson!'

'My good sir,' objected Mr Sinclair, 'I can't possibly assent to a contest for money. But if she can dive I will give her an engagement. Who is the girl?'

Then Father pointed at me, and I stood up, removing my hat.

'Why, it's Daisy Belle!' gasped a woman. 'It's the girl who swam the Thames!'

CHAPTER FIFTEEN

On the following Saturday we returned to the Aq for the public challenge. As I walked along the promenade this time I barely looked at the birds in their hanging cages or the glorious fish in their tanks. All I could think was, would I make it? We reached the diving area and Mr Sinclair showed me into a dressing room behind the stage where I changed into my costume. Father thought it best if I dressed like Professor Poisson, he said it would make the crowd take me more seriously that way, and so I wore blue tights and bright white trunks. A great cheer rang out as I emerged back onto the stage and walked to the ladder where Father stood, and as I started to climb I could feel the crowd were agog with excitement. I would not use the ropes like Professor Poisson had done, instead I would step my way up to the second platform, for it would take longer this way and the anticipation would slowly mount. But when I reached the first platform I nearly lost my footing, and as I steadied myself I heard the men below laughing and the muscles of my legs began to twitch. The worst thing in the world was to be laughed at. I had to show a girl could do it. Yet never in my life had I dived from such a height: it was one thing practising on makeshift boards suspended from the gallery at the Lambeth Baths and quite another to be here at the Aq. As I started to make my way up to the second platform, step by careful step, the band ceased playing and absolute silence fell on the crowd.

'Ladies and gentlemen,' cried Mr Sinclair, 'what you are about to see here this afternoon will prove or disprove the equality of the sexes. For the first time in the history of the *world*, a woman will compete with a man... She will dive from up there – sixty feet high! Down into there – an eight-foot tank! The tank is not padded in any way, ladies and gentlemen. The success of the diving is entirely down to skill.'

I reached the second platform and took a deep breath, stepped from the ladder and onto the plank. Then I eyed the tank, as small as a bathtub below. I thought of when Father had first taught me to dive, how

I had learned that danger clears the mind. I knew that if I didn't dive well, if I missed that tank or went too deep, then a few minutes from now I would be no more.

I saw Father gesturing with his hands at either side of his face and I couldn't think what he was trying to tell me. I knew the main thing was to keep my body rigid and not allow my legs to curl, and to judge correctly how and where I would land. There were only two ways to do this dive; I could hit the water with my arms outstretched and end on my belly like Professor Poisson. Or I could dive in head first. With the tank so shallow I must hit it at an angle, and whatever happened I did not want to land on my face. Still I stood there, practising the leap in my mind. But I was so high up that for a moment I couldn't tell if I were standing tall and straight or leaning too far forward. Dive, I said to myself, just dive.

I could still see Father; he seemed to be pinching his cheeks and finally I realised what he was trying to say: don't forget to smile. So I opened my mouth and put a big smile on my face, bounced on the platform and lifted my arms. I thought of the fish I had seen the week before, and the whale, felt a sense of exhilaration that I at least was free. Then off I flew, my body turning in a wondrous curve as I streaked through the air. I saw nothing, I heard nothing, it was as if I were underwater. Then I sensed a blur of colour, heard a roar of noise and after that I had only one thought left; when would I feel the water? I stretched my legs and arms, arched out my back and hit the water with a slap. I was under. It was over, I had done it. Not a single part of me had touched the sides of the tank, although my head had been just inches from the bottom. I came triumphantly to the surface, my legs as soft as jelly.

'A near perfect dive,' said Father, helping me over the side of the tank and covering me with a cloak, and I waved to acknowledge the deafening applause, such had been the pent-up excitement.

Then I ran back to the stage, panting and laughing and dripping, and stood there to watch Professor Poisson.

'And now,' cried Mr Sinclair, 'our diving *man* will attempt the dangerous feat.'

But the Professor looked annoyed. He hadn't even started to climb the ladder; instead he was standing with his arms tightly folded over his chest. 'The lady's platform is nearer to the tank than mine,' he said in a petulant voice. 'And her platform is a good foot or two lower than mine.'

The crowd murmured their disapproval. They had come to see a challenge and they had paid good money. Was the man going to dive or not?

'The courage is oozing out of his toes,' said Father, at which several gentlemen laughed.

'I will not do my dive,' said Professor Poisson, 'because it is not equal unless her platform is heightened a few feet.'

At this I just could not help myself. I had done the dive from the platform provided, I had completed my part of the challenge and now he must do the same. 'Very well!' I called out. 'If you can manage your dive then after that I shall dive from your platform as well.'

'Manage the dive?' demanded Professor Poisson. 'Haul up my platform!' he shouted to Mr Sinclair. 'Haul it up right now to seventy feet and I'll do it from there.'

Mr Sinclair looked exasperated. 'That would take far too long; the platforms are of equal height. Do your dive or the trial is over, we're not here for a dispute.'

So at last Professor Poisson did his dive, the same way as I, a straightforward headfirst plunge. The crowd applauded him of course, but not as much as they had for me. A girl had done what a man had done; the feat no longer had the wonder it once had.

The Professor left the tank, I climbed up his ladder, smiling and waving to the crowd. When I reached the platform I gave a bow and blew down a kiss, then I held my hand to my forehead as if I were so afraid of the height that any moment I might swoon. The audience laughed and cheered, the band struck up, and with a final wave I hurtled through the air to complete my second dive.

'Marvellous,' said Mr Sinclair as I got out of the tank after a perfect landing. 'Absolutely marvellous.'

'I told you she could do it,' said Father.

'Indeed you did,' said Mr Sinclair, wiping sweat from his face. 'She has broken the record without breaking her neck. You have an engagement. If she can dive from the platform into the tank twice a day then the pay is ten pounds a week.'

Ten pounds a week! Our debts would be repaid; we wouldn't have to leave our home after all and I couldn't wait to tell my mother and brothers the news. Then Mr Sinclair took Father to his office to discuss the terms and I was about to return to my dressing room when a reporter called my name from the side of the stage.

'Miss Belle. Please! Some questions...'

I looked down at the pool of water forming round my feet. 'Would you mind waiting until I've changed?'

'I shall not keep you more than five minutes,' begged the reporter. 'Please, tell me, if Professor Poisson was to increase the height of his dive, would you do the same?'

'Certainly I would.'

'But surely that jump would be too perilous for a girl?'

'It is a headfirst plunge,' I corrected him, 'not a jump.'

'But do you not consider it a dangerous feat for a girl?'

I looked at him with irritation now. This was the same question I had been asked after my first swim in the Thames, and he seemed to have forgotten that I had just demonstrated not one perilous dive but two. 'It is a dangerous feat for anyone,' I told him, 'and for those who are untrained it is certain death.' And with that I turned on my heels and went to change, feeling very pleased with myself. I would rather swim than dive but still, I would be a rich young woman now. But what I should have remembered from Captain Matthew Webb is that what goes up will always come down, and that included me.

CHAPTER SIXTEEN

I stayed at the Aq performing my daily dives until one morning I came to work to hear that the beluga whale had died. It was Mr Sinclair who told us as we stood backstage, shaking his head gloomily, more at the loss of money than from sadness at the fate of the whale.

'Terrible,' said Father. 'Now what will you do?'

'Bring another I suppose.'

'Or,' said Father, stroking his chin, 'how about trying something else?'

'Like what?'

'Well, what you need, sir, is to manufacture a new sensation.'

Mr Sinclair nodded.

'So, instead of bringing another whale...' Father looked at me as if he'd just had a novel idea, 'why not have a mermaid?'

'A mermaid?' laughed Mr Sinclair. 'Whatever do you mean?'

Father pointed to where I stood and I smiled and tried to look agreeable, although he had not mentioned anything of this to me.

'But,' said Mr Sinclair, 'what would she do?'

'Well, swim of course, she can stay in the whale tank all day.'

'All *day*?'

'Two days,' said Father, growing excited now, 'three if you like! Have you ever seen anyone perform submerged in a tank? No. And she can hold her breath for minutes at a time. You, sir, will have your very own mermaid.'

'Aside from holding her breath what will she do?'

'All manner of things,' said Father, 'just you wait.'

I was sad about the whale; it had come such a long way and I remembered how mournful it had looked as it lunged and lurched around the tank, how I'd been sure it wanted to tell me something. But I had also not forgotten when I'd first looked at the fish on the promenade, and realised a tank could serve as a stage, and wondered if I could join them. Father said with a mermaid show I would be paid even more;

my nest egg was growing by the day and wasn't I happy about that? 'For now you can have a new outfit,' he said. 'We'll make you a mermaid tail.'

But I didn't want a mermaid tail. How would I swim in a tail?

'You can have two bikes when this is done,' he added. 'How about roller-skates too, a different pair for every day of the week? You can have anything you like.'

'Anything I like?'

'Yes.'

'Can I go to America?'

Father looked surprised. 'Well you certainly can, if you wish.'

That very evening after we'd left the Aq he beckoned me into his and Mother's room. 'See Daisy?' he asked, crouching down and pulling a large trunk from under the bed. 'There you go.' He lifted the lid and I stared at the trunk, full to the brim with coins. 'There's your money. I'm keeping it safely for you.'

'Can I have some now?' I asked but when I reached forward he clasped my arm to stop me.

'You have no need of it now,' he said, closing the trunk. 'I'm your father, I provide everything.'

My mermaid practice started the following week. The annex was closed to the public and only Father and I were allowed in the room. It wasn't as brightly lit as when the whale had been here; instead it was a little spooky. I climbed up and sat myself on the edge of the tank, dipping in my feet. Then I leaned down and felt the water with my hands, splashed it on my face. The tank had been cleaned of course, and it was not as deep for Father had lifted the height of the floor, but it seemed to have a very fishy smell and for a moment I wondered if the whale had truly gone.

'In you get,' said Father. 'Jump in for now, later we'll rig up a plank so you can dive.'

I had never been in a tank before and it was a strange feeling being so contained, aware of the glass walls all around me, knowing I could never strike out or cover any distance.

'Have a swim, get used to the thing,' Father called, 'but stay near the sides so people can see you. We'll add some salt later to give you more buoyancy.'

So I set off in imitation of the whale, resting my head against the glass, flapping my hands, pretending to lunge, moving up and down, across and back. After an hour or so I had a break and the oddest thing was, once I was out of that tank I wanted to get back in again: it was already feeling like home.

Things went well until the afternoon; I had even started to learn a new routine, when all of a sudden I felt a cramping in my stomach.

'What's wrong?' asked Father when I stopped swimming and hung onto the side.

'Nothing,' I mumbled, aghast at the idea I had my monthlies. We'd have to wait a week or more, and if we weren't seen to be rehearsing then Mr Sinclair might have second thoughts. He might even cancel the show.

'If nothing's wrong,' said Father, annoyed, 'then keep swimming.'

'Let me get out for a minute to rest.'

'No. You've only been in there a few hours! Whatever it is will pass. Don't let me down, Daisy.' Father leaned over the side, his expression stern. 'My reputation's riding on this.'

Your reputation? I thought. It was I who was in the tank! But I did as he said, let go of the side and swam around for a while and eventually the pain did go away; it had been a false alarm and I continued until it was night. The next day I was back in the tank and for the next two weeks instead of diving I practised my mermaid routine.

Just before Christmas Father announced the news: his daughter Daisy Belle would stay afloat at the Royal Aquarium for sixty hours. New Year's Day dawned dull and showery, and even if the weather hadn't driven people inside, there would still have been a large number of visitors wanting to greet the New Year at the Aq. We arrived before dawn to make sure everything was in place and to meet the referee, the same grey-haired man who had first accompanied me on the River Thames. Then members of the press were invited into the annex, including Robert Winkle, and given tea and buns. Just before eight, Father called three ladies into my dressing room to confirm I had no concealed floating supports. Once that was done I came out in a long floor-length cape, my hair tightly plaited, wearing a new costume of navy blue; for it was best I wore as dark a colour as possible in case it faded after so long in the water. What the spectators could not see was my mermaid tail, woven of silver and blue, in which I had to shuffle along with my feet held together.

But whether I would be as popular as the whale remained to be seen and at nine o'clock the room was half-empty, except for the press and Aq employees arriving for work. I heard the clock chime and the birds in their cages on the promenade waking up, then at ten o'clock the audience began to arrive. There still weren't as many as Father had expected and I could see him glancing worriedly at the door, but when I removed my cape there was a round of applause as the people saw my tail.

'Behold!' said Father, 'this marvellous sight. Half-woman, half-fish.' Then he picked me up and put me on the small plank that served as a diving board.

'Are you doing this for money?' a man with a booming voice called out as I stood there preparing myself. 'Because if you are, then there's a sovereign for you, girl,' and he flipped a coin into the water.

I was so annoyed at this. I was not a beggar in the street to whom he could toss a coin, I was going to swim in a whale tank not a wishing well. So I dived in a little off centre, deliberately plunging to my left, and when I came up I was delighted to see I'd made the man soaking wet. Off he went muttering oaths and that, I thought, was the last I'd see of him.

Then the bell sounded and I began swimming, keeping my mouth closed as salt had been added to the water and it wouldn't do to swallow. I had practised repeatedly with the mermaid tail and while at first it had felt as if a child were holding on to my legs now I found it quite easy. It gave a wonderful speed as I moved round the tank and when I wanted to come to the surface it propelled me as fast as if I were indeed half-fish. But still few people came to watch and it was a lonely swim; perhaps we had started too early. Then at 11 o'clock the annex finally began to fill and Father decided it was time to perform.

'Ladies and gentlemen!' he announced, taking his place on the plank. 'I introduce to you Miss Daisy Belle, heroine of the Thames, companion of Captain Webb, and the world's most daring diver. Walk up! Walk up to see how the London mermaid lives *below* the water!'

I turned a somersault, sank to the bottom and laid down flat, just as the whale had done. I stayed there, perfectly still, my eyes closed, counting in my head. One minute went by and then two. I opened my eyes and looked up. All around the tank people had gathered, men, women and children, craning forward with open mouths. I knew they were wondering why I hadn't come up. Had I run out of oxygen, was I dead? I felt a sway above me where someone was splashing the water with a hand or a stick. I didn't have much time left; I needed to come up. So I kicked down with my tail and shot to the surface.

A lady screamed, the children shouted, 'Look at the mermaid!' and began running around the tank, pointing.

I put my head fully out of the water and piped up 'Good morning!' and the children were so shocked that I could speak that one began to cry.

'Ladies!' cried Father, 'gentlemen, this amazing mermaid can breathe *under* the water just as you have seen. Now watch while she eats a banana.'

'A banana?' laughed a gentleman standing by the ladder. 'How can she eat under water? She will suffocate. It's not possible!'

But of course it was, and I had practised long and hard to make it seem as effortless as I could. Father tossed me the fruit and I caught it in one hand, then sank the rest of my body down with one knee resting on the bottom. I lifted my other arm out of the water, peeled back the banana skin, broke off a piece and quickly carried it under. The trick was to fill my lungs just before I descended, and then to give a gentle exhalation as I placed it in on my tongue. The audience was captivated; I could see them pressed up against the tank, several tapping on the glass. All I had to do now was to repeat the process until the banana was eaten, then I rose out of the water, whereupon Father came down from the plank to relieve me of the skin.

'Now,' he told the spectators, 'a sponge cake!'

Again I submerged myself and lifted out my hand, took the cake and ate that piece by piece, and finally up I shot, to hearty applause.

'Daisy,' called Father, 'are you thirsty?'

I nodded my head vigorously.

So he handed me a small lemonade bottle, half-filled with milk and sealed with a cork. I took the bottle down, pulled the cork out sideways with my teeth, then blew a little air through my nostrils and began to drink. Again this was well suited to a tank because in a bath it would be difficult to see what the swimmer was doing, but I had to manage my breathing perfectly and keep myself on the bottom all the while. Then finally I rose up, with the empty bottle securely corked, again to loud applause.

At dinnertime Father floated a tray of meatballs across the water, but by now I was hardly hungry and had to make a show of eating. There was then a lull as others went to eat their dinner too and I swam around for an hour or so. But by early evening the annex was so full they had to close the doors. Finally I had my first hour's rest and I was so grateful when I got to my dressing room and could remove my tail and free my legs, wash my salty face, apply some lotion and powder. At last I could use the toilet and lie down on the bed, my skin as soft and pliable as a newborn baby's after ten hours in the water.

But almost at once I was being woken up. 'Daisy!' It was Father, shaking me by the shoulders. 'Rouse yourself.'

I opened my eyes, unsure where I was, thinking I might still be in the water and if I was then where had the people gone?

'Put this on,' he said, handing me a dry costume and a new mermaid tail, 'and let's get back to the tank.'

I stared at him; my mind seemed to have slowed to a halt.

'Now,' ordered Father. 'I'll wait for you outside, you have five minutes.'

So I took off the dress I had been wearing while I slept and put on the costume and the new tail, but it took me a long time to get my legs and arms where they should be. Then I shuffled back to the annex where I heard the people shouting, 'The mermaid is back!' before Father picked me up and placed me a little dazed on the board.

By 11 o'clock I had been back in the water for several hours, the audience had left, the lights were all put out except one and it was peaceful but for the clock chiming the hour and the occasional screech of an owl. It was now that Father served champagne to members of the press, to keep up their interest and their spirits, but by midnight even they had gone. So he and Robert Winkle and the referee enjoyed a steak supper, then Father said Billy was on his way to keep an eye on me for a while; they all needed a bit of a rest.

I fell asleep after that, taking short quiet breaths and hooking my heels onto the side as I'd learned to do as a child. When I opened my eyes the men had gone and I was alone. I did a couple of somersaults, just for the chance to use my limbs, and swam around swishing my tail. It was then that I got the fright of my life, for there on the other side of the glass were two blue eyes looking in at me. I thought I was dreaming, that it couldn't possibly be true, when one of the eyes winked at me and I shot to the surface with a yelp.

'Aren't you bored?' asked the girl standing by the side of the tank, 'in here all alone?' She had very short hair, parted on the side like a man's, and her eyes were large like a child's. She was wearing a white satin tunic over bright white stockings and in her hand she held a straw hat. 'Miss Violet Mitchell,' she gave a bow, 'gymnast extraordinaire. You've probably heard of me. I was in the water show last week. Until fat-face fired me.'

I laughed and nearly swallowed water. How cheeky she was! 'Why did Mr Sinclair fire you?' I asked.

'Because I did this,' she said, and as bold as anything she put her hands on her hips and stuck out her tongue. 'And then this,' she said, and made a rude gesture with her fingers. 'Oh I'm sick of being a performing seal. They hired me as a gymnast and then fat-face wanted me in a water show in a see-through costume! The things they say to you, well I'd had enough. He says he's going to sue me, well let him if he thinks my services are no longer required.'

'What are you doing?' I asked as Violet hauled herself onto the edge of the tank.

'I'm getting in with you,' she replied, spitting on her hand and slicking down the parting in her hair.

'You can't!' I cried. What if the referee should find out, and the press – then the feat would be over and all my hours of swimming wasted. Nothing had been said about anyone joining me in the water, the whole performance would be invalid. But Violet had already landed in the tank with an enormous splash and was laughing like a child. 'Will you teach me, Daisy, to be as good a swimmer as you?' she asked and then she caught me round the waist and did a little dance, and despite my fears that someone would come in I realised I was having fun. Then the door opened and Billy ran in. What we were *doing*? Were we mad? Father was on his way and so was the referee! Violet must get out at once. My brother offered a hand to help, but there was no need for she scrambled out as agile as anything, and I saw the admiring look on Billy's face as he watched her run out of the room.

By the second day there were several hundred people waiting to be let into the annex of the Royal Aquarium. News of the mermaid had spread and Mr Sinclair put two men on the door to keep the crowds moving. I enjoyed myself that morning, chatting with the spectators and answering questions, and there was quite a fuss when Lord Aylesford arrived with his friends just in time for my first performance of the day. He was an impressive-looking man but for his fishlike, bulbous eyes. He crouched down on the walkway by the side of the tank so he was looking up at me and he seemed to enjoy the view from there.

'Ladies and gentlemen,' announced Father, 'I present to you the world's most famous mermaid, Miss Daisy Belle, who has been in this tank for over twenty-four hours! She will now write her name.'

'Write her name?' laughed the Lord. 'How does he think she's going to do that?'

Father didn't reply, only slid a piece of slate and a stick of chalk on a tray across the water. I ducked down and quickly wrote my name in letters as large as possible, before pressing the slate against the sides of the tank to show what I had done. The children laughed as I blew them bubbles of kisses and the ladies clapped. As I came up for air Lord

Aylesford doffed his hat and leaned over the tank. 'You must intro-duce me to your father,' he said. 'I want to congratulate him on his floating capital.'

'There he is,' came a reply, 'over there, chuckling over the gate money. There's been five thousand people in to see his daughter since yesterday.'

Five thousand! Father must be very pleased, I thought, and I was just about to ask if it were true when Mr Sinclair came into the annex and fixed two large signs on the wall, which read, 'Do not speak to the mermaid.'

I swam in silence for the next few hours, sometimes floating on my back, and after dinner I dozed again. The annex was hot and the water very warm and I began to lose my sense of direction as I floated face up on the surface for minutes at a time. When this alarmed some of the spectators, Father said I would be examined by a doctor and he took me to the dressing room and laid me down on the bed. My mouth was burned dry from the salt and my stomach and legs were badly chafed, but despite this I fell asleep at once.

When I woke the doctor was there, rummaging in his bag, and I winced as he applied some lint.

'How's her temperature?' asked Father.

The doctor felt my forehead and declared that it was fine.

'And her pulse?'

The doctor put a finger to my wrist and nodded; that was fine as well.

But I didn't feel fine; I could barely sit up. 'Let me sleep a little longer,' I begged.

'No,' said Father, 'two cups of strong coffee and back to the tank.'

'I'm tired,' I said.

'Of course you are, not long to go now.'

'Please let me sleep a little longer.'

'No.' He handed me a cup of coffee, pouring in some tonic. 'There's no time. Drink that and get back in the tank.'

The second night went much like the first, only with a great deal of gaiety among the press when Father handed out the champagne.

Tomorrow would be my final day and they would have a good story to write. In the morning there was great excitement when the Princess of Wales arrived with the little princesses, and the band struck up the National Anthem and the bells rang out as the royal party made their way to the annex. In came the Princess, holding a large bouquet in her hands, and the people jostled to see her. So I put a big smile on my face and I swam and dived and promenaded the bottom of the tank with my hands. Then Father slid the tray towards me containing the next and final part of my act. I trod water, picked up a piece of cloth and sank to the bottom, took the already threaded needle and began to sew. At last what Mother had taught me was being put to good use and the Princess was so amused that she threw her bouquet right into the tank.

'Excellent,' I heard Father say, 'patronised by the Royal Family, we'll put that on the next poster.'

At rest time he gave me more tonic, and when I returned to the tank the anticipation began to mount. The bell was sounding every five minutes now, people whistled and cheered and with a last burst of energy I began to turn somersaults as fast as I could. Then the clock chimed and a great roar went up. I had managed 60 hours in the tank.

But when I grasped the side, about to pull myself up, my arms were so weak that my fingers slipped. My sight went dark as if the lights had been dimmed and I felt a tightness around my tail. Something was pulling me under. Perhaps it was the whale. It hadn't gone at all, it was still here. All this time it had been in the water with me and now it had me by its teeth. I let out a shout, my mouth filled with water, and then Billy's arms were around me and pulling me out.

CHAPTER SEVENTEEN

It was several weeks before I recovered from my tank performance and I lay listlessly in bed, waiting for my skin to heal and my strength to return. Mother said it was no wonder that I was weak if I chose to spend three days in a whale tank, but she was happy enough with the money I'd received. I had that odd sensation that sometimes comes after success, when you've done a thing you set out to do and now there's no more to be done. So I didn't mind when Father said he was planning a new show and he wanted Billy and me to swim together again. It would be a leisurely interlude, he said. I wasn't to worry. It would be nothing too taxing and not longer than an hour at a time. The important thing was to build on my success. 'Don't let people forget you, Daisy,' he said. 'Whatever you do now, they will come.'

Father's timing was excellent, because Billy was only too keen to perform again, thanks to Miss Violet Mitchell. Mr Sinclair had had a change of heart – Father said he feared a court case – and she had been rehired as a gymnast in the main hall. My brother couldn't keep his eyes off her, as she swung twice a day from the trapeze in her white satin costume, shouting 'Coo-ee!' before somersaulting through the air. When she had her breaks Billy did everything he could to get Violet's attention. At last he had someone he wanted to appear before and he couldn't wait to get into a tank and show her what he could do. I was glad, for it was thanks to Violet that my brother's love for swimming had returned.

But this was not the only reason for his new enthusiasm. Father wanted us to enact a series of aquatic myths and now Billy had the chance not just to swim but to tell a story. My brother was full of ideas: I could be a nymph helping boats through rough storms, Charlie and Tom-tom being the sailors. I could be a siren drawing men to the rocks with my enchanted singing, or a hideous sea monster with live eels attached to my hair. He wanted to tell the story of Oceanus who ruled the oceans and his sister Thetys who ruled the rivers, and when they married and had three thousand children buckets of small fish would be added to the tank. But Father ruled this out, and so did

Mr Sinclair. It was one thing for a Greek god to marry his sister, they said, but it wasn't the done thing now. Billy was also keen that little Minnie had a part, for she had begun to ask if she could come to the baths. Father liked the idea too; he said my brothers were getting too old to attract much attention and a young girl would be just the thing. But Mother wasn't having any of it and wouldn't let Minnie out of her sight. In some ways I began to feel sorry for my sister, when she complained and cried, 'Why can Daisy go out and not me?' My sympathy didn't last long, however, for she gave me sly pinches when Mother wasn't looking and I was relieved to leave her at home and go to the Aq. I had been replaced in my mother's affections and no success of mine would ever bring back the bond we had once shared. But I had my swimming, I was working with Father and I told myself I didn't care at all.

It was agreed that the show would begin with Neptune, then Venus, and as the days went by the story would darken and the tank would be turned into the underworld to tell the tale of Orpheus and Eurydice. I wasn't happy about this; I didn't mind dressing up and swimming with Billy and my other brothers again, but I didn't like the idea of the underworld. I couldn't quite explain my fear, but I hadn't forgotten the feeling in the whale tank that the sad white monster was pulling me under. I didn't want to be in the mythical realm of the dead, yet every time I made an objection no one listened to me. Didn't I know, asked Father, that by the end of this I could have whatever I desired? Didn't I trust him and hadn't I seen the trunk full of money? Hadn't I said I wanted to go to America? So now, I just needed to perform.

We would not use the whale tank for these shows, for a new whale was on its way from the coast of Labrador; instead we would perform in a specially built square tank. This would be set against the wall in a large room near the annex, with the audience seated in front and unable to walk around the sides. Father would have a canvas passageway built to allow Aq employees to carry in the props, while pipes at either end could let more water in. Billy was excited about the upcoming shows and every day he brought Violet in to see how the set was progressing. They were inseparable now, and I had never seen my brother happier.

After months of preparation, it was opening day. A silk curtain was draped over the front of the tank and it was only when people had taken their seats that this was thrown off to reveal me lying on the bottom like a river sprite. Billy stood on a rock behind me dressed as Neptune, his head and shoulders out of the water, with a flowing white beard and a three-pronged spear. He had wanted to dress Charlie and Tom-tom as bulls and have them sacrificed, but Father had said no, he had seen a mosaic somewhere and he had an idea of how the tableau would look. All we needed was to dress up and look pretty.

Then Billy recited lines from Shakespeare as I stayed there lying on the bottom. He spoke whatever came to mind, as long as it was aquatic and suitably dramatic. 'My bounty is as boundless as the sea,' he cried, and then he lifted the spear. 'Will all great Neptune's ocean wash this blood clean from my hand?' My favourite was from *The Tempest*; I loved the sound of the words as they rolled from my brother's lips: 'Full fathom five thy father lies; Of his bones are coral made; Those are pearls that were his eyes; Nothing of him that doth fade.' There was no knocking on the glass this time; everyone sat still on their seats and when I rose up and we swam a few strokes together it was met with polite applause.

Midway through the first performance Violet arrived to watch. I had just come up for air when I noticed her standing in the shadows near the door to the room. She had her back to me and was standing with Father, wearing the blue cloak she wore in between shows. I thought this was a little strange for she had been unwell and I had been told she had taken a break from performing. I could see Father's face, inclined to one side, listening to whatever it was Violet said. She laid her hand on his arm, dipping her head as he planted a kiss on her forehead, and I was pleased that Violet was already becoming part of our family.

But the next time I came up for air I realised it wasn't her at all. Instead it was a stranger who turned towards me, with a pale white face and ringlet hair, wearing a much prettier cloak than Violet would ever wear.

I was so shocked that I forgot what I was supposed to be doing, until my brother issued instructions and we continued the scene. But I didn't want to sink under the water now; I wanted to keep my eyes and ears on the lady. How did Father know her and where had she come from? I thought of other ladies too, the one with red lips who had come looking for him the day he'd slapped me at the Lambeth Baths, the lady who had linked her arm with his when I arrived at Greenwich Pier, and our first visit to the Aq when I'd thought he was giving a stranger directions down the promenade. Was this the same one or not? The gestures I'd just seen were intimate: a hand on an arm, a kiss on the face. What was she to him and why didn't I know who she was?

That evening she was there as well; I saw her right at the end of our performance, standing between Father and Robert Winkle. She was dressed this time in a fur-collared coat, throwing back her head to drink champagne. She wasn't even watching the show in the tank.

That night when I came home Mother was very anxious. She asked me, as she always did, where Father was and this time I had no idea. For the first time in my life I was as curious and worried as my mother. It stabbed away at me, wondering who the lady was and if I had seen her before. If only he hadn't kissed her. Did he not think I would see, did he not care that everyone else would? Now it was my turn to question why Father had always been so eager to offer swimming lessons to ladies and why he'd hired Miss Mane from Brighton. Was this why Mother hated the baths? It wasn't me she didn't trust, it was Father.

I couldn't bring myself to ask him. I didn't want to admit my fears even to myself. I just wanted the lady to go away and not come back. Perhaps she was a relative, perhaps any day now Father would bring her home and introduce her. Or maybe she was Robert Winkle's friend and not his at all.

I couldn't sleep at all that night; I tossed and turned, unable to rest. Early the next morning, while Mother was giving Minnie breakfast and Father had gone out, I sneaked into my parents' room. I had been thinking about it all night long, who it was that paid for the champagne and the lady's fine clothes. When I pulled the trunk from under the bed and opened the lid I knew what I would find before I saw it: half the money was gone.

Father was waiting when I arrived at the Aq for the second day of our show and he frowned when he saw me. 'Why so late?' he asked.

I didn't reply but I was aware that my fingers trembled as I took off my cloak.

'And why so anxious? Are you coming down with something?'

I shrugged. I had barely slept. All these years I had blamed Mother. I had dismissed her concerns and believed her to be jealous of my success. Now I saw that Father cared for no one but himself. I was his performing seal, and so was Billy.

'Get yourself ready then,' said Father, 'and have a drop of this to calm you down.'

I took the bottle he offered and the drink tasted both bitter and sweet as I tipped it to my mouth.

'Better?' asked Father.

And I was. The effect was so soothing, my breath became slower, my heart no longer rushed, and I took another drink and then another until Father said, 'That's enough. Now remember, you're to lower yourself into the tank feet first and slide down into the scallop shell. Swim over it a few times then stand in it, carefully as it's only made of plaster, and your brothers will lift the shell to the surface.'

So I put on my costume and after the audience had settled themselves into their seats I lowered myself into the tank, plunging down towards the shell. Plenty of fish had been added to the water, as well as two turtles, but they seemed very shy and had gone straight to the bottom, keeping their heads tucked out of sight. When I saw the pearl gleaming there inside the scallop shell it suddenly came to me that I would simply curl up and put my head on it like a pillow. I don't know why I thought of this, but as I got into the shell and made myself small I had such a feeling of tranquillity. I didn't have to think about a thing; I just laid down my head and closed my eyes. I stayed there as a minute passed and then another, savouring that moment before the body and the mind slide into unconsciousness. I thought I heard a shout from outside the tank and I ignored it. Such a relief it was, not to think. I was lying still and yet I felt that I was flying.

I could sense the fish around me, weaving in and out of the shell, and I began to hear them too. They were chattering to each other like children, and when I opened my eyes they seemed to have grown very big and I had shrunk very small. Then they were very small and it was I who was big. I looked down and saw a turtle put out its head and smile at me, and on its back was a water sprite with skin the colour of the sea.

Then Billy was in the tank. He had his hands under my arms and was trying to pull me up. I was laughing at this, only soundlessly, and trying to say he should leave me where I was. As he began to pull me up I felt overcome with dizziness and the fish grew louder, snapping their jaws and rattling their teeth as if to eat me.

'What's wrong with her?' a woman cried, as my brother lifted me out of the tank and I fell against him, shivering.

'She stayed under too long,' said Father. 'That's all. Nothing to worry about.'

Back home that evening he was furious. 'Why did you do that?' he demanded as I lay in bed covered with blankets. 'You know how dangerous it is, if you don't come up for air.'

I tried to tell him that it hadn't seemed dangerous at all, that perhaps I had drunk too much tonic.

'Why did you stay under so long, what were you playing at? Didn't you hear me telling you to come up? Three minutes is the maximum, after that you'll hallucinate. Look at the state of you. I had to cancel this afternoon's show, what do you think of that? And tomorrow you know it's the underworld scene.'

I wanted to say I didn't want to do the underworld scene, but I was too tired to speak.

'Daisy,' Father leaned over me, grabbed tight on my arm, 'I want you back in that tank tomorrow and if you ever, ever…'

He didn't finish his sentence; he didn't say what would happen if I did that again.

'Who is the lady?' I asked.

'What lady?'

'She was there yesterday, standing next to you.' And I knew, by the way he began searching in his pockets and by the look in his eyes, both furtive and challenging, that I was right. She was my father's mistress.

CHAPTER EIGHTEEN

The next day when I arrived at the Aq the tank had been transformed. The floor was painted black and a wooden ceiling had been fitted on the top. To begin with the room would be very well lit, while I walked waist deep in water gathering flowers as if in a meadow. Then once I had been bitten by a viper the tank would be covered with a silk curtain and I'd get out through a trap door while the scene was changed into the underworld. Water would be piped in from either side, filling the tank to the top, and I would dive back in, with Billy dressed as Orpheus.

At ten o'clock, with the room full to overflowing and the tank covered from view, I opened the hatch door and climbed in. I was tired but I knew what I needed to do and soon it would be over. The curtain was removed to show me swimming prettily around, then an eel was sent down through the hatch door and I pretended to be bitten. I lay on the bottom, put my arms by my side and died. I felt the water move as Charlie slid into the tank, allowed him to put a coin into my mouth, and then the lights went off. Under the cover of darkness and with the curtain back in place, I rose up to climb out through the hatch.

I held my hands palms up and gave a strong push at the ceiling. But the hatch door didn't move. Perhaps I hadn't found the right place; maybe it was further to my left. I peered up, but it was too dark to see and so I began to feel my way around the ceiling. But everywhere was solid wood; where had the hatch door gone? I told myself not to worry, if Charlie had just climbed through the hatch then I could too. And after all, any moment someone would open it; they would need to change the scene, to add the black rocks and white fish to inhabit the underworld.

Then I felt the water on either side of me begin to roll and swell, bubbles popping against my skin. They had started to fill up the tank. A light came on in the room and I could see the indistinct figures of people moving on the other side of the curtain, like characters in a shadow puppet show: a man puffing on a cigar, another taking off his hat. It was interval time and the audience were milling around, chatting and stretching their legs. Then I saw a gap in the curtain and pushed myself up against the glass, waving my hand to attract attention. They were filling the tank with water and I was still in it! But no one took any notice; Father was urging them to take refreshments and a band was about to play.

The water swelled still higher and I grew worried now. It was gushing up to my chest and soon it would reach my neck. I hit my fist against the glass and saw one figure move away from the others. I was sure it was the man with the booming voice who had thrown a sovereign into the water the morning I had started my swim in the whale tank. He knew what was happening, I was certain he did, he was peering right at me through the gap in the curtain. Then he smiled and turned away.

Why did no one realise I hadn't come out of the hatch door? Surely they would alert Father? He must have thought I had come out, no one had told him that I hadn't and the attendants were waiting for his instructions.

Then I saw him, a familiar silhouette walking towards me. He had something in his hand, a sandwich perhaps, and he was in the process of taking a bite. And next to him, holding his arm, was the lady with ringlet hair. They stopped with their backs to me just by the gap in the curtain and she laid her head gently on his shoulder. Still he ate his sandwich, gesturing with his other hand to a man in front, pointing to something else. He was making a joke! My father was making a joke and entertaining a lady while I was trapped in a tank.

'Help!' I shouted as loud as I could and desperately now I banged on the glass. But no one heard, such was the noise of the band. I was forced to take a large gulp of air as the water rose above my mouth; soon it would cover my head. Had Father forgotten me, or was he trying to teach me a lesson? I had stayed down too long in the scallop shell and now he was showing me what could happen if I truly ran out of air. I remembered the day at the Lambeth Baths when he'd pushed me under the water and forced me to hold my breath. Just weeks ago when I'd felt pain in my stomach he had made me continue swimming, and when I'd been so exhausted in the whale tank he'd ordered me to get back in. Was he setting me some sort of test? How dare he play with me like this? It was my life that was in his hands; was I nothing to him? Angrily I rose up to the ceiling, searching again for the hatch door. Then the water passed over my head and there was nothing to do but to close my eyes and count. A minute went by and then, so slowly, another. Three minutes had passed and all I could hear was the sound of my own blood rushing in my ears. Just like the fish, I had no way out.

Then boom! My ears were deafened with a noise like the echo of a firing cannon. I felt myself enveloped in a whirlpool; rocks hurtled past, slamming against me, as I was sucked into a mass of water. I tucked my head to my chest, it was like the strongest tide in the world and I had no choice but to go with it. I felt a crack on my head, needles piercing my skin. The glass had burst and I was being sucked through a hole in the tank.

There were screams as the water threw me onto the floor; spectators began to flee in panic, crashing into each other as they made for the door, showered with falling glass. And there I lay like a dead fish on the shore, the floor turning red with my blood.

The glass had been too thin, there had been too much water, something had not been properly secured. The water pipes had been turned on too early, the hatch door had been stuck and the handle had fallen off. I never found out what exactly was the cause.

I was put on a stretcher, taken home in a cab. Billy carried me up the stairs and laid me on the bed while a doctor was called. Little Minnie cried and asked, 'Why is Daisy all cut up?' and I closed my eyes, squeezed them as tight as I could, as the doctor took his tweezers and began to pull out the fragments of glass. 'She will have a scar,' he said as he bandaged up my forehead.

Billy never left my side; he held my hand and wouldn't let go. 'I should have known,' he said, 'I should have realised something was wrong.'

When Father came into the room I refused to speak to him and turned my head to the wall.

The doctor gave me medicine, and for a few hours I slept. But when I woke my heart was racing. I was sure it was morning but the room was dark and there in the shadows was a turtle sitting on the end of my bed. I fell asleep again, dreaming of fish that looked like leopards, and heard the soft voice of my brother whispering, 'Full fathom five thy father lies.'

I woke for the last time just before dawn and lay in bed, thinking clearly now. I had just one thought on my mind: I'd had enough. My performing life was over. I was not going back to the Aq. I would never get in a tank again.

I began to shiver, pulling the blankets around me. Swimming was the only thing I knew. If I left the Aq then what would I do? Could I train other girls to swim, would Billy help me? All I knew for certain was that I needed that money in the trunk before Father spent the rest of it on his mistress.

Two days later, left alone to recover from my injuries, I crept into my parents' room. I kneeled down, pulled the trunk towards me and opened it. There was the remaining money, and the gleaming guineas were mine. I picked up handfuls, each one enough to get me away from London, to start a new life, and I poured them into a purse. I tried not to think about the future, whether I would see my brothers again, if Billy would be able to join me. I would miss this house and this city, the place where I'd lived for so many years and learned to swim and found fame. But whatever happened, I would be in charge now. I didn't need my father. Instead I was taking the money that was rightfully mine and there was only one place I could go: I was running back to Margate.

CHAPTER NINETEEN

The moment I had the money in my purse, I hurriedly packed my clothes and costumes, aware that at any minute someone might return. A door slammed downstairs, I heard the sound of laughter, and I dashed out into the street, hailing a cab just turning into the road. But I didn't even know which station I needed; I had to ask the driver. I had done nothing on my own before; everything had been arranged for me. All I'd had to do was obey. I'd wanted the crowd's applause and Father's approval and so I had done what I'd been told, even when I'd been afraid. But I'd been nothing but his puppet and he'd spent my money on his ladies. He had betrayed Mother and he had betrayed me. I was the one who swam the Thames and dived at the Aq, yet what good was any of that now? The money I had made had gone into his pockets, not mine. This was my nest egg and I was leaving. I was 20 years old and determined to be free.

The cab dropped me at Charing Cross, the station full of wealthy families moving out of London for the summer, nannies herding children along the platform, servants struggling with trunks. I was hungry but the refreshment room was closed and I hadn't thought to bring even an apple with me. I limped a little as I walked, my legs still bruised from my escape from the tank, and it was difficult carrying the bag with my arms so sore. I kept my face down; someone might know me and ask where I was going, but I doubted Father would come after me today. He would never forgive me for running out on him and ruining the next show.

At last I was settled in the carriage; the engine started with a heavy throb and with a blast of the whistle the train pulled off. Two little girls sitting opposite began asking their mother questions, wanting to know how long the journey would be, while beside me an elderly lady fell asleep with her mouth open. I tried to rest as well but it was impossible and as we entered a tunnel I clutched my bag tightly. It was all I had and I was afraid that in the darkness someone would steal it.

When the train arrived at Margate it was early evening and as I left the station and came into the open air I felt like a four-year-old child again. How could I have forgotten the smell of the place, the salty lingering seaweed smell that lifted my heart and told me the sea was near? And the sounds, the clang of the fishing-boat masts and the noise of the seagulls as they shrieked and cackled and laughed? I sped up my pace, no longer limping as I reached the King's Stairs, and there were the sands ahead of me, the very same bathing machines lined up on the shore. It was nearing the end of a long warm day, the tide was out and the sky was periwinkle blue. I came down to the beach and saw a group of children crabbing with buckets under the pier and a solitary man standing in a rock pool, his trousers tucked up to his knees. The sand was pitted with footmarks from the people who had spent their day here, half-collapsed sandcastles decorated with seaweed and shells, fragments of crabs, a forgotten umbrella and a left-behind spade.

Then at last there I was with my first love, the sea. It stretched out as flat as glass and if I could have reached the horizon in a boat then surely I would fall off the lip of the world. I could see so far ahead and all around; there were no fixed landmarks to distract my eyes, no factories or church spires or chimneys, just the sea and the sky and the sails of a distant hoy heading for London. I had that feeling that comes when a person faces the ocean; I was an insignificant nothing and it filled me not with fear but with joy.

The water was calm and strangely green but for a sprinkling of silver from the sinking sun. I sat down on the sand to take off my boots, then held them in my hand as I walked towards the waves, rippling and folding in on themselves. 'Come in,' said the sea, 'how can you resist?' But I did, for I couldn't get in and leave my bag and money on the sand. And how long could I stay here until Father found out, and what would he do when he did?

I stood there until the sun had set, while the seaweed on the beach turned as black as rock and the sea became the truest, deepest blue.

Soon the rats would come scattering onto the beach and later still a smuggler might emerge from a cave; it was not a safe place to be at night. So I left the beach, the boats in the harbour lighting my way back across the sand to town.

I was sure that Auntie Jessie would take me in. She wouldn't turn me away at this time of night. She had never got on with Father – they had quarrelled about everything, and I felt certain I could trust her not to say where I was, at least for now. Then perhaps I could rent my own room, although I didn't know where or how. What would people think of me, a lady all alone? But I didn't care. I had money in my bag and that was enough.

I asked a gentleman the way to Love Lane, where Auntie Jessie rented out her rooms above an eating-house, and when she opened the door for a second she didn't know who I was. Then she gave a cry of surprise and as she held her arms out towards me I gladly returned her embrace.

'Have you come alone, Daisy Mae?' She leaned back, looking over my shoulder.

I nodded, feeling a knot in my throat for no one had called me by that name for a very long time.

'All this way?' she asked. 'Where's your father?'

I didn't answer and Auntie Jessie sighed and beckoned me in.

She didn't ask me any more questions that night; she seemed to understand what might have happened. It was almost as if she'd been expecting me. She gave me a supper of fish and bread and then made up a bed with one of her daughters and bade me good night. But oh, the wind! How could I have not remembered the wind in Margate? It was like sleeping at the bottom of a chimney as it whirled and howled outside. I should have been happy; I had made it this far. I'd no longer be anyone's performing seal. Yet all that night I lay awake next to my sleeping cousin and listened to the wind and thought of my family.

I remembered happy times with Father, all the hours in which he had trained me, how I'd learned to float and swim and dive. He'd been so delighted that day he'd lifted me out of the water when I swam the River Thames. I'd wanted him to be proud of me – surely he had been and maybe he still was. It wasn't his fault the glass had broken; he hadn't known I was trapped in the tank. Perhaps the lady I had seen meant nothing to him and he'd spent my money on something else. Maybe right now he was looking for me. Perhaps when I woke in the morning I should go back. I had been too impulsive, I would have to return.

Early the next day I felt myself drawn out of the house, my costume on under my dress, heading to the ocean. I was pleased to see that the sea was rough, and I took off my clothes, not minding if anyone saw me, and ran towards the water. The sand was sticky beneath my feet as I waded in and then, when I was deep enough, I leaped in.

I swam breaststroke at first, heading out towards the horizon, smiling to myself when a wave approached and I had to sink my head to go through. And that's when I knew this was where I was meant to be, not in a bath or a tank, because the sea is alive and I'd forgotten that. And what a noise it made, a hiss and a spit, a splash and a tinkle, as it held me and caressed me, pushed and slapped, and all the time there I was, secure in the midst of such power.

I was not performing now. I was not in a show; there was no one to watch me. I could do what I wanted. So I swam on, laughing now, riding up the crests before they crashed. The tide was on the turn; the waves were pushing me towards the shore while the ocean was intent on carrying me out. When I felt myself growing tired I turned on my back to rest, watching a cauldron of clouds rushing towards the cliffs. Then at last I returned to shore, aware with every stroke I took that the current that was trying to steal me back. I laughed again, invigorated. I would stay in Margate; I would never go back to Father.

But after I returned to my auntie's house I was spiritless and it was a feeling that didn't lift for many days. I sent a telegram to Billy at the Aq to tell him where I was, but warning him not to breathe a word to anyone at home. The next day he replied that he would join me in Margate, he would do anything I wanted, he would help me organise a show at the Marine Palace Baths. But Violet was pregnant, he said, I would need to wait until she had the baby. I was so happy at this news, to think that my brother would become a father, but as I paced the streets of Margate there was still one question always on my mind: did our father now know I was here?

I was sure Auntie Jessie hadn't told him, but someone else might have spread the news. I needed to take more care. I thought I saw him everywhere, a solitary figure strolling along the pier just after dawn, or standing in the shadows by a street lamp on the corner of Love Lane come nightfall. And when Violet did have her baby and Billy came to join me, then Father could ruin our plans if he chose. He could make sure that no one in Margate would hire us.

The town was even busier than it had been when I was a child: everywhere were lodging houses, inns and hotels, and at bathing time in the morning the foreshore swelled with life as children shrieked and splashed. The streets of Margate, the pier and the promenade, were full of colour and bustle and I knew it was a perfect place to organise a show.

That summer Billy's son was born and they called him Percy. Soon my brother would be on his way to Margate and I began to grow excited by what we could do when he arrived. It would be a new start for us; for the first time Billy and I would decide how to perform and keep the takings for ourselves. But still I could not shake off my constant worry, for whatever we did and however successful our new seaside show, how long would it be before Father appeared to stop us?

CHAPTER TWENTY

I stayed in Margate throughout the summer, helping Auntie Jessie with her rooms. I tried to be as useful as I could, waiting on a succession of single ladies, who plotted excursions over tea, and cleaning up after families who placed their children's salty sandy boots on the windowsills to dry. But I was restless and my money was running out.

One afternoon in September I was strolling aimlessly along the beach near the Harbour Arm when I saw a party of gentlemen in a rowing boat. They were traveling parallel with the shore and making quite a racket, splashing the oars in a drunken fashion. One of them stood up; he had a bottle in his hand and was making a toast. Then another two stood up and the inevitable happened: a gentleman at the back fell in.

I stood quite still for a moment, expecting that they would stop the boat and put out an oar to help, but instead they were paddling round in circles. Was it all a game, I wondered? Hadn't they noticed what had happened, or was the man in the sea a good swimmer? But he couldn't be; I could see him floundering, his head rising and sinking, and from somewhere behind me came the cry of 'He's drowning!'

I had never rescued anyone before, but I had watched my father and Billy countless times and my movements seemed to be instinctive, as without even stopping to take off my boots, I ran to the sea and dived in.

I kept my face high in the water, aiming for the spot where the man had fallen in, and when I saw a patch of bubbles ahead I knew it was air escaping from his clothes. I dived down with my arms outstretched, sweeping my hands from side to side until I found him. The man's hat had come off and I grabbed at his hair, twisting it like a rope in my hand and pulling him to the surface. The water was deep and although the sea was calm I couldn't let him go under again because I might never find him. I could feel him being dragged down by the weight of his clothing, and my own skirts were wrapped tightly around my legs. But the incoming tide would help us; if he would just let me keep hold of him I could drag him to shore.

Then he began to struggle and turned himself around. I lost hold of his hair and his legs entwined themselves so tightly around one of mine that I could barely move. If only I could lose a limb like a starfish, then I would gladly have let go of my leg. I felt a sharp kick from one of his boots and then his hands were on my shoulders and I was conscious of the sheer strength of him as he pushed me down. In order for him to stay up, he would do anything to keep me under. I was locked in an embrace with a drowning man.

Then his hands were around my neck and I felt his whiskers brush against my skin as he forced us both down again. We moved against each other in a terrible dance, cheek to cheek, his arms still round my neck, he trying to get to the surface and I seeking a way to break his hold. I grabbed at his whiskers, as bushy as seaweed, and when I felt one of his hands move I latched onto it with my mouth and bit as hard as I could. The hand went limp, my neck was released, and as we came to the surface I heard myself gasping: we had only just made it in time. I turned on my back, pulling his body up between my legs; at last he had stopped fighting. Then I kicked as hard as I could, heading back to the beach.

It was now that I became aware of the gulls swooping overhead, a boat sounding its horn, even the faint sound of people on the shore. I wondered where the man's friends were – why hadn't they brought the boat to help? Still I kicked out with my legs, using both arms to keep his body on mine. He was a young man, I thought, strong and determined. How happy his family would be that they hadn't lost him to the sea. I looked down at him, grateful that he was no longer struggling, that he trusted me now. And that was when I realised that something was wrong. He was lying against me as still as a corpse. I sensed the water growing shallower and I stood up, struggling with the weight of him, unable to bear what would come next.

Then up ran the foolish gentlemen from the rowing boat. 'Dob!' they shouted, 'Dob McGee!' Relieving me of my burden, they took him by the arms and legs and dragged him to shore.

'Put him face down!' said one as they laid him on the sand.

'No, on his side!' said another.

I looked down at the man they called Dob McGee, expecting his skin to be blue with foam around his mouth. But instead his face looked strangely restful, he even had colour in his cheeks, and I fell to my knees, pulling frantically at his clothing until his neck and chest were free. I saw his eyelids tremble, his nostrils twitch, and when I put my face to his mouth I felt a gentle salty breath.

The people on the beach were shouting, asking for blankets and dry clothing, if anyone had any spirits. A few moments later a man was kneeling on the sand binding Dob's hand with a handkerchief and I watched as the cloth turned blood red.

Someone threw a blanket around my shoulders and I became conscious of my soaking clothes, my boots full of water. It was a sunny day but I was shaking as if it were the middle of winter.

'Bring smelling salts!' a man cried.

'Get the snuff,' said another.

I didn't know if they were talking about Dob or me, but when I looked down at him again he was awake. His face was turned towards me and there I was, staring into a pair of deep-set eyes of such a strange colour I couldn't decide if they were brown or green. Then, as I was looking at him, he winked.

'Dob!' shouted one of his friends, and as he looked around at the people on the beach, he tried to sit up.

'Don't,' I told him, 'don't try to get up too soon.'

He turned his head to the other side, began coughing fit to burst, then he lifted his hands and flexed his fingers. He began patting himself all over, his chest, arms and legs, as if trying to find where he was injured.

'You fell in the sea,' I told him, 'but you're fine.'

He looked at me with a puzzled expression now. Did he know what had happened and where he was, had he understood what I'd said, was he even aware that he'd winked at me? Then he pushed himself up to a seated position and his friends gathered round, slapping him on the shoulders, offering brandy, saying what a fright he'd given them. But Dob didn't reply, he was still patting at his coat pockets until at last he brought out a sodden notebook and brandished it in his unbandaged hand. 'Ruined!' he said. 'Utterly ruined.'

Was he mad? I thought. A few minutes ago he had nearly drowned in the sea and now he was worried about a notebook! Then he fumbled inside his waistcoat and this time he brought out a pocket watch. 'It's stopped,' he said, looking up at me and shaking it in his hand. 'Hmm... it must have stopped at the precise moment you rescued me. Look,' he shook the watch again, 'a quarter past two, the moment we met.'

The police arrived with a stretcher then, followed by dozens of running children. 'Wait!' cried Dob as the crowd pushed me to one side and that was the last thing I heard before they wheeled him away.

CHAPTER TWENTY-ONE

The very next day when I came out of my auntie's home on Love Lane, there was Dob McGee sitting on a wall. He was playing a mouth organ, sliding it across his lips, and on the cobbles sat a cat, watching as if enjoying the tune. It was 'My Bonnie Lies Over the Ocean' and it was such a sad lament to bring back a loved one that as he reached the chorus I stood there as mesmerised as the cat. I wondered how he had found me so soon. Was this really the man who just yesterday had tried to push me under the sea in terror for his life? Now here he was, as fit as a fiddle.

I closed my auntie's door, and Dob jumped down from the wall. He wore a coat the colour of wheat and as he landed on the cobbles it waved apart to show an emerald vest. His hat was new and so were his boots; he looked like a gentleman of some means. But although he was smartly dressed everything about him was a little rakish and a little askew. His necktie was carefully knotted but lay to one side, and when he took off his hat there was a loose lock of hair hanging over his forehead. He saw me look at the hand that held the mouth organ and then my gaze fell to the other, tucked away in his waistcoat pocket, and I remembered what I had done and the handkerchief on the beach red with blood.

'I'll survive,' said Dob. 'Only the doctor says I am not to play the piano for a while.' He laughed to show that this wasn't something he did. 'Please,' he said and held out his elbow, 'will you walk with me? I owe you my life.'

It was as casual as that. I took his arm and off we went down Love Lane.

'So,' he said, as we turned into the market place, busy with holiday-makers buying supplies, 'you ran away from the Aq?'

I stopped, surprised, and released his arm.

'One of my friends recognised you. Don't you think I know who you are? Daisy Belle! The diver who proved the equality of woman-hood! I saw you once, at the Lambeth Baths with Webb.'

I nodded; that seemed an age ago.

'But I was so far from the pool I didn't see your face.'

I waited to see what else he would say, anxious that he might make a comment on my costume or some trivial thing that would make me wish I'd never agreed to walk with him.

'Your stroke I remember, a very fierce breaststroke, far more skilful than Webb's.'

I nodded, because this was true, and when he offered his arm again I took it.

'I heard something about an exploding tank at the Aq. Did they not feed you there?'

'Sorry?'

'Were you so hungry yesterday that you had to bite off the tip of my thumb?'

I laughed then, I couldn't help it. 'It was only because you wouldn't let go of me.'

He smiled too and we stopped and exchanged the oddest of looks. There we were, standing in Margate's market square, surrounded by people in their holiday best when only hours before we'd been under the sea battling for our lives. I thought of his arms round my neck, the strength of him carrying me under. How I'd pulled him up between my legs and nestled his head beneath my chin as I'd set off back to shore. I could still feel the weight of him, the fear when I thought he was lost.

'I heard you were badly cut at the Aq,' said Dob. 'You must be very brave.'

I shrugged.

'You have a scar,' he said, and as he leaned closer I felt heat rise through my body and I could smell his cologne, a mix of lime and rum.

Then a fiddler ran by screeching out a tune, a donkey cart came careering towards us, and we resumed walking up Duke Street to the pier. Everyone on the parade seemed to know Dob and several times we had to stop as he answered questions. Yes, he was fine. No, a little water never did anyone any harm. Yes, indeed this was the lady that had saved him. Not once did he show any shame at having almost drowned or having been rescued by a lady. Instead, he had turned it into a triumph. And I could see, as we continued heading east-ward out of town, that Dob was the type of man other men wanted to impress and women wanted to be noticed by. He seemed to draw people to him, to make their voices a little louder and their expressions brighter. And all the time, even when he was standing still, he never stopped moving, his hand drumming on a hip, fingers jiggling in a pocket, boots tapping on the cobbles.

He told me he was from Manchester where his father was a doctor; he'd had a carefree life until his mother Hettie had died and then he'd moved south. 'I thought I'd become a vet,' he said, 'so I went to London to be a student. But I had a terrible secret…'

'Yes?' I looked at him a little worriedly.

'I hated the profession! So then I became a sports journalist.'

'A sports journalist?' I laughed. 'And you don't know how to swim!'

He looked a little bashful. 'I think I may have found someone who could teach me. I was thrown in the canal as a child and it was enough to put me off for life.' But he'd loved sports since he was little and had often snuck away from home to watch a fight in the street. His first ambition had been to be a boxer. Did I know, he asked, what it was like to have a childhood ambition?

I nodded; of course I did.

'When I was ten years old I was set to fight an older boy who was the terror of the area. It took two days for the winner to be decided.'

'And it was you?'

'It was. Father wasn't amused. It wasn't manly to organise a fight in a field, and I was banished to the top of the house and put in solitary confinement for a week. I didn't even get the chance to patrol the neighbourhood,' said Dob with a smile. 'I was a hero and an exile all at the same time. If that's fame, I thought, I will have no more of it!'

And we laughed then, how we laughed, as we started to climb the pathway up the cliff.

'Why do they call you Dob?' I asked.

'My middle name is Robert, and my *nom de plume* is 'Robert the Devil'! The report I wrote yesterday was ruined. They will not be happy with me back in London.'

So that was why he had been so upset, I thought, as we reached the top of the cliff where ripening corn rippled in the breeze. It was a drowsy autumn day; below us the sea shimmered like a new coin, the beach a curve of untouched sand. Dob stared out to the ocean, then he picked up a stone and dropped it lazily off the cliff and when he turned to face me his voice was soft. 'I could have stayed there forever, you know, down in that sea yesterday, being held by you.'

We looked at each other in silence then and I knew at that very minute that we were linked, Dob and I. A current ran between us, and wherever one of us went the other would follow. My brother Billy would like him, I thought, and Violet too. He couldn't swim but he was a sports journalist, he knew our world. He knew what it was to compete and to race, to try to be the best.

'What were you celebrating in the boat yesterday?' I asked.

Dob smiled, jangling some coins in a pocket. 'An engagement.'

'Oh?' My face fell and I turned away, ready to walk back down the cliff.

'My brother is to marry,' said Dob. 'He has found true love, our mother would have been delighted. Whereas I...' He took his mouth organ out of his pocket and began to tap it against his leg. 'I am still searching. So, what is there here for you in Margate?'

'It's my home,' I told him. 'It's where I was born.'

'But what will you do, now you're not at the Aq?'

He sounded very interested about what I had planned and for a moment I wanted to tell him all my fears and dreams, how I'd left London and didn't know what I would do next. But I couldn't, we had only just met. 'I thought I might do a show here.'

Dob shook his head as if this wasn't good enough. 'Is that what your father wants?'

I didn't answer; what did my father have to do with this, why was he asking about him? 'It's my decision,' I said, 'not his. I've run away.'

Dob smiled. 'Ah, an independent girl. But what will you do? You're a champion swimmer. The mermaid of London. The naiad of England! You could do anything you put your mind to. Surely there is something you'd like to do?'

And I thought, he understands me. He admires my drive. It was fate that brought us together and allowed me to rescue him. If I hadn't been on the beach, if I hadn't left Father and been here in Margate, then would Dob be standing here now?

'What do you want most in the world?' he asked. 'Fix your mind on it and you will get it.'

I smiled a little sadly. 'You can't have everything you want in life.'

Dob laughed. 'Why not?' Then he winked at me and played a few chords of 'My Bonnie'. 'This island is too small for you. You've done the baths; you've done the Thames and the Aq. What's next? Have you ever thought of America? They are mad on swimming over there.'

'Are they?' I asked, as if it were nothing to me. But America had been my dream for a long time. Father had promised I could go and he had lied, and as I set off following Dob down the cliff I wondered: had I rescued him or was he going to rescue me?

CHAPTER TWENTY-TWO

Nine months after we met, Dob and I set sail for New York. I had remained in Margate since the day I'd pulled him from the sea, while he had returned to London. Billy had joined me, along with Violet and their baby Percy, and together we rented lodgings. We kept ourselves busy, Billy and I, with seaside shows, plunging twice a day from the head of the pier and displaying our skills at the Marine Palace Baths. Father knew where we were, but he had not come after us. Instead he was pretending he did not care. He was certain, said Billy, that in time his children would come back to him.

Mother was aghast that my brother had not married the mother of his child and one evening while Violet was putting Percy to sleep I asked her about this.

'Why would we marry?' she replied. 'I don't want to put up with things the way my ma did.'

A part of me agreed with her; I didn't want to end up jealous and fearful like my mother, but then that had been Father's fault, not hers. 'What did she have to put up with?' I asked.

'Everything,' said Violet. 'He wouldn't even put jam on his own bread. Men change when they marry. They woo and pamper you, then they turn into a husband.'

I looked at little Percy, asleep on his parents' bed. He was growing into a restless child, wanting to walk before he could crawl, to argue before he could talk. But now here he was, as peaceful as anything, and I wondered if I would ever have a child. I don't know where the thought came from, because I couldn't swim if I had a baby, so what was I thinking of? Yet the more I looked at his soft, sleeping face the more I felt a yearning for one.

It was difficult to be apart from Dob but he sent me weekly telegrams, had flowers delivered to my door, showered me with flattery and praise and made me feel I was the centre of his world. The times we were together were fleeting but this made them even sweeter, the trips he made to Margate and the evenings we shared on the promenade. I looked forward to these visits with the excitement of a child, eager to tell him how I was, to answer his questions on my swims. How big was the crowd that had watched that day, how much had they been willing to pay?

Then Dob's father died and Dob inherited his estate, and when he asked me to marry him I sealed my reply with a kiss. Despite what Violet had said about marriage, and despite my mother's life, I knew that Dob was different. And after we had married, then we would make the journey to New York. There were plenty of opportunities in America, said Dob, he already had contacts in the sporting world and I could take my pick from any number of women I wanted to swim against. This was what I wanted, he asked, wasn't it? And indeed it was, for I had not forgotten the day I had nearly swum against Emily Parker in the Thames.

Only once did I hear from my parents during this time. Father sent a telegram. He must have realised our performances were a success and that we were not after all coming back to London. The telegram bore just three words: All is forgiven. And I was angry because it was Father who should have been asking for forgiveness. I had done nothing wrong but take the money that was already mine. I heard he had left the Aq and was back at the Lambeth Baths, but without his daughter or eldest son the crowds were far smaller than they once had been and I was pleased about that.

'You wouldn't go back to him, would you?' asked Dob.

'Of course not,' I replied, although sometimes at night I did dream of such a thing, that we were back to how we once had been, swimming together again. But I was stubborn and so was Father, and Dob said, 'Good, because he doesn't have your best interests at heart.'

We had a quiet wedding at Auntie Jessie's house. Billy gave me away and I thought of Mother and how she used to say, 'What man will want you?' But she was wrong, a man had wanted me, and he had wanted me as a swimmer. I would have liked Mother to have been at the wedding, but she would not have come without Father and this was my day. I didn't want him there to cause a scene. Auntie Jessie was sad about this and begged me to tell my parents, but Dob supported me; we would keep this marriage to ourselves.

He gave me a plain gold ring with our initials and the date engraved inside, along with the time we had met, a quarter past two. Once his friends had congratulated the groom and we had cut the cake, I couldn't wait to change into my travelling clothes and be gone. Dob had arranged the tour; he would be my manager now, and he'd advised me to use my maiden name. 'That is what people know you by,' he said. 'Let them still call you Miss Daisy Belle.' Billy was happy to take a back seat from making arrangements; he was concentrating on his new family now.

Auntie Jessie was there to bid us goodbye when we left for Liverpool. She helped us load our luggage onto the train and then she slipped a small flask of brandy into a pocket of my holdall, saying, 'You never know when you might need it if you get seasick.' I laughed and told her I was a swimmer, I would never get seasick.

Little Percy was excited, although he wasn't quite old enough to appreciate the adventure. But he was beginning to speak now and he knew three words, 'mama', 'papa', and 'America!' He couldn't wait to start exploring the ship; he was a child full of questions just as I had been, inspecting the wash basin and the round windows, turning the electric light on and off, struggling to get up into his mother's bed.

Dob had taken two second-class cabins but if things went well, he said, we would be coming back in a first-class stateroom. The ship was magnificent, with funnels and sails and fluttering flags, and as we stood on the deck to bid England farewell Dob played his mouth organ and I linked my arm in his, eager to start our new life.

But while we were told it would take ten days to reach America, it felt like a hundred to me. Everyone else was able to get up and walk the deck, to play cards and leapfrog, to have their meals and enjoy themselves, but from the moment we set sail I was confined to bed miserable with nausea. I couldn't understand why Dob, who feared the water, fared so well. Perhaps it was because I was happy within the sea but not riding on top of it; if only they could throw me overboard, I thought, I would swim to New York instead.

My husband was very patient during my sickness; he didn't press me for anything. And I felt sorry for him, because this was not the way our honeymoon should have been.

A kind stewardess said I would be fine by Monday, but Monday came and went and there I was, still sick on my berth. 'What can I fetch you?' she asked and I could think of just one thing – if only she could fetch me land. I lay there holding myself while the ship pitched and rolled, the sea outside the porthole bespattered with foam, the waves sending thundering blows to the sides of the ship. By day I listened to people hurrying to and fro, shouting and singing snatches of songs, heard the clash and clang of dishes, the urgent orders for food. Then at night while Dob slept I listened to the sounds of scrubbing and the occasional foghorn that drowned out everything else.

After a week, the ship's doctor paid a visit and urged me to come up on deck or I'd be in no fit state to do anything else. I struggled into my clothes and Dob helped me along the passage up to the promenade. Oh, the fresh air and the sight of the sea! I didn't know why I had stayed in my cabin so long, as I sat on the deck with a rug wrapped around me and the great ocean all my own, watching the last hour of light over the Atlantic. A steward bought me a hot drink and asked if I were a stowaway, for no one had seen me on the voyage at all. No, I told him, I'm Daisy Belle and I'm going to America to swim. I was quite proud of myself, certain from everything Dob had said that a warm welcome was waiting, and I was happy to leave the seaside shows behind.

The next day I woke feeling refreshed and I was up on deck along with everyone else as we started to enter the harbour and steam towards the island of New York. I took my husband's arm; our married life had not started as it should and now in America it would.

'Where is Sandy Hook?' Dob asked a steward.

'Why, you've missed it sir.' The steward gestured behind us. 'It's that hook of land at the tip of New Jersey.'

'What is Sandy Hook?' I asked.

'It's where you'll be swimming from,' said Dob.

'It is?'

Dob laughed, 'Yes, from Sandy Hook to Rockaway in New York.'

I smiled and put my face to the breeze, surveying a waterway as vast and busy as the Thames. We passed a tall lighthouse and then ahead of us was a line of sandbanks and church steeples rising into the sky. I glanced at my brother standing next to me; he was wearing his best suit and looked healthy and ruddy from our voyage. 'Here we are,' said Billy, putting his arm round my shoulder, 'this is it, little tadpole: America.'

CHAPTER TWENTY-THREE

When we stepped off the boat a dozen reporters were waiting on the wharf, surrounded by passengers rushing to collect their belongings and hurrying to be reunited with loved ones. 'Aha,' said a man at the centre of the group, 'the celebrated swimmers from England! Mr Richard Fitzgerald, pleased to make your acquaintance.' He wore alligator shoes and a waistcoat that dazzled the eye, and in his mouth was the largest cigar I had ever seen. 'You must call me Dickie,' he said, pausing to spit on the ground, as all American men seemed to do. Then he held out his hand, saying he would take us in charge and escort us to our hotel. But first we needed to answer the reporters.

'Miss Belle!' called a short man, a camera clutched against his chest. 'What do you think of this country?'

'Oh,' I said, 'I have only just arrived, but I think everything looks... so bright and cheerful.'

The reporter laughed. 'How funny do you talk!'

And I thought, it is not me who talks funny, it is you. I couldn't believe I had come all this way to hear people speaking this strange sort of English.

'Miss Belle!' cried another reporter. 'Can you really remain in the water an entire day?'

I was about to reply when Dob answered for me, 'She can remain in the water three whole days, as she did at the Royal Aquarium. And mind you include the nights as well!'

'Without being tired?' asked the reporter.

'Certainly,' said Dob, 'if someone watches and keeps her awake when she feels drowsy.'

He smiled at me and I smiled back, though I felt a little confused. Dob had never seen me at the Aq, we hadn't known each other then; and it wasn't true, no one had had to keep me awake.

'I could stay in the water floating and swimming on my back for a week,' I told the reporter, 'if I wanted to.'

He chuckled and scribbled in his notebook. 'Don't you get cold?'

'No,' I told him, 'I never feel cold in the water.'

141

'But where do you get the muscle from?' He raised his eyebrows and looked me up and down. 'A pretty young girl like you?'

I pushed up a sleeve and flexed my right arm. 'Do you see,' I asked, 'what a muscle I've got?'

'That's enough,' said Dob, moving to stand in front of me.

But Dickie Fitzgerald was delighted with my gesture and so were the journalists, who began to shout out more questions.

'What do you think about swimming from Sandy Hook?' asked one, 'when you don't know the currents and there's only a one in a million chance you'll make it?'

I tried not to show my surprise, that he'd known about my intended swim before I did. So I kept my face calm and looked him in the eye. 'I can do it. If I set my mind to it.'

'Can he swim?' asked the reporter, pointing at little Percy who was struggling to get down from Violet's arms.

'Why of course he can,' replied Billy, taking his son and lifting him up in the air. 'He can swim nearly as well as I could at that age.'

'So the science runs in the family?'

Billy smiled. 'The fondness for water is hereditary.'

I caught my breath then, for he sounded so like our father and we were in America now, I didn't want to think about him.

'Mr Belle!' cried one of the reporters, turning his attention to my brother and firing off a barrage of questions. What was his weight, his height, his fastest time? Which stroke did he prefer, who did he intend to beat in America?

'Gentlemen,' said Dob at last, 'I think we'll have to leave the rest of this enjoyable chat for later.'

'One more question for Miss Belle!' shouted the man with the camera.

Dob put up his hand to cut him off. 'She is tired.'

'I don't mind,' I said.

'I'm sure you don't,' said Dob, lowering his voice. 'But perhaps you could be more ladylike.'

He spoke so gently that it took me a moment to realise what he'd said. I felt my face flush as the words sank in, hoping the journalists hadn't heard. What did he mean? I was as ladylike as I knew how.

'One final question for Miss Belle!' implored a reporter standing at the back.

I smiled and waited; whatever Dob said I would be polite and reply. He would ask me about my diet and training regime, he would want to verify the length I'd swum in the Thames, or the height of my dive at the Aq. 'Yes?' I asked.

'Your hair, Miss Belle. However do you curl it like that?'

Then out we were on the streets on the way to our hotel and I forgot about the reporters, eager to take everything in: the shop windows, the people in the park, the traffic on Broadway. But New York had a dry choking heat that was like being smothered in blankets and soon I was desperate to reach our hotel. Lunch was laid out for us, cakes and buns, huge pears and oranges, jugs of creamy milk and plates of fried ham. How the Americans loved their ham, they seemed to have it morning, noon and night, and Percy was overjoyed with the feast.

'Mr Fitzgerald's very friendly,' said my brother, peeling an orange. 'I like him.'

'So does your sister,' said Dob.

I saw the way that Billy looked at my husband and I glanced away, not wanting to see the dislike in his eyes. I'd exchanged barely two words with Dickie Fitzgerald. I had demonstrated neither like nor dislike, I had simply been civil. Then Dob laughed and passed me a slice of cake and I decided that my husband meant nothing by his words. Billy had been wrong to take offence on my behalf. And perhaps I had been over-familiar with Dickie Fitzgerald. I didn't know the ways of Americans; I should not have pushed up my sleeve. Dob was looking out for me and that was only natural.

That night we shared a bed for the first time. In Liverpool we had stayed in one room with Billy and his family, while on the ship I had been ill. But now we were alone. Dob had been a gentleman since the day we'd first met, he had done nothing that my mother would have frowned upon and that was why I had trusted him. I was excited now as I undressed and got into bed, full of anticipation of the night to come. But then Dob turned off the lights, saying it was better that way, and I was surprised; did he not want to see me? I felt the bed sag under his weight, and I waited for him to join me, to hear the sweet words he had spoken in Margate. I felt the roughness of his whiskers, the heat of his body on mine. And yet all the time he moved above me he spoke not a single word. Then it was over and the only sound inside the darkened room was the tick-tick of a clock.

I lay there for a long time afterwards, staring at the ceiling while Dob fell asleep. I listened to the noises of New York, horses' hooves fading as they passed along the street outside and the sudden piercing sound of a clarinet. It seemed to me that I was as far away from my husband as a woman could possibly be, and that there had been no love between us at all.

The following week Billy and I gave a small exhibition intended mainly for the press. It was in a sizeable pool in the east of the city, and there were quite a few ladies in the audience, with powder all over their faces, necks and arms, which Violet and I thought very strange. Dickie Fitzgerald introduced me as having come all the way from England, which drew great applause, and the people cheered even more when they saw me emerge in a sailor suit. It was Dob's idea: I was to plunge into the water, unfasten my clothes at the bottom, and reappear on the surface wearing a simple shirt and black silk drawers. How my mother would hate this, I thought, as I bowed to acknowledge the cheers, to think I was undressing in the water for everyone to see! But that didn't matter, I didn't care. I was in America now and if this is what they loved then I would give it to them. And then I would swim.

CHAPTER TWENTY-FOUR

For the next few weeks we performed all over New York and each time the reception was even better than the last. At the city's Natatorium we were introduced as champion swimmers of the world; by the time we arrived at a bathhouse on the Hudson River we were champion swimmers of the planet. The Americans were an exuberant audience and the applause was not scattered as it was in England, but long and almost continuous. They were thrilled to see Billy devouring sponge cakes and smoking a pipe, and Dickie Fitzgerald laughed and said, 'Pshaw! If a man can eat, drink and smoke under water during this awful hot weather then why come to the surface and be roasted?' But the Americans seemed to find my performance even more fascinating, as I propelled myself through a hoop, dived for pearls, and changed out of my sailor suit.

We visited a swimming school and sat in the gallery to watch a lady called Miss Bennett teaching girls to swim. Her pupils gathered by a flight of steps, all ages and sizes, dressed in brightly coloured costumes from rose pink to vivid scarlet, before running fearlessly into the water. Then I saw the most wonderful thing: a mother and daughter swimming together like a duck with her duckling. I glanced at Billy and he raised his eyebrows in reply; neither of us could ever imagine our mother doing such a thing. Miss Bennett reminded me a little of Father, the way she introduced her pupils, and when she told the crowd that young women were more likely to catch a husband by saving his life than by spending his dollars Dob laughed the loudest of all.

Finally came a girl who swam what they called 'the prayer', holding her clasped hands above her head. It was said to be a useful style for steamboat collisions, for the swimmer could pray for help while paddling forward. I didn't think it would be much use myself, but again Billy and I exchanged looks; perhaps we would use this in our routine as well.

'She seems very strong,' I said, still watching the praying lady in the water, admiring the taut muscles of her arms.

'She is,' said Dob, 'that's Sarah Rosenheim. She has just challenged you to a swim at Atlantic City next week.'

Why hadn't he mentioned this earlier? For the first time in my life I'd be swimming against a woman like me. I craned forward to get a better look; she certainly cut a fine figure as she got out of the pool and I could see she was a favourite with the crowd. But could she race, was she fast and strong enough to beat me? There was a murmuring among the spectators then, I could sense a new excitement in the air as this time a man appeared at the top of the steps. He took his position at the far edge of the pool, and as he flexed his arms and rolled his shoulders, I felt the oddest flutter in my chest. Then a voice called for quiet. 'Ladies and gentlemen! Put your hands together for Johnnie Heaven!'

I sat bolt upright in my seat. Had I really travelled across the ocean only to see the man I had once swum with at the Lambeth Baths? I watched as he dived into the water and set off across the pool. I saw the way he reached forward with his right hand as if to catch something and then drew himself up and over. His eyes were closed, just as they had been that morning at the baths when I'd slipped down into the water to join him. I remembered his broad back rising and falling and how I had sped up my stroke, about to overtake him when Mrs Peach had turned on a light. That had been the day I'd first wanted to see more of the world outside my father's swimming kingdom, and now here I was in America.

'Like the look of him, do you?' asked Dob.

I didn't answer; it was the man's swimming I was admiring and why shouldn't I?

'Careful,' said my husband and he put out one arm, resting it between the rail and my chest. 'If you lean any further you'll fall in.'

'Did you ever see such an all-fired sight?' exclaimed a voice from behind. 'He's certain to cross your English Channel this time.'

I turned around to see a gentleman chomping on a cigar. 'Has he tried it before?' I asked, for I had not heard Johnnie Heaven's name since that morning at the baths.

'He sure has,' replied the gentleman. 'Four years ago. He lasted a whole six hours. Last year he gave up in terrible weather.'

I returned to watching Johnnie Heaven in the pool. He looked like he could swim all day and I admired his perseverance. He had set his heart on something and had failed, but now he was trying again.

'Shall I introduce you?' asked Dickie Fitzgerald when the swim was over and I was clapping along with everyone else.

I looked around for Dob but he had left his seat to talk to a reporter and so I allowed Dickie to lead me down from the gallery. We walked along crowded corridors, past shivering girls with their chaperones, and I kept my eyes out for my rival Sarah Rosenheim, hoping to catch a glimpse of her. Then we came to an open door and Dickie gestured inside. Johnnie Heaven was sitting on a wooden bench, a towel looped around his shoulders like a scarf, both arms resting on his knees. He had a compact figure, more so than I had remembered, with fine brown curly hair plastered against his forehead. How dark his eyes were, how fetching were the freckles high up on his cheeks. He saw me at the doorway and he smiled with such a cheeky expression that even though I knew I shouldn't, I walked in.

'I saw you swim,' I said, feeling foolish now as I heard the door close behind me. He didn't remember me and why should he?

'Why thank you, ma'am.' He smiled again but stayed exactly where he was and I wasn't sure what to make of this. Did I want him to stand because I had entered the room?

I'd heard he wanted to try the Channel, I said. I was from England and I'd like to do it myself. I wanted to wish him good luck. Johnnie Heaven looked up and I felt his eyes like a lighthouse letting out a beam; perhaps he did remember me.

'Do you swim, ma'am?'

'Yes, I do.'

There was a scuffling noise then from under the bench and a young child crawled out, his shorts covered in dust. 'Oh Moses!' Johnnie Heaven rolled his eyes. 'I told you to stay outta sight, kiddo. We're playing hide and go seek.' He laughed and picked the boy up, tickling him on the stomach. 'See this lady here,' he said, 'she's a swimmer. And this here is my nephew. He wants to be a swimmer too.'

'Are you strong?' asked the boy.

'Yes,' I told him. 'I am exceedingly strong.'

'Who taught you to swim?'

'My father,' I faltered for a second. 'Professor Belle.'

'Ah,' said Johnnie Heaven, 'the Lambeth Baths. Of course. I swam there once myself... So you must be Daisy Belle. And what swims will you be doing over here?'

'Atlantic City,' I told him. 'I shall be racing Sarah Rosenheim. And then I shall swim from Sandy Hook to Rockaway.'

Johnnie Heaven gave a low whistle. 'No one has ever managed that crossing.'

I laughed. 'Are you issuing me a challenge?'

'Daisy!'

I whirled around to see Billy standing at the open doorway with Dickie Fitzgerald. 'Dob's looking for you.'

I became conscious then of what I was doing, standing unaccompanied in a changing room with a half-dressed man.

'Your husband?' asked Johnnie Heaven, pulling slowly at the towel around his neck.

'Yes,' I said, aware that my face was uncomfortably hot.

Then Dob was at the doorway too, and Dickie was introducing them. 'This is the fella you've just seen in the pool, our Channel hopeful.'

My husband made a curt gesture from the waist and Johnnie Heaven laughed. 'I ain't a Lord, you don't need to bow to me.'

Then Dob scowled and said it was time to go.

That night in our hotel room as I sat before the mirror letting down my hair I knew my husband was angry. I should not have gone to meet Johnnie Heaven alone, Dob was jealous and I had annoyed him.

'How very slow you are to undress,' he said, as he lay on the bed watching me. 'You are very quick to remove your sailor suit in the water, not so quick when your husband is waiting for you.'

'The sailor suit was your idea.' I put down my brush, trying to keep my tone light.

'Yes, but you didn't need to have agreed to it so readily.'

'But I did it to please you,' I objected, standing up to face him. 'You said it would be good for the show and I agreed.'

Dob laughed, a mirthless sound. 'You are very keen to please men, aren't you Daisy? Well then, are you coming to bed?'

I looked at him, startled by the coldness in his voice. I had worn the sailor suit to please my husband, and yet here he was looking at me like this.

CHAPTER TWENTY-FIVE

A week later we headed south to Atlantic City and it would have been a pleasant train journey if only Dob had not been so sullen. He had barely spoken a word since we boarded, except to criticise my hat and complain about the heat. Perhaps, I thought, it was the weather that had spoiled his mood. He had wanted us to come to America, it had been his idea, and now we were here nothing seemed to meet with his approval, including me.

'Is she fast, Sarah Rosenheim?' I asked.

Dob scratched at his whiskers. 'Would you be racing her if she were not?'

'I wonder what she's like?'

'You are not to speak to her,' he said, 'you're not here to make friends but to beat her.'

I shifted in my seat with impatience; surely I could be friends with someone and still race against them. 'What is the wager?' I asked.

He raised his eyebrows but didn't reply.

'Is it large?'

'A thousand dollars.'

I sat back, shocked. A thousand dollars! We both knew he had no such sum of money should I lose.

'We're in America,' said Dob, 'we've come to win.'

And I thought, *we*? It was I who was racing, not him.

The next morning we joined Dickie Fitzgerald on the beach and as we walked along the city boardwalk, past the restaurants and fancy hotels, I could almost have been in Margate. Everywhere were holidaymakers, strolling along to see and be seen. We saw a woman in a wheeled chair being pushed by a laughing man and Violet said she had half a mind to hire one too. But the further on we walked and the more I looked at the sea the less carefree I became. It was not a good day to swim, the surf was rolling in and all the waves were capped with white.

A small crowd had gathered around Sarah Rosenheim on the pier and she turned round as I approached. 'Daisy,' she said, as if we were in the habit of meeting like this, and she offered her hand with a firm shake.

'Pleased to meet you,' I said.

Sarah laughed. 'You are just so quaint!'

'Now then, ladies.' Dickie Fitzgerald cleared his throat and spat on the ground. 'We've got everything well fixed, this sea will blow over in a while and then we'll start on the second fire of the cannon. You are to dive from there—' he pointed at two planks jutting out over the side of the pier. 'Then you swim back and forth in view of the shore. When you get to the buoy, that's when you swim back. Five miles either way.' He rubbed his hands together and spat again. 'Now girls, neither of you must lay a hand on anything for support… and don't you even put as much as a tip of a toe to the bottom.'

We both laughed; we would be out in the sea and it was unlikely that if we put our foot down we would touch the bottom.

Then Sarah took off her cloak and so did I. I caught sight of her sloping shoulders and the way her suit was cut off at the arms and knees.

'Are you ready?' she asked, looking me up and down. 'In that cumbersome outfit of yours?'

'Why of course I am,' I told her. 'And if you ever come to London you'll need a more ample bathing costume than that.'

Sarah laughed. 'Oh, they are very particular over the pond are they?'

I was about to answer, enjoying the banter, already thinking of what I would say next, when Dob muttered 'Daisy' in a warning voice. He had told me not to talk to her. Perhaps he was right, I thought, as he left the pier to take his place on the judges' boat. Talking with Sarah might distract me from the challenge. So I held my tongue and looked out at the sea and at the waves slapping at the foundations beneath us. Then two men approached, each with a bucket, and asked if we were ready to be greased. I flinched as they began applying the lotion to my legs, rubbing it in as if I were a goose at Christmas.

'Porpoise oil and lard,' said Dickie Fitzgerald. 'Don't you know it? Didn't you use it in the Thames?'

I shook my head.

'It will keep you warm, and ward off the sharks.'

I laughed a little nervously; no one had mentioned any sharks.

'How was the Thames?' asked Sarah Rosenheim, holding out her arms as the men began to grease her too.

'Very unpleasant to drink,' I told her. 'But then it's never safe to talk while swimming in case you get a mouthful.'

'Well that's funny,' she said, bouncing on her feet. 'Because they never can stop me talking when I'm swimming. And they can't stop me chewing gum neither.' At that she held out her hand and her trainer produced a strip of gum the colour of slate. She rolled it up with her fingers, popped it in her mouth and started to chew.

'Five minutes from now, ladies,' said Dickie, ushering us forward. 'Take your places please.'

So we stepped onto the planks and Billy came to stand behind me, kneading away at my neck and my shoulders as Father used to do. It was time to be serious; there would be no more talking now. Sarah and I stood side by side, so close we almost touched, then a cannon boomed and all along the shore the people began to shout and cheer. When the cannon boomed for the second time we both leaped in.

I came up at once and set out as fast as I could, but my rival stayed so long under the water I thought she would never appear. Then there she was, right next to me, smiling and chewing away on her gum. We travelled parallel, she closer to the shore than me, and as we did great swells of sea came rolling over us. Soon I was riding up and down on the waves like a girl on a see-saw, spitting salt water at every breath, and the judges' boat was hidden in a shower of spray.

I was glad it was only five miles each way for I'd never raced in the sea before and already I was using up my energy just battling the waves. I saw the buoy ahead of me, we were halfway at least, and then I realised that Sarah was no longer by my side: she was overtaking me now. I heard the people on the boat cheering and told myself to ignore the waves and focus on the race. But I saw how fast she was

swimming, lengthening the distance between us, and I knew that if I
didn't catch up soon then it was possible I never would.

Suddenly I saw Sarah's head plunge down and her back rise out of
the water, writhing from side to side.

'Heavens!' someone cried from the boat. 'She's doubled up, what is
it?'

'She has a cramp,' came the answer, 'she's sunk!'

Her head appeared out of a great wave and I saw the anguish on
her face as she tried to keep on swimming. But she was rolling under,
back and forth, and I knew it was no cramp of the arm or the leg; it
was cramp of the stomach. The boat had reached her now; she could
barely lift her hand to touch the oar and with a great deal of shouting
she was pulled on-board.

'Is she all right?' I called, swimming towards the boat as it dipped
up and down in the waves.

'Swim on!' shouted Dob.

I shook my head. I would not continue on my own when my competitor was in pain; there would be no triumph in that. The race was
over.

'Swim on!' Dob shouted again.

'I shan't,' I called, 'it's not a fair race.'

'A thousand dollars!' he hissed, hanging over the side of the boat,
waving me on with his hands, 'a *thousand* dollars!'

I saw Sarah trying to stand up, and I knew what she was doing; she
wanted to be back in the water. I felt her desperation as keenly as if it
were my own, and so I put out my hand and deliberately touched the
boat; the race was done.

'Daisy won,' said Dob as I was pulled on board.

The judges looked surprised.

'She did,' Dob insisted, 'she swam the longest.'

But the judges disagreed; neither of us had completed the course
and I was disqualified by touching the boat. We could repeat the swim
on Saturday, they said, if the water was smooth and the weather better. No, said Dob, it was not possible; they knew that, we couldn't
stay. We would take our money elsewhere: we had to go to Sandy
Hook.

Back on the shore he waited impatiently outside a bathing hut as I changed, and the minute I came out he started marching along, muttering about cigar-chomping swindling Americans.

'Why did you give up?' he asked.

'I didn't give up. I chose to stop. How could I have swum on when Sarah could not?'

'And that makes it all right?' Suddenly he grabbed me, his hands digging hard into my arms. 'Don't provoke me, Daisy. You made an utter fool of me. I told everyone you could do it. I wagered a thousand dollars. Then you *chose* to stop.'

But he hadn't lost any money, I thought, the wager was off. The only person to have lost money was Dickie Fitzgerald for meeting our costs.

I felt his hands move down my arms and tighten around my wrists and as I let out a cry a group of people on the boardwalk stopped to watch.

'Why did you accept the challenge?' asked Dob, 'if you couldn't do it?'

'Let her be,' said Violet, coming up behind us, and Dob let go, thrust his hands into his pockets and walked on alone.

CHAPTER TWENTY-SIX

Dob and I left Atlantic City two days later and took the train north to Sandy Hook, while Billy and the others carried on to New York to be there when I arrived. I was nearly mobbed by well-wishers at Sandy Hook; it seemed that everyone was ready to wager that I would do the swim. Word had spread that I had outlasted Sarah Rosenheim in a terrible sea and this was a straight sixteen miles to Rockaway Beach. Dob did not speak about what had happened at Atlantic City, there was no mention of my having given up the swim. He was cheerful and charming once more.

We waited days for the right conditions and each morning I went down to the beach where the air smelled of pine and the sand was thick like clay. I listened to the rustle of the grasses in the dunes and looked out towards the bay, wondering when I would be allowed to begin. Dob seemed to understand my restlessness; he did not bother me with questions, only encouraged me to train every morning for as long as I liked. Then at last we had a perfect day; the blue waters sparkled and the breakers curled in a lazy fashion as I stood on the thin spit of shore waiting for the boat to arrive.

'How long do you think it will take?' I asked the boatman, while the reporters boarded and Dob loaded the provisions.

'That's up to you.' He gave a hoarse laugh. 'But I'd try it as fast as you can if I were you.'

Then a gentleman came running along the beach waving a telegram, and for a second I was fearful, convinced it would bear bad news.

'What is it?' asked Dob after I had read the telegram and folded it into my hand.

'Nothing,' I told him. 'Just a message of good luck.'

'You have the skill, Daisy,' he said, 'you don't need good luck.'

I got on the boat and settled myself below in the cabin, the telegram still tight in my hand. I caught sight of myself in a mirror on the wall and saw that I was smiling as I slipped the message from Johnnie

Heaven into a crack behind the glass. After the swim, I would retrieve it.

Then we pulled off and a little later the engines stopped. It was time to come up. I could hear the reporters' chatter as I appeared on the deck. 'Oh I agree that women should know how to swim,' said one, 'but as a sport it should be purely masculine.' Then another joined in, 'I reckon these women hold some very fishy records, even more fishy than the swimmers themselves!'

The men fell silent as I made my way through them, keeping my expression calm and heading for the stern. The day was burning hot, there were barely clouds in the sky and I tried to think of nothing but the cooling water below me. What did it matter what the journalists thought? I would soon prove them wrong.

So in I dived and the water was delightful, as smooth as buttermilk and so clear that I could see the sand beneath. 'Throw me my hat,' I called to Dob as I came up to the surface, 'it's so hot I'll wear it while I swim.' The sea was the best place in the world to be on a day like this and I slipped through the water with barely any effort at all. Before long the people running along the shore grew smaller, a buzz of insects danced around my ears, and then ahead of me was the bay dotted with vessels.

'Slow down,' called Dob as a ferry packed with passengers came into view.

But I didn't want to; I was revelling in my speed.

'Slow down!' he called again. 'Don't waste your energy.'

But I wasn't wasting it; I was using it. Ever since we'd arrived in America he'd been telling me what to do, and now I'd just about had enough. So I ignored him and carried on. Soon I heard a man shout, 'You've left New Jersey, you're in New York now!' and I grew thirsty and paddled next to the boat to ask for lemonade. Again I set off with a strong fast stroke; it was a little cooler now with wisps of cloud in the sky and when my hat blew off I simply laughed and continued swimming. Then a man called, 'Look out, jellyfish!' I dipped my head under and saw their tentacles hanging down, sweeping the water like the fringe of a rug. I stopped and tried to swim around them. But instead I found myself gliding through and over them and it was a horrible sensation, their tentacles as sticky as jam. I felt a sharp sensation as if a knife was slicing across my skin and let out a cry.

'What's wrong?' called Dob.

'I've been stung.'

'Stop the swim!' he shouted, holding up his palms to the judges.

'No!' I said, regretting I had told him. 'It doesn't hurt,' although it did. I carried on, trying not to think of the pain in my arms and the fact my eyes were turning raw from the sun and the salt. Not long to go, I told myself. I wasn't racing anyone, I had no time to beat, it didn't matter after all how long I took, only that I made it. 'Give me chocolate!' I called to Dob, and as the boat bobbed next to me I saw there were only two men left standing on the deck.

'Where has everyone gone?' I asked.

'Lying in the cabin,' called the boatman, 'as sick as dogs.'

'In a sea as gentle as this?' I laughed, glad that the men who had doubted me were so indisposed. Then I reached a bell buoy bobbing in the water, its warning bell ringing. Rockaway Beach was only a few miles away; the shore was plainly in sight. I felt calm now, almost as if I were moving in my sleep as fish swam by, silver bodies leaping into the air with glimmering yellow fins.

But then the character of the water began to change; I was swimming as strongly as ever yet when I looked at the boat it seemed to be rolling just where it was.

'What's happening?' I asked.

Dob waved that I should come nearer. 'It looks like the tide has changed.'

'The tide?'

'Yes. It's impossible. You will never reach the shore.'

'I will,' I told him, for I couldn't stop now, the land was in view. I would stand on that beach even if I had to crawl in on my knees. But my stroke was growing more uneven; each time I pulled myself forward a far stronger force pulled me back. 'Give me a drink and I'll be fine,' I said, but my body was moving backwards now, I was actually losing ground and the wind had picked up, turning the sea to waves.

'It's impossible,' said Dob again.

'I'll wait it out,' I cried, stopping to tread water.

'It will be another six hours before it turns and dark by then, you can't.'

'I can. I'll keep afloat and swim in when the tide changes.' If I had to tread water for six hours to try to stay in one place then I would. I felt the boat come nearer and I kicked my legs to move away, but when I looked up again the vessel was even closer and Dob was leaning an oar over the side. I turned to swim away and heard him shout, 'You'll have to stop.'

'No,' I cried. 'Let me go on.' But then a wave slapped at my face and I coughed and gasped for air.

'Grab her!' I heard Dob shout as I came to the surface and saw the oar was just inches from my face.

'No!' I shook my head. I would not be grabbed. There was no way in the world I was stopping now. 'No,' I said again as a wave thrust me up against the boat and the oar touched my hand.

I was almost forced from that water, there seemed to be arms clutching me from every side as I was pulled against my will onto the boat, and strongest of all was Dob. I sat down, utterly stunned. What was I doing in the boat? I should have been there in the water finishing my swim. The boatman put a blanket around my shoulders, offered me a drink. I shook my head, I didn't want sympathy. I wanted to swim. Why had we set off at the time we did if the tide was going to change? Why had nobody told me?

When we reached the pier at Rockaway I stood up in the boat and saw the seasick reporters crawl out from the cabin. The beach was busy and the crowd who had gathered to watch my arrival began politely to clap. I felt people pat me on the shoulder, asking if I were all right; saw Billy and Violet pushing their way through the spectators to reach me. But it was my husband I was watching as he strode off to join a huddle of men. Why had he touched me with the oar? How dare he ruin my swim? And what business could he possibly be doing now?

I went into a bathing hut to change, angrily removing my costume, and when I came out Dob was standing on the sand, puffing on a cigar, shaking hands with the boatman and looking pleased with himself.

'Why didn't you know about the tide?' I asked.

'They didn't tell me.' He shrugged his shoulders. 'Never trust a Yankee.'

'But I could have gone on.'

'No, you couldn't,' Dob tossed away his cigar. 'You were on the point of collapse.'

'I was not! I sat up in the boat! I climbed out of it alone.'

'You would have drowned, Daisy. You were sinking and barely conscious. It was for your own good.'

'That is a lie.' I stood there facing him, unable to understand why he wasn't more upset. Why was it I who was angry? He had wagered that I would make the crossing and I hadn't. 'My father would never have done that!' I cried. 'He never would have misjudged the tide. Did you *want* me to fail?'

Dob laughed. 'Your father? You're comparing me to your father?'

And that is when I knew, as he opened his waistcoat and I saw his thumb resting on a bundle of notes in his pocket. He had not wagered that I could do the crossing; he had wagered that I would fail. I could have gone on and he'd stopped me. That was what he had been doing on the shore, receiving his winnings.

Dob returned to New York that afternoon; he had business to attend to and would be back in two days. Billy took me to our hotel and it was only when we reached my room that I remembered what I had left on the boat. It was too late to retrieve it. As evening fell I headed to the beach and stood in front of the rippling sea. I had tried to do my best, I always had. I had stayed strong and worked hard and done what was demanded of me, and now I had failed. I wondered what people would say, how the reporters would relish writing their reports, and suddenly I wanted to jump in that sea and give up the fight. Let it carry me away, let it take me where it wanted, back to Sandy Hook, or across the ocean home.

But then I had another thought: where was that fearless child who had paddled on her own in the ocean at Margate? The girl who had dived from the dome of the Aq and swum in a tank? She would never be beaten and nor would I. Dob had taken revenge for my refusal to continue against Sarah Rosenheim. He had betrayed me, but that did not mean he would win.

I looked up then to see a figure walking towards me along the shore, a man in bold striped trousers and a blue bow tie. He came nearer with strong buoyant steps, swinging a hat in his hands, and then nearer still until I could see his face.

'Oh Moses,' said Johnnie Heaven, stopping a yard away from me on the sand. 'I don't know that I ever saw such a thing. I couldn't bear to watch.'

'Were you here?' I asked, 'on the beach?'

'I was here.' He nodded. 'Waiting to see your triumph.'

'The tide turned. I was stopped.'

'I know, I saw it all. I felt shipwrecked at the very sight. You were so close, so close! I was going to swim out and join you.'

'I wish you had,' I said, 'perhaps then I wouldn't have failed.'

'Failed?' Johnnie Heaven sounded surprised. 'Do you regret not making a fortune?'

'No!'

'That's just as well.' He bent down and picked up a shell. 'Because the only real fortune worth finding is to have an aim in life.'

'Such as crossing the Channel?' I asked.

'Exactly.' He handed me the shell, as light as a biscuit, bleached white from the sun. 'It's a sand dollar,' he said. 'It is to remind you of this day. Your failure was not your fault.'

I felt tears at the back of my eyes and wiped them away with my sleeve. 'If my husband hadn't touched me with the oar I could have gone on.'

'I know you could. You could have reached Rockaway and swum back to Sandy Hook!' Johnnie Heaven laughed, and then his face grew serious. 'What were you thinking, as you were standing here just now?'

'Oh, I thought I should fling myself into the sea.'

'It is a fine night,' he sighed, 'for a swim.'

I was about to tell him I hadn't been thinking of swimming, but then he sat down on the sand, began taking off his boots. 'Shall we go in?' he asked. 'Shall we swim together again?'

'Again?' I laughed.

Johnnie Heaven smiled, a slow smile full of promise. 'Do you think I've forgotten the Lambeth Baths?'

And I looked at him and thought, why shouldn't we swim? The night was warm; there was no one here to see us. So I sat down next to him and took off my boots and dress, and then we walked in together. The water reached my ankles, then my shins and my waist and a second later in we had plunged, coming up at the exact same time. I turned onto my back, laying myself flat on the sea, and so did he.

'There is something about water,' said Johnnie Heaven, 'that makes you feel yourself,' and I nodded because I knew exactly what he meant. We floated there for a while, splashing a little with our hands, admiring the moon in the sky and the silhouettes of flying birds. I turned on my front, did a somersault or two, and then we both set off, swimming towards the horizon. The sea was black and motionless and each time my face came up so did his, our arms raised at the very same time. I kicked a little stronger, overtaking him now, for if he thought I couldn't beat him he was wrong. Then we both stopped, panting and laughing, and when his wet hands touched my face I felt as if I had been dipped in sugar, my skin prickling to life.

I found his lips with mine and threw my arms around him and the sea held us up as we kissed.

'Daisy Belle,' he said, as I let him go, 'never forget that you are the most wonderful woman in the world.'

The next morning I woke alone just before dawn. I knew what I had done was wrong and I didn't feel condemned at all, because every inch of him had been a joy to me. I kept my eyes closed, remembering the way we had dressed on the shore and how gently he had brushed the sand from my clothes. I could feel him now, even though he was gone, sense the warmth and the pleasure he had left in the room. 'Let me look at you,' he had said, as he laughed and whispered in my ear, 'let me look at you.' It was as if I had been swimming, pushing strongly against a tide then finally letting it carry me away.

When I opened my eyes the sand dollar was on the bedside cabinet, placed on top of a neatly folded sheet of paper. I opened it up. There was only one sentence inside, a simple question, but that was enough. I heard Percy chattering in the hallway, Billy knocking on the door, and I pressed the paper to my lips, closing my eyes again. Yes, I told him, I will meet you next summer in Dover.

CHAPTER TWENTY-SEVEN

We returned to England not in state cabins as Dob had promised but in the same small berths. There was none of the adventure of our outward passage; even little Percy was subdued. I said that I was seasick although I was not, but I preferred to stay alone in the cabin, keeping my precious letter to myself and rereading the words to keep my spirits up. I didn't know where Johnnie Heaven had gone after that night at Rockaway, but I read of his training swims in New York and I was certain that he was waiting until I was free. For now, I had no choice but to leave America with my husband. I had refused to undertake any more swims, but I could not refuse to go home.

I lay for hours at a time on my berth, venturing out only at night when the wind was fresh and sharp, the clouds had blown away and the stars began to burn in the sky. I heard the cry of 'All's well!' that accompanied the sound of the bell and I didn't know if all would ever be well as I watched the horizon rising and falling. 'Don't worry, little tadpole,' said Billy one night, 'it will all turn out all right in the end.' He knew, I thought, somehow he knew about Johnnie Heaven, and he hated Dob as much as I.

My husband stayed away from me, as he had done for weeks, and I was grateful for that. The days of our courtship in Margate were over, and I was a different person now. We spent a night in Liverpool before returning to London, and the countryside seemed very sleepy-looking to me, green fields and old red farms, children gathering blackberries who stopped to wave as we went by. When we arrived at Rugby, Dob handed me a newspaper and I gave it to Billy, not interested in any news. Even when I heard my brother let out a muffled gasp I had no inkling of what was to come.

'It's Father,' he said, pointing at the paper.

I was so wrapped up in my own thoughts that I didn't know what Billy meant; perhaps Father was putting on a show but why would either of us care about that?

My brother put the newspaper on his lap and I saw he had tears in his eyes.

'What is it?' I asked.

'It's Father,' he said again. 'His funeral took place yesterday, at Nunhead.'

'Funeral?' I didn't seem to be able to understand the words, was only half-conscious of little Percy climbing onto my lap. 'But that's impossible.' I stared at Billy, waiting for him to correct himself, to say he had been mistaken.

But he picked up the paper and pointed at the report. 'It says there were many splendid wreaths for the famous swimmer Mr Jeffery Belle. And a large number of well-known sportsmen.'

'But how?' I asked. 'How can that be?'

'Pneumonia. He was taken ill with pneumonia two weeks ago.'

We looked at each other, my brother and I, both with the same question: what had we been doing then? Why had we not known, why had some sixth sense not told us?

'It says the end was very sudden,' Billy sighed. 'He died ten days ago. The day we boarded the boat.'

'But why didn't they wait for us?' I asked. It was then that it hit me and I had such a sense of loss that I didn't know what to do with myself. All this time, even when I'd run away from him, I had known I would see Father again. Even when I'd torn up his telegram and refused to reply, and when I would not invite him to my wedding, I knew that one day we would be reconciled. I was so full of regret. He was still my father; he had trained me and he'd had faith in me. I couldn't have done what I had done without him. Despite what had happened, he had given me so much and I wished he were alive so I could tell him, so that I could say those three words back: all is forgiven.

Had he known we'd gone to America? He must have done, he would have read about our arrival, our performance in New York. He would have kept up with the news of my swim against Sarah Rosenheim, and known of my failure at Rockaway. But he didn't know the truth, and now he never would. He would have thought his littlest frog Daisy had been beaten by the tide. I glanced at Dob and he looked away. Had he known, I thought, had someone told him Father was ill? And I sat there, rocking gently from side to side as the train carried on, nearing London, taking us to the place where my father no longer was. Why had he left me, why now?

We rented two gloomy rooms in Kings Cross and when I asked if we couldn't afford better Dob said the money had all gone on expenses. I stopped myself from asking what had happened to the income from my swims that he had made in America. For what was the use; I was penniless now. Each night Dob slammed the door on the flimsiest of excuses, pulling up the collar of his coat so he looked more like a sewer rat than the man I'd first met. Then he returned in the early hours smelling of brandy and perfume and I lay there beside him, glad that he had no interest in me. Billy and Violet urged me to leave; they were returning to Margate and I should come too. But grief had fogged up my mind. If I ran away, Dob would find me; I was his wife. And if I ran away, I would never get back what I was owed. I took off my wedding ring, our names and the time at which we had met engraved inside, and decided to throw it away. But then I changed my mind, for what I needed more than anything was money. I must swim and I must find money.

Three days later Billy wrote from Margate to say that Mother was there. She was staying with Auntie Jessie and Minnie was with her. Mother had sent a telegram when Father had fallen ill, she was distressed that we had never replied. Billy explained we had not received any telegram, but when she hadn't heard from us the burial had gone ahead. Father had left no money; they could not afford to wait. I should have gone to see her then, but my body seemed unable to do the simplest of things, overcome with tiredness and a nausea as severe as on my outward journey to America.

One afternoon Dob came home and asked, 'Do you think you can still dive?'

'Of course I can still dive.' I was sitting listlessly at the window and didn't even bother to turn around. I hadn't eaten that day, I felt a strange weakness inside and my mouth tasted of burned milk.

'Well here's the thing.' Dob thrust his hands in his pockets. 'I bumped into Robert Winkle...'

I turned around in surprise. Robert Winkle? I'd not seen him since I had performed at the Aq. I thought of how Billy and I used to call him Mr Kettle and nearly smiled.

'He told me about the bathing pond on Hampstead Heath,' said Dob. 'Do you know it?' His eyes were eager; I could see he was excited and trying not to show it and I shook my head, uninterested.

'There's a diving display in two weeks' time, twelve girls from nearly every county in England. See?' He brought out a showbill and held it up.

Still I didn't reply.

'They have the highest diving board in the country. And they want you to open the show.'

'Me?' I stood up and took the showbill. 'They want me to dive at a pond?'

'If you dare. It's the deepest in London, and many a diver has met their death at the Hampstead pond. The offer is a thousand pounds, with the prize money and wagers, enough to see us retire.'

Us? I thought, I would not let one penny of that money out of my hands, it was I who would retire. 'Why so much?'

'Because,' Dob came up behind me and laid one hand on my shoulder; I could feel his thumb pressing into my skin, 'you will be bound.'

'Bound?' I shrugged him off. I didn't like the smell of him; he seemed to carry a scent of rotten eggs.

'They want your ankles and wrists tied with rope.'

'Why?'

'Why?' Dob laughed. 'Because no one has done it before and they need a sensation to open the show.'

I told him I wasn't interested, I didn't feel like diving at the moment. He taunted me that I had lost my nerve, pacing around the room, trying every which way to persuade me. And I let him, although I had already decided I would do it. Finally I agreed, on one condition: Dob must sign a declaration that the prize money would be in my brother's name. That was ridiculous, he said, there was no need. We would share the money.

I shook my head. 'Then I shan't dive. You must sign the papers and the money must go to Billy. Then I will give you half.'

'Fine!' said Dob, 'if that's that you want.' I think he would have agreed to anything at that moment, never believing the money would not be his. And as for me, if I had to leap into a pond bound at the hands and feet then I would, because this one dive would set us all free.

CHAPTER TWENTY-EIGHT

A week later we were sitting in a hansom cab on our way to Hampstead Heath. 'Ten thousand at least,' said Dob with a lick of his lips as we inched our way through the crowds. I didn't reply but looked out at them keenly, sensing their expectation, boys running with flags held high, gentlemen with jaunty boaters and ladies with sun-scorched faces. Still the people came, the new arrivals spreading themselves out until the grass could barely be seen. A man lashed at a donkey, his cart laden with sacks of coconuts, another frantically pushed an ice-cream barrow, everyone racing for the best place. It was a fine sunny bank holiday and if there was an entertainment to be found then the crowd was here to find it.

We drove onto a causeway and there was the bathing pond, a circle of water enclosed on three sides by trees of vivid lime. At the far end was a neat boatman's hut nestled among the foliage. Then my eyes lifted to the diving platform and the top board suspended seventy feet above the water. Soon I would be standing there to prove myself for the last time. After this, I would never need to dive again.

I heard the wheels of the cab rattling on the stones as we turned off the causeway and onto a lane, then we pulled to a stop and I climbed out. At once Dob was beside me, walking quickly in that impatient way of his, his left hand tucked in his waistcoat pocket. He had his other hand resting around my waist and I was forced to stop as he greeted the people he knew; we might have been away in America but Dob was a popular figure still. We came to a tent, its entrance decorated with garlands of yellow flowers, where the other girls were changing and I could hear the happy chatter from inside. Then there was the burst of a trombone as a brass band arrived, marching with a flash of medals and silver sashes down to the jetty on the water.

'Here she is,' called a reporter lounging by the boatman's hut. 'They may have lungs smaller than a man, but by God are lady swimmers blessed with natural life belts!' I gave a wan smile as Dob released me, entered the hut and closed the door. It was silent inside as I readied myself, removed my clothes and put on the costume that Dob had had specially made. But the neck I'd found too high and the day before I had cut into the cloth with a pair of scissors because I wanted my throat quite free. Then I bound up my hair with a satin ribbon and drew a cloak around my shoulders. I thought I heard a whisper in my ear, 'Dive pretty, Daisy. And don't forget to smile,' and I whirled around, half-expecting Father to be there. What would he think of this, his daughter diving bound into a pond? Would he think I had lost my mind or would he understand and wish me well? I so wanted to ask his advice on how I should perform this dive. But Father was gone; I was alone now.

I checked everything was in place for afterwards: a bowl of clean water, lotion and powder. In half an hour or less I would be back in this hut, and then how my life would be changed. I bent over my clothing, looking for the letter I kept always in a pocket sewn into my skirt. But as I slipped my fingers into the cloth I found the pocket was empty. I was about to search through the rest of my clothing when the door flew open.

'Why have you cut it?' asked Dob.

I touched the neck of my costume, feeling my fingers tremble.

'To better show your décolletage?' Dob walked in. 'Here,' he said, 'wear this.'

In his hand he held a golden crown, its arches decorated with shining stones. I put out my fingers to touch it; there was something about the crown I didn't like, but I couldn't argue, not now. I had to be fearless today, even more than usual, and if he wanted me to wear it then I would.

'They're waiting,' Dob said. He pushed the crown down on my head and I was surprised at how heavy it was. 'You're their queen, Daisy. Don't disappoint them.'

For a second we looked at each other, Dob and I, and I found myself searching his face for the man I'd once known. I saw him lying on the Margate sands after I had rescued him and the way he had winked at me. And the next day, when he'd been sitting outside my auntie's house and he had listened to me and fuelled my ambition. But that day when I'd saved his life it hadn't been my skill he'd admired; he had seen the opportunity to take advantage and seized it with both hands. The man I'd first met had never existed; Dob had felt contempt for me all along. He had betrayed me at Rockaway and now I was going to betray him.

'Remember,' he said, 'once you've made the dive stay under for as long as possible, make them gasp and wonder where you are. After three minutes I'll raise the alarm and then the boatman will pretend to come looking for you.'

I nodded, agreeing to everything. Then I stepped out of the hut and walked purposefully beneath the flower-decked arches down to the water's edge. There I stopped and blew a series of kisses, and from all around the pond came the most delicious sound, the crowd erupting in cheers. Then I climbed up the steps of the diving platform, step by careful step, leaving the earth behind.

There was a great hush as I stood at the top, and I savoured that moment when a crowd from above looks like shiny pebbles on a shore. But then a young girl raised her hand, a man glanced up and took off his hat, and that is when I saw the individual people, each with their own lives and loves and lusts. I searched the crowd for Billy, who had arrived from Margate two days ago, and saw him standing at the edge frowning. I looked as well for Robert Winkle, but he was nowhere to be seen. Perhaps this had never been his idea after all.

I waited while my husband climbed up the steps behind me, thick coils of rope slung over one shoulder, heard the distant cries of 'Oh!' and 'Ah!' as he joined me on the platform. Slowly Dob removed my cloak and for a second, as he glanced at my costume stretched tight across my stomach, I thought he knew what I had suspected weeks ago: I was going to have a child. I felt giddy at the idea, anxious that he had found the letter hidden in my dress. I watched him cast the cloak to the ground and it fluttered slowly down, getting smaller and smaller, until a gust of wind picked it up and threw it across the water.

There was a smile on Dob's face as he slid the ropes off his shoulder and held them up to show the crowd. Then he kneeled down on the platform like a knight before a queen and slowly, deliberately, started to tie my ankles. He stood up and began to bind my wrists, the rope snaking around my flesh and digging into my skin, each tug watched with interest from below.

171

Once he had finished I cleared my lungs, took a number of quiet breaths and shuffled my feet onto the board. I waited until Dob had climbed down the steps and then I thrust up my arms, waiting for the sound that would send me hurtling into the air. 'Introducing...' came the voice of the announcer, his words distorted by a megaphone, 'England's one and only... fresh from her success in America... bound hand and foot... the highest plunge ever known to man... Ladies and gentlemen, our very own DIVE-IN-ITY... Miss Daisy Belle!'

I looked down at my stomach and said a whispered prayer, 'This is for you, my baby.' When the dive was over then we could leave.

I inched my feet forward until they projected over the side of the board. I needed to kick out just enough to turn my body over; I must not leap too far up or out when both my hands and feet were tied. There was a brief, powerful silence, that moment of poise before the flight when I had to battle with a voice that urged me not to jump, not to be so foolish, and I had to remind myself why I must do it.

I flexed my wrists as best as I could; if I kept them straight as I touched the water then I would go directly down. Then I would surface and rise to the top like Neptune's daughter to receive my applause. The gun fired and I had no doubts now, my muscles would remember what to do. But as I hurtled through the air and hit the water I felt my neck thrown back and something snap. A moment later I had sunk like a stone.

I tried to right myself, to thrust my bound hands up towards the surface, but I was struggling against gravity and the world had gone upside down. I held my breath, kept myself perfectly still and waited for my body to rise up naturally – but instead I sank further down. I felt a weed slip around my neck, the quiver of a fish somewhere nearby. Then I opened my eyes and saw nothing but swirling water the colour of tea. What had gone wrong?

I stopped fighting; it was soundless in the pond but for my heart pounding in my ears. My lungs began to fill with water; my limbs became as heavy as mud. But my mind, how it raced with thoughts and images. I was standing on the deck approaching New York, submerged in the whale tank at the Royal Aquarium, learning to float at the Lambeth Baths. I thought of joyful days on the Margate sands with Billy and then I closed my eyes and I had the strangest, the most glorious impression of green, like fields or gardens, and I was a tadpole again, alone in an ocean paradise.

Suddenly there was a disturbance in the water; something in my world had shifted. I heard a boom like distant thunder and a great splashing from above as an object, solid and heavy, hit against the pit of my back. It was the blade of an oar. The boat had found me. I had the sensation of someone leaning down towards me, of being hauled up and out of the pond, spluttering and gasping as I emerged into the air. Then I was lying on the bottom of the boat, looking at the sky, aware of the planks beneath me and the musty smell of wet wood.

'What happened?' I asked.

But neither Dob nor the boatman replied.

'What have I broken?'

Again they didn't reply. Was it my arms, my feet? I tried to check my body, to see how badly I was hurt and as I did the boatman leaned over, his face above mine, with warm brown eyes and a white moustache. Then I saw his shocked expression, watched as a red flush spread up his neck and into his cheeks. That was when I felt the pain, radiating from my neck, across my chest, and down along both arms.

'What do you think?' asked Dob.

The boatman turned to one side and I heard him retch over the edge of the boat.

I tried to move my head, aware that something was pressing down on me, and I looked at the boatman with pleading eyes. I felt his hands come down, heard his heavy breathing.

'I can't,' he said, 'it's stuck fast.'

Suddenly I knew what might have happened. That moment when I'd hit the water and felt something snap. Had the weight of the crown broken my neck?

The boatman rowed us back across the pond, and I lay there helplessly, listening to the creak of the wood and the rhythmic scrape of the oars. I felt the boat bump against dry land, heard a child scream, 'She's dead!' and looked up to see two men peering down on me.

'Get a stretcher,' said one.

The other shook his head. 'There's no point.'

I thought I heard the sound of a lone bugle playing the starting notes of 'The Last Post' and I began to cry, tears rushing down my cheeks, unable to wipe them away. Just before I passed out, I thought of my baby. I had risked everything for the future of myself and my child. Now we would never get to Dover. We would not even survive the night. My dive was the end of all of us.

CHAPTER TWENTY-NINE

There is little I remember of the days that followed, or perhaps I don't care to. I recall waking one morning to hear the hospital chaplain saying prayers, and the sound of a screen being dragged down the ward and placed around my bed.

'Can she feel that?' the doctor asked Dob, tapping my right foot with a little hammer.

'Yes,' I said. Then I glanced away, distracted by a lady crying from a neighbouring bed, and when I looked back the hammer was above my other foot. He'd tapped it when I wasn't looking, and I hadn't felt a thing.

'It is doubtful,' said the doctor, 'that your wife will recover.'

'What has happened?' I asked.

The doctor looked thoughtful and I could see that he wasn't sure. 'She appears to have fractured the bones in her neck. The spine may be damaged and hence the legs. Rest and prayer, that's all that can be done now.'

'Will I walk?' I asked.

He shook his head. 'It is doubtful.'

'Will I swim?'

'Swim!' The doctor laughed. 'I should hardly think so.'

I thrust off the blanket and tried to grab the rail of the bed, desperate to show that I could at least sit up. That was when I realised that my body was bound to a board of wood, with bandages tied around my waist, my chest and neck.

'Hysteria,' said the doctor. 'There is nothing we can do for her here. She must lie flat until the baby comes.'

'The baby?' asked Dob and I saw the colour drain from his face.

'Yes, it is still possible she may have a healthy child. Rest and prayer,' the doctor tapped my husband on the arm, 'rest and prayer.' I heard the click of his boots as he moved away and I wondered how he knew. Had I told the nurses when they'd examined me? Then Dob was leaning over the bed, a snarl on his face. 'Whose baby?'

I looked away.

'Whose baby, Daisy?' he asked. 'It's a puzzle, isn't it? A very *dirty* puzzle. For a man to hear his wife is having a child from another man. But you're still my wife, and that means what's yours is mine. Even if you are nothing but a damned whore.'

I didn't see my husband after that. I was of no use to him now, unable to swim or dive. Only Billy cared for me, and Violet came to join him, leaving little Percy with Auntie Jessie. Day after day they massaged my legs, applied lotion to my sores and tried to relieve the pain. 'Take her home,' the doctor told them, 'there is nothing to be done for her here.' But I could hardly move and I had no real home.

Every night I had the same dream; I opened my eyes in a sunfilled room and there in the doorway stood Johnnie Heaven in his fine striped trousers. He began to walk towards me, getting nearer and nearer with strong buoyant steps and then just as he reached me, I woke up. Had he read about my dive, did he know what had happened and would he come to see me? It was impossible; he was over the ocean in America and even if he did know, what good was I to him or anyone else?

As the days went past I knew what I had to do and one morning I asked Billy to bring me pen and paper. I had a letter I must write; I could no longer get to Dover or anywhere else. I must set Johnnie Heaven free. He mustn't wait for me; he could follow his dream and swim the Channel; he could start anew with someone else. I told him I had changed my mind. I'd had an accident during a dive but now I was fully recovered. I was staying with my husband. He should forget about me.

When I put down the pen I felt the oddest sensation, as if a fish were in my stomach. But determinedly I sealed the letter and asked Billy if he could find the address of the swimming school in New York. He took it without further question, saying he would try his best.

My brother and Violet did everything for me. They rented a room in Lambeth, where Billy began to teach swimming in the afternoons, while Violet dressed and fed and washed me as if I were a child. The pain in my neck lessened as the weeks went by and I was no longer tied to the board. My right leg hurt if it was touched, but the other had no sensation at all. I had to keep my strength up, said Billy; I must exercise my arms as best as I could and he fashioned me a corset to keep me straight. But the left side of me remained far weaker than the right, and while I could freely use my arms there were days when only the fingers on my right hand would do as they were told. The one thing that gave me hope was the thought of my child. She had survived the dive, and now I must do the same.

The following spring I caught an infection and Billy took me to St Thomas' where from outside the window I could see a view of Westminster Bridge. That was where I had stood as a six-year-old and said I wanted to swim the Thames. And I had; no one could take that away from me. Big Ben was my companion during those endless nights, announcing the hours to a sleeping world. In the morning I smelled the river through the open windows and sometimes, in the gloom, the patients before me all wrapped in blankets looked like a row of boats on the shore.

One day it started snowing and when I woke I was aware of a hush in the ward. I felt an odd shortness of breath and as I pushed myself up I realised I was panting. By the end of that day my baby was born.

I lay in the bed, cupping my hands around her head, feeling the heat of her body against mine. I stroked her skin, as shiny as a wet pebble, looked deep into her black eyes, and when she shivered and grew goosebumps it was like touching a starfish. I didn't sleep at all that night; full of wonder, studying every inch of her, counting each freckle high on her cheeks. What would I call her? I couldn't decide. Every day I thought of a different name. Perhaps I would call her Cloelia.

Two weeks later I woke from a fitful sleep; it was nearly dark in the ward and silent but for a lady coughing. I wanted to feed my baby, it had been hours since I had seen her, and so I called a nurse who was walking past. 'Can you bring me my baby?' I asked. 'She needs to be fed.' But the nurse continued on her round. I rattled the side of my bed, trying to get attention, asking another nurse, but she too walked by. 'Why will no one answer me?' I called. 'I need to see my baby.'

'Now then,' said the matron, marching into the ward, 'hush.' She tilted her head to one side and pursed her lips. 'Hasn't anyone told you? Baby has gone.'

'Gone?'

'Yes, an hour ago while you were sleeping.'

'Gone where?'

'Why, with her father.'

'Her father?' I looked around the ward in wonder.

'Yes,' said the matron, 'Mr McGee took her home, to get everything nice and ready for you.'

'No!' I cried. 'No! He's lying! Tell him to bring her back.' I felt as if I were plunging from a great height with no water to break my fall. I clasped the edge of the bed, frantically trying to get up, wanting to leave the ward, to run after her. I thought of what Dob had said the last time I had seen him, *what's yours is mine*. He had taken her. He was still my husband and he could do whatever he liked. I had no claim to my own child, not if he knew about Johnnie Heaven.

All that night I waited and waited. I told myself Dob was punishing me for my affair, that was all. Then he would bring my baby back. Once she started crying with hunger, he would return. Every time someone entered the ward I was flooded with hope, but daylight came and Dob did not come back.

The nurses said my sobbing was disturbing the other patients and when Billy came I'd been restrained, my arms tied to the bars of the bed to stop me moving. I was drained of blood, quivering from the lack of my child. 'He took her,' I told Billy, 'Dob came and he took her,' and my brother held me in his arms as he promised me, 'Then we will find her. Trust me, little tadpole, we will find her.'

CHAPTER THIRTY

Billy and Violet moved me to Margate that summer to be reunited with little Percy, but I could have been anywhere for all I cared. I took no notice of my surroundings. I rarely went to the sea and everything seemed grey to me, the promenade and the people, the pier and the sands, even the ocean itself. Nature had lost its colour; I was living permanently underwater and I couldn't have got to the surface even if I'd tried.

Mother was still living with Auntie Jessie, but when my brother took me to see her we had little to say to each other. She was ill and bedridden now and she lay there dressed in her mourning clothes, saying, 'It won't be long before I join your father.' Mother had always considered diving a dangerous thing to do and now, I thought bitterly, she had been proved right. I wanted to confide in her, to tell her everything that had happened, about my love for Johnnie Heaven and the loss of my child. But each time I opened my mouth to speak she simply closed her eyes. My sister Minnie had left Margate and moved north to be with Charlie and Tom-tom. Billy said they were performing in aquatic shows but my interest in galas was over.

By now I had recovered enough feeling in my right leg to be able to take a few steps with the aid of a stick, but it still caused pain to move from lying down to sitting, and from sitting to standing was even worse. Billy bought me a bath chair in order to wheel me occasionally around the town. But I hated the way it creaked and I didn't like how people stared, seeing me as peculiar, the way they nodded to their companions as they passed and glanced back wide-eyed. I only wanted to be in quiet places where I couldn't be seen.

One night there was a storm which raged for hours, the wind blowing in terrific gusts all through town. Boats in the harbour broke from their moorings, swamping and sinking or drifting out to sea. Chimneys fell in the market square, uprooted trees lay on the ground and the pavements became running streams. Margate was in danger of being destroyed, and so was I.

Billy began to teach at the Marine Palace Baths and Violet did too, and in between he did everything he could to find my child. He made frequent visits to London, went to every address at which Dob had been known to stay, wrote to every newspaper, contacted every person in the sporting world. But Dob McGee had disappeared. He could have changed his name, he could have left the country and gone to Australia for all we knew, and there was nothing we could do about it at all. As each month passed and as the months turned into years, I wondered: was my baby walking now, was she talking? Did Dob treat her with love? Was she even alive?

In the spring of 1886 we returned to London. Billy had been appointed swimming instructor at the Essex Road Baths and he tried to get me to join him. I could sit in the gallery, he said, or he could position my chair at the poolside and I could watch from there. Look at little Percy, just five years old, wasn't it wonderful the way he raced and performed? But I didn't want to be anywhere near water, for I would only long to be in it and to feel my body come to life again. So as the months passed and we settled into our new home, it was Violet who taught the women and girls to swim, while Billy organised galas and travelled around other London baths to see what they were up to, just as Father had once done.

One evening my brother came back very excited and said he had a trip planned for me. 'I've told you I don't want to go on any trip,' I replied, not moving from my position at the window where I stayed for most of the day looking out over the square.

'Well, you are,' said Billy, 'because tomorrow we're going to the Hornsey Road Baths.'

'Why would I want to go there?' I muttered angrily.

'Because ladies have a pool to themselves on Wednesdays,' he said, 'and girls can swim there all day long if they wish; they even have a swimming club. Don't you remember the girls in America, wouldn't you like to see this new pool?'

I didn't answer. That was the day I had seen Johnnie Heaven and I didn't want to think about him.

But Billy was insistent; a gala was being arranged at the Hornsey Baths and they wanted me to present the prizes. 'Everyone still remembers you, Daisy,' he said.

'What do they remember?' I snapped. 'My failed dive in a pond with a crown on my head?'

'There's no harm in going to have a look,' said Billy. 'The girls' instructor is keen to meet you.'

'It's a long way to go for a look,' I objected, although in truth it was only two miles.

'Why?' asked Billy. 'Don't you think you can make the journey?'

The next day he hired a cab and the driver roped my chair to the back; it clung there precariously as we drove through the streets of Islington. I hadn't been out for a very long time and I couldn't help but notice the life all around me as people bustled to get to their destination, never stopping to think how easy it was to move from place to place.

When we arrived at the Hornsey Baths, Billy wheeled me in through the gatehouse and then he handed me my walking stick, took me by the arm and led me in. It was a pretty bath, although very small, and I had to admit there was a pleasing lightness about the place. There was also plenty for the bathers to do, with a chute and springboard, a hanging trapeze and rings on a rope. The bath was full of girls, splashing and floundering and making a racket, but it didn't look too clean to me; there was floating fluff and streaks of dye, flakes of mud brought in on people's shoes. Surely, I thought, it was time to change the water. But this didn't bother the girls, it was a sunny spring morning, they had their own pool and they were having fun. I felt my body relax, felt a spark of interest now.

'Do you want to stay and watch?' asked my brother.

'Perhaps,' I said, 'for a little while.'

Billy positioned my chair in an alcove and I glanced at a group of girls standing in the shallow end performing arm movements. The water was so cloudy that nothing could be seen of their bodies below their waists; they could have had mermaid tails for all anyone knew. Every shout and laugh was multiplied, as it always is in a bath, echoing off the tiled walls and the iron rafters. *Whoosh* went a girl down the chute and behind her came three more.

'No more than two at a time!' shouted a female attendant, hurrying along the poolside, just as one particularly large girl attempted to crawl her way up the chute. Then my brother tapped me on the shoulder. 'Here's Mr Millichap. The girls' instructor.'

I looked up to see a stout red-faced man wearing a none-too-clean white coat.

'Miss Belle,' he said, 'delighted and honoured to have you here. *Down* the chute not up!' he shouted at the girl still crawling up the slide. Then he sighed. 'It's not easy teaching girls. Some learn in three weeks, others have scarcely mastered a thing. That one over there,' he pointed to the far end of the bath, 'she learned in a couple of lessons.'

I looked at the girl, holding onto the rail kicking her legs; she appeared about to give up.

'But that one,' he said, nodding to a girl standing by the side, 'if she won't get in soon I'll have to push her.'

Push her? I thought; you will do no such thing. How would a girl learn the joy of swimming if she were pushed?

'If you had any idea how much trouble it gives having a girls' bath,' sighed Mr Millichap again, 'all the stray hairs… Get *off* the chute!' he roared. 'Would you mind watching them race, Miss Belle? It won't take long.'

I was about to say I had to go, I was tired and would come back another time, but Mr Millichap was already heading off along the poolside. 'Take me home,' I told Billy, 'I've had enough.'

'Wait!' he said, in a voice so urgent that it made me wonder what was wrong. Then he pointed at a girl sitting on the diving board below the gallery. She was a plump little figure with curly brown hair, and she was tugging impatiently at the sleeves of her knitted one-piece costume. There was something about the way she sat so self-contained on that diving board, with her legs a-dangling, that sent a flush of recognition through my body.

'Do you see her?' asked Billy.

I nodded, unable to speak.

'I noticed her when the superintendent showed me round the girls' pool. She is so like you, Daisy, I thought I'd seen a ghost.'

The girl stood up then and held out her arms like a fairy about to take flight and I caught my breath, my heart in my mouth as it used to be when I dived. How sure she was of herself, how fearless she seemed as she bounced on that board with a big smile on her face, looking around to see who was watching. And I knew the impossible had happened this morning at the Hornsey Baths. After all this time, after years of fruitless searching, Billy had found my child.

'Is it really her?' I whispered. 'Who is she with? Where does she live, how did she come to be here?'

Then I saw the girl fall into the bath with a horrible splash. But she hauled herself out quite easily, the sodden costume sagging down, looking very pleased with herself. As she passed the alcove on the poolside she gave me a look of curiosity. Only it was not my chair she was looking at, it was me. How I longed to announce myself, to reach out my arms and pull her in, to tell her who I was. But I knew that I couldn't. If I was to steal her back, then I must wait and watch. I must be very careful until the time was right.

'That was good,' I said, my voice raised as the little girl went by, loud enough to make her stop.

She stood there flushed with pleasure, her hair plastered against her forehead, eyes as dark as ink. How shiny was her skin, how pretty the freckles on her cheeks.

'Only,' I said, 'you need to start a little nearer to the edge of the board.' Instantly I regretted that I had pointed out a defect in her dive, when what did it matter how she did it?

'I know how to dive,' said the little girl in a stubborn fashion.

'Do you really?' I asked, amused, for she was clearly a child not intimidated by adults. 'And who taught you?'

'My Pa. He got me a teacher.'

I felt a stab of fear then; was he here? Was he right here at the baths this very minute and could he see me? I looked around, scanning the poolside, glancing up at the gallery, but I could see no one who looked like Dob.

The girl looked at me and suddenly smiled. 'My name is Hettie.'

Hettie? I felt my heart tremble with fury; my child had been named after Dob's mother.

'I'm four and a half and I have a brother and a sister but I'm the old-est.'

'You are?' I asked, trying to sound unconcerned. But who were these other children, and who was their mother? 'And do you like to swim, Hettie?'

'Yes. But sometimes I'm scared.'

I felt a tug on my heart. 'Why, what are you scared of?'

'That I'll hit my head on the bottom.'

I laughed, the first time I had laughed in years. 'Have you ever seen a kitten fall, from a chair perhaps? Because if you have then you'll know a kitten always lands up on her feet, and you will too if you're taught right.'

Then off Hettie went and I watched as she took her place on the board, inching further to the edge this time, and she looked across at me before diving in.

'That was much better,' I said, and she smiled with the easy open-ness of a child being praised.

Then Mr Millichap was clapping his hands for attention. Practice was over and it was time for the races to begin; whoever succeeded would be in the gala next week. Billy went up to the gallery to watch, while Mr Millichap shouted out instructions to the girls and they lined up by the poolside, tall and short, stout and thin, eager and anxious, all about to get in the water.

'Today, young ladies, we have a very special visitor, Miss Daisy Belle, a former world champion.' He bowed in my direction and I heard one or two of the girls begin to titter. They didn't believe I had ever been a champion, how could they, this lady in a bath chair?

'Miss Belle will present the prizes at next week's gala,' said Mr Mil-lichap, 'and now she wants to see what you're made of.'

I watched the older girls jump in and swim the length of the bath; some had a ragged style, gulping and giving up and clutching the rail, while the rest struggled gamely on. Then it was the turn of the younger girls and I saw Hettie putting on a hat, impatient for her race to begin. I felt such a rush of love for her then because there she was, a creature who had grown inside me, and now it was as if I was looking at myself.

The girl to her right was fat and built for battling the waves, while the girl on the left needed to build her confidence for she was already asking whether she was standing in the right place. 'Do I dive in from here?' she asked. 'Do I swim the whole way?' But Hettie just wanted to get in. That was her first mistake; she was so keen to begin that she entered the water clumsily and the other girls were already swimming off. Hettie was determined to catch up, and very quickly did, but then she made her second mistake. She so wanted to know if she was winning that she wasted time by looking constantly left to right, and didn't even see the stout girl coming up behind her. By the time she'd grabbed the rail another girl had caught up too and Hettie came third.

She was so disappointed. Her shoulders slumped as she got out of the pool and when I called her over I tried to be kind. 'Sometimes,' I said as she stood there dripping next to me, 'failure is more interesting than winning.'

But this meant nothing to Hettie; instead she was growing tearful. 'I was nearly last.'

'No you weren't, you were third. You'll still be in the gala. And whoever likes someone who is always first?'

She was not convinced, scratching at her leg and mumbling, 'I'm glad my Ma didn't come.'

'My mother never saw me swim,' I said and immediately wished I hadn't.

'Why not?'

I opened my mouth and then closed it again; this wasn't a conversation I wanted to have. 'It's better to experience failure early on, then it won't be such a shock when it comes. Proper training is essential, you can't win without it.' Goodness, I thought, I sound exactly like my father, and for a moment I could have sworn I smelled cigar smoke in the air. 'I was four years old when I first performed in public, so a little younger than you.'

'Were you really a champion?'

'Oh yes, I was a champion. But that was a long time ago, and when I was little, girls weren't allowed to swim.'

'Why not?'

'Perhaps the boys were afraid we would beat them.'

Hettie laughed at this, a childish giggle. But then she shivered and I saw she was cold.

'Do you have a towel?' I asked, 'Your own towel? You don't want to catch any diseases.'

She shook her head, teeth chattering.

'Hettie!' called Mr Millichap from the other side of the pool. 'Stop dawdling and go and change.'

The other girls came rushing past us, the people in the gallery began to leave and Billy came down to join me. But still Hettie stayed where she was. 'What if I'm last in the gala?' she asked.

And suddenly I knew what to do. 'Well,' I laughed, 'if that's what you're worried about I can teach you to swim much faster if you'd like?'

She eyed me carefully, perhaps about to say she didn't need anyone to teach her, and I worried I'd been too eager, too direct.

'Do you know what, I first learned to swim at the seaside. Have you ever been to the sea?'

Hettie shrugged. 'What is the sea?'

'What is the sea? Well, I will tell you if you want. I was the fastest girl in England you know, the first to swim the River Thames. I dived higher than anyone. I even swam in a whale tank.' I spoke quickly, the words tumbling out because I had to get and keep her attention. I had to make my very own child want to see me again.

'What's that?' she asked, pointing to my forehead.

'This scar?' I lowered my voice. 'I got this on a dreadful day when I was in a tank… and it exploded.'

'Really?' Hettie looked amazed.

'Yes,' I said, leaning forward and taking hold of one of her hands, 'and I can tell you all about that as well, and how to be the fastest swimmer ever, when I come back next week for the gala. Would you like that? Will you be here?'

CHAPTER THIRTY

And Hettie said yes, she thought she might, and then off she skipped after the other girls to the changing room.

CHAPTER THIRTY-ONE

I pestered Billy to take me back to the Hornsey Baths several times over the following days and he refused. We need to think this through, Daisy, he said. But for the first time in years I had a purpose and for me there was nothing to think through. We had found my child. I so wanted to know what it was like, the home where she lived. Did Hettie have everything she needed? Was there happiness in the house? Was Dob a kind father? Was there a woman she called mother, and did she treat her as her own? But Billy had not been able to find out anything more about Hettie. He could not even establish where Dob lived or worked, or how he'd earned his money once he was no longer my manager.

I spent every minute thinking how to win her favour. I needed Hettie to trust me more than anyone else. She was a swimmer; I'd seen how she loved the water and how keen she'd been to win. If I offered to coach her, would Mr Millichap allow it? But although I pestered Billy, I understood why he was reluctant to take me straight back to the baths, for if Dob learned of our visit then we would lose her again and no court of law would ever give her back.

So I spent those days pacing my room as best I could, determined to build up my strength. Billy set me exercises like Father used to do; it was as if I were in training again. My brother had me lifting weights; he fixed pulleys to the ceiling for me to grasp with my hands, and while at first I cursed myself and everyone else I did begin to feel a little stronger in my arms.

The following Wednesday we returned to the Hornsey Baths for the gala, arriving well before starting time. 'Let us wait here,' I told Billy as he fetched my chair from the cab and set it on the pavement opposite the baths. 'So we'll see her when she comes.'

'Daisy,' he leaned down towards me, 'we can't. Let's get inside. What if —'

Then a cab pulled up near the entrance to the baths, out stepped two gentlemen and, by the time the cab pulled off, a lady and three children were walking down the road towards us. The next thing I knew Billy had hold of my chair and was wheeling me away. 'I told you,' he said, 'we should have come later when the place is full.' I turned my head to see Hettie standing on the pavement, her hair plaited in pigtails, dressed in a pale blue dress with a sash. Then the lady took her hand and as I watched them go in all I could think was, that child is mine and it should be *me* taking her by the hand and leading her into the baths.

The pool was nicely set out for the gala, with coloured bunting hanging from the gallery and a table on a stage laid out with buns and lemonade. The moment I was settled in my place Hettie came running up with a cheery, 'I'm going to win the race!' Her pigtails were very neatly done, I thought, and I wondered if the woman she might call mother had tied them. Had it hurt a little as she divided Hettie's hair with a comb, telling her to keep still as she jerked her head, or did she have a gentle touch? How very black Hettie's eyes were, how beautiful the shape of her nose, how wonderful the way she smelled so faintly of soap. But oh, how it hurt to realise how little I knew about my own child, to have missed all those years when she was growing up. I knew nothing about what she liked or feared, how she slept or what she loved to eat.

'Are you racing against them?' asked Billy as a group of girls came marching in with club badges on their costumes.

'Yes,' said Hettie, 'and I'm going to win. Pa says a winner can have a lot of money.'

'Does he?' I asked, and I bit my lip. This was why he had taken her. Dob would want to make money from Hettie's skills just as he had with mine.

The audience began to make their way to their places and I saw Hettie looking up at the gallery. 'My Ma is here today,' she said with evident pride.

'And your father?'

'No. Pa is away.'

'Oh,' I said with relief. 'That is a shame.' So it was all right, I thought, we were safe for now, we could stay. 'Where is he?' I asked, but Hettie was distracted by a young soldier making his way past, hopping on a crutch.

'That man doesn't have a leg,' she said.

'No, he doesn't.'

'So he couldn't swim.'

'Oh yes he could,' said Billy, 'whatever a person's body, they can swim. I once knew a man called Captain Camp, he had one leg and he was a wonderful swimmer. Saved many lives too.'

'Pa has rescued lots of people,' said Hettie, moving to stand in front of me; her head just level with mine.

'Has he really?'

'Yes, don't you believe me? When he was in America he rescued a lady in the sea and a shark bit him on the thumb!'

'Well,' I said, 'what a lucky lady. So, are you all ready to race?'

'She most certainly is.' I looked up to see a well-built woman with auburn hair, her eyebrows so pale it was as if she had none. There was a pinkness about her eyelids that made me think of a mouse, but there was nothing mouse-like in her manner; she stood very tall with her chest held out and one hand clasped behind her back. 'I'm Bessie Hope.' She bowed slightly. 'I'm the new instructor.'

I looked at her in surprise; what had happened to Mr Millichap? I was a little jealous, at the idea that a woman would be teaching Hettie now. I didn't want my child to like her too much – and what if Miss Hope didn't realise Hettie's potential, if she had no idea of the right way to instruct? I had decided I would ask Mr Millichap if I could coach the girls, but what if now I were not even allowed to watch?

'I understand you saw Hettie last week,' said Miss Hope. 'She shows grand promise.'

I nodded. 'Indeed she does.'

'And can I ask—' Miss Hope brought her hand round to her front and I saw she was holding some picture postcards. 'If it's not a bother?'

'What are those?' asked Hettie.

Miss Hope selected a card and showed it to her, a handsome man in a one-piece bathing suit, his arms folded across his naked chest.

'Who is he?' Hettie giggled. Perhaps it was his white stockings.

'Captain Webb,' said Miss Hope, 'surely you've heard of him?' Then she showed another postcard, a strong young woman standing high up on a board with a hoop in one hand.

'Who's that?' asked Hettie.

'Don't you know?' laughed Miss Hope. 'This is her, right in front of you.' Then she turned to me. 'I couldn't believe it when I heard you'd be presenting the prizes. I saw you when I was just a girl. We came all the way from Glasgow. I will never forget that for the rest of my life. You were my inspiration. I was a Scottish long-distance champion, and now I'm teaching the next generation.'

I smiled at Miss Hope, grateful that Hettie was to be trained by someone as skilled as she. Then I looked at the picture thoughtfully, admiring my younger self. 'I was an ornamental swimmer then,' I said.

'An ornament?' asked Hettie.

'No,' I laughed, 'not exactly. I saw a woman once when I was young like you and she had a hoop and I copied her. Miss Mane from Brighton, she was my inspiration.'

'Why did you have a hoop?'

'Ah, the hoop,' I smiled, 'that was Father's idea. I used to swim through it and turn somersaults too. He was a very clever man, my father, because whenever there was something new, he'd be the one to find it.'

'Might I ask you to sign?' asked Miss Hope and she handed me a pen; and carefully, as if I'd almost forgotten how to spell it, I wrote my name on the front of the card.

Then it was time for everyone to get ready and Miss Hope asked if I would like to accompany the girls to the dressing room. After they had changed and lined up to be inspected, she gave them all a pep talk, saying to try their best but to remember that while winning was important, being a good sport was paramount. She was just explaining the order of the races when there was a commotion at the door and a voice asking 'Hettie? Is Hettie here?' and in came a woman followed by a little girl and boy. My heart started beating so loudly I thought all the girls could hear it, for here she was, only a yard away from me, the lady whom Hettie must call her mother. She and the two children looked like peas in a pod, with blue eyes and thin pale faces, and I wondered what Hettie made of this, that she was so clearly the odd one out. I found myself assessing the lady critically, looking for something to dislike, from her narrow cheeks to her long skirt and the way her shoes click-clicked across the floor.

'Hettie,' she said. 'I can't stay. Your sister doesn't feel well.'

I looked at the girl standing by her side; she seemed the picture of health to me.

'Please Ma,' begged Hettie, 'you promised you'd watch.'

'Your daughter will swim a very good race, I'm sure,' said Miss Hope. 'She has talent.'

'Well, I don't know where she gets that from,' said the lady, her eyes flicking briefly towards my chair and then away again.

'Please Ma,' begged Hettie once more.

The lady sighed in a put-upon way. 'Oh for goodness' sake Hettie, it's not as if you're going to win.'

I was so horrified at this that I looked down and studied the floor, not wanting to see Hettie's reaction. But when I glanced up her face was not tearful as I'd expected but flushed with anger, and her little hands hanging at her sides were curled into fists.

'Don't forget to dry your hair properly afterwards,' said the lady, 'and wait for me here.'

A little while later we returned to the pool and as Hettie took her place with the youngest girls I saw her glance up to the gallery in a hopeful fashion. I knew what she was doing, wanting to believe that her mother had changed her mind and stayed to watch. How eager she was for her attention, I thought, and how unlikely she was to get it. I could see that Hettie was not the favourite child and I wondered what Dob had said to make the lady take her in. I felt so sorry for Hettie then, that she wanted to perform in front of someone who could not care less. Her distress hurt as if it was my own and I longed to make everything right.

Then the gun fired and Hettie dived in to swim. She didn't look up, she took no notice of the others; instead I could see that anger was spurring her on. So she passed the girl who lacked confidence, and then the stout girl, and then the girls from the other club as well. And all the time Miss Hope was on the poolside, her voice rising higher and higher as she rushed along the bath urging her pupil on. When Hettie reached the end, a yard ahead of all the other girls, I was the first to clap. I was so proud when it came time to present the prizes, to know that when they called Hettie's name it was I who would give her the medal. Up she came to where I sat by the table, next to Miss Hope on the stage, the audience clapping as she bowed her head, and as I placed the medal on a ribbon around her neck I was absolutely certain that this would be one of many. But I also knew that this wouldn't do; I had been lucky that Hettie's mother hadn't stayed to see the races, to hear my name announced and then return home to tell Dob. Perhaps he already knew. Hettie had said he was away, but perhaps she had told him. I had to get my child away from the baths. We needed somewhere more private and there was just one place that came to mind.

'Hettie,' I said, gesturing her back, aware that the other girls were lined up behind her waiting their turn for a medal. 'How would you like it if you were to swim somewhere else and not at a bath?'

'In the sea?' she asked hopefully.

'No, not yet. I was thinking of a different place all together. I was thinking of a pond.'

'A pond?' she laughed.

'Yes, a lovely cool pond with ducks and fish.'

'Really?' Hettie looked delighted. 'I can swim in a pond?'

'If you like,' I said, although I had no idea if this was true. But after I had given out the remaining prizes and the audience was leaving I asked Miss Hope if I could have a word. 'I would like to help you coach the girls,' I told her. 'Especially Hettie.'

Miss Hope beamed. 'I was hoping you might say that.'

'I think it would be good for her to gain experience with open water…'

'Yes, you're absolutely right.'

'Perhaps we might go to the bathing pond on Hampstead Heath?'

I half-expected Miss Hope to ridicule the idea but instead she said she knew the pond well and there were ladies' hours on a Thursday. It was an excellent plan and she would bring the girls there herself.

Billy thought I was mad. How was he going to get me onto Hampstead Heath, had I any idea how difficult that would be? But most of all, why on earth did I want to go back to the pond? It was hard to explain myself. I told him it would be a safe place for us and he cried, 'Safe! You nearly died at that pond.' But that was Dob's fault, I reminded him, and mine for agreeing to wear the crown. Didn't he want to see his niece learn to love to swim outdoors? Where else could she do this in London, if not the pond? Perhaps then she could swim with Percy, I suggested, just like we had swum together as children. Hettie was a born swimmer; he could see that. He had found my child; he must understand that I had to see her again and that it couldn't be at the baths. By the time we got home Billy knew there was no more use objecting. We would go to the pond.

CHAPTER THIRTY-TWO

The very next Thursday, just before ladies' hours, my brother took me to Hampstead Heath. It was quite early still, few people were out but for men arriving for work at the fairground site, and there was a feeling of pleasure to come, the promise of rides and coconuts. How gentle the pond looked that day, as Billy pushed me down to the causeway and towards the water, how pretty the golden elder on the banks with their creamy-white flowers. The trees had grown more mature since last I'd been here, but there ahead of me was the very same diving platform. I felt a little shiver, remembering how determined I had been as I'd climbed up its steps ready to risk everything for one single dive.

We turned along the path, following the wooden fence that lined the lane, and I sensed that the day would lift; it would soon be warm. The boatman was waiting for us by the gate, leaning on his boat hook, and for a second I thought it was the very same one and I wanted to clasp his hands and thank him for saving my life. But it wasn't him at all; instead he had a shock of white hair like Father Christmas. My brother greeted him and they shook hands; he was a friend of a friend and that was how we'd been allowed to come just before ladies' hours.

Billy parked my chair by the boatman's hut, overlooking the grassy bank where a dozen men lounged, smoking and chatting. One stood up, walked to the jetty and dived in. It was several minutes before he came up but then I saw him swimming on his back, both arms held up in the air, sending ripples over the pond like a plough across a field. I too wanted to strip off and plunge into that water, its surface dancing with midges and scattered with tiny white feathers and summer leaves. I caught a sudden flash of turquoise as a kingfisher flew into the air but as I turned to point it out to Billy the bird had gone.

At the far end of the pond a man was floating on his back, his stomach like unbaked bread in the air, while a group of boys were shouting and ducking each other under. It had been a long time since I'd seen men swim and it struck me that people become children in the water; it didn't matter whether they were lords or rat catchers because in the pond they were equal. I watched the bathers with a bittersweet feeling. I too wanted to see the bottom of things, the roots of trees, the grass on the banks, the wet underbelly of logs, to feel the water as smooth as ink and the smell of bracken as I broke the surface.

Then I heard the sound of childish laughter and the squeak of the gate and Hettie arrived. Miss Hope led the way holding two girls by the hands, half a dozen following after, like a goose with her goslings.

Billy told the girls to change in the hut and as the door squealed open I could see the air inside floating with fluff as if someone were blowing dandelion seeds. I heard a creak and a sigh as if the hut were talking to itself and I could picture myself on the day of my dive when I'd lost the letter from Johnnie Heaven. How worried I'd been, not knowing where it had gone, but I'd also been looking to the future. What had happened that day had nearly ruined my life, yet by bringing Hettie here perhaps I could look forward again.

She was the first to emerge from the hut, all ready in her costume, and gazing in wonder at the pond. 'A duck!' she said, 'I can see a duck!' and she was so excited that it looked as if she were about to rush straight down the bank.

'No ladies in the water until ten o'clock,' said the boatman, holding out his hook in both hands as if to bar the way.

'Oh, they're only children,' said Billy.

'Even so,' said the boatman, 'rules are rules. Wait 'til all the men have finished and made themselves decent.' He studied the girls one by one. 'Do any of you know how to swim?'

At once Hettie had her hand in the air.

'How old are you, Missy?'

'I'm nearly five.'

'Nearly eighty-five?' asked the boatman in a teasing voice. 'Ever swum in a pond?'

Hettie shook her head.

'She's a strong swimmer,' said Miss Hope.

'Is she now?'

'Hettie can easily swim the length of this pond.'

'And can she sing "God Save the Queen" while she's doing it?' The boatman laughed and put down his hook as he cupped his hands. 'Time, gentlemen, please!' he called out to the last swimmer in the pond. 'Avert your eyes, ladies,' he said, as the man made his way to the jetty.

'I want to dive from there,' said Hettie, pointing at the platform.

'Later,' I told her, 'you're not ready for that yet. First you need to learn how to swim in a pond, it's not like the baths you know.'

'What are those?' She pointed at three grey cygnets sitting on a patch of water lilies next to their mother.

'Those are baby swans, so be respectful when you're in the water because the mothers are very protective.'

'Are there really fish in there?'

The boatman nodded. 'Watch out for the pike, they can give you quite a nip. And don't go anywhere near the whale.'

'A whale?' Hettie's eyes grew wide.

'There aren't any whales,' I laughed, 'although do you remember how I told you that once I swam in a whale tank?'

But she wasn't listening; all the other girls were standing obediently in line but Hettie had started walking down the grassy bank.

'Hey!' called the boatman.

But she was mesmerised; she had reached the jetty now and any moment would be making her way along it.

'Hettie!' I called. 'You have never been in a pond before and you must wait while I —'

But still she didn't respond and the further she went down the jetty the more annoyed and worried I grew because I couldn't come after her.

'Hettie,' I called again, 'will you wait!'

And that's when she did it: one second she was on the jetty, the next she'd tipped forward and jumped in and the boatman was running and shouting and red in the face. The water closed around her as if she'd never been there and for a moment I was full of terror. What had I been thinking of, bringing her here when she didn't understand the dangers?

Then Hettie's head popped up. 'There's no bottom!' she cried.

'Come out at once!' I shouted as her head went under again. 'Hettie!'

Then the boatman was on the jetty, lowering his hook into the pond, sweeping it around, trying to catch her.

Again she reappeared, laughing. 'I can't see my feet!' But this time the boatman had caught her. He hooked the back of her costume and began to drag her out like a stork carrying its young, before depositing her on the jetty.

A moment later she was running up the bank, shivering and waving at the other girls. Then she saw my face and stopped.

'You shouldn't have done that,' I said.

Hettie looked abashed and stared down at the grass.

'You will never be a proper swimmer if you don't do as you're told. If you ever want to dive from that platform then learn to listen. Don't take more risks than you need to, Hettie. If I tell you to wait then you must wait.'

I heard the sound of men's laughter from somewhere behind and I turned my head to one side to hide a smile, because despite my scolding I knew full well that I would have done exactly what Hettie had just done, unable to resist the lure of a pond. Then Miss Hope handed me a towel, and I drew it around Hettie and pulled her close.

'Why do we have to wait until the men have finished?' she asked.

I didn't answer, only continued to dry her hair.

'Did you ever beat a man?'

'Did I ever beat a man?' I laughed. 'Oh yes. I could dive higher and swim longer than any man and if you do as you're told then that's what I'll teach you too.'

'I want to go in again,' said Hettie.

'No, not now. Not when you wouldn't listen. You will have to stay here while the other girls have their turn.'

'I'm going to tell my Pa I can swim in a pond.'

I released the towel, letting her hold it herself. 'Does he know that you're here?'

'No.'

'Well,' I said, 'shall we keep it a surprise until you are able to dive from that platform?' And as Hettie went back into the hut to change

I looked around at the water and the banks and the causeway, and I wondered how long we could be here before Dob found us.

But I was right to take Hettie to the bathing pond on Hampstead Heath, for she loved it there and as the weeks went by so her stamina increased. The boatman got used to us, as long as we came early then he let Miss Hope's pupils swim whatever the day of the week and sometimes he even made the men and boys wait until they had finished. I think he was impressed with Hettie's perseverance and the way she was so full of bounce and smiles.

I took so much pleasure in her pleasure at the pond, wanting her never to lose the wonderful freedom and ease she felt when she swam. I could enjoy the water through her enjoyment, despite my frustration that while Miss Hope could run and pace the girls I had to stay in my place at the top of the bank. One morning I told Hettie to continue swimming even though she said she was tired, because I wanted her to know that feeling of power that comes from a long swim, a feeling that every girl should know.

It was then that I began to dream of water again. There had been a time when I used to dream I was swimming and woke so unbearably sad that the following night I would not want to sleep at all. But now I dreamed of so many places, of the Margate sands and the Lambeth Baths, of the River Thames and the bays of New York. Yet in all these dreams, of seas and pools and rivers, there was still something missing for I was never *in* the water: I was always a spectator, just as I was with Hettie.

CHAPTER THIRTY-THREE

One morning Billy and I arrived at the pond late and there were men behind us coming for their swim. But I made my brother stop awhile so we could watch through the trees, for this was the day I had decided to tell the truth. Because that little girl who made her way across the pond as happy as a seal, the little girl who would soon be waving to me from the water, is you of course. My daughter. The baby who was stolen from me, the child who Billy found at the Hornsey Road Baths. This is your story as much as mine, Hettie; this is the tale I wanted to tell you.

But there was no private time in which to speak that day and the moment I arrived I heard you cry out to the other girls, 'Miss Belle is here! I told you she would come.' Then you clambered out of the pond and up the grassy bank to stand next to me. 'Can you swim?' you asked, tugging on my arm. 'They don't believe me.'

'Me?' You hadn't asked what I was able to do before. You hadn't queried why I was in my chair; you even seemed to take it for granted. 'Not in this I can't,' I said.

'But I thought you don't need legs to swim.'

'That's true,' said Billy, pleased that you had remembered his story about Captain Camp.

'But how would I get in the water?' I asked. 'I can't walk down that bank. And even if I could, then how would I get out?' I tried to sound light-hearted, but it was something I'd been thinking of long and hard as I did my exercises at home and built up the muscle in my arms. Was it possible that I could swim again, could I find a way?

'What if someone carried you?' you asked.

I made a face; I didn't want to be carried by anyone. 'Well, they would have to be very strong.' I looked at you, standing there trying to persuade me, and suddenly I could see Johnnie Heaven in every single part of you, from the curl of your hair to the way you bounced on your toes, and I squeezed my eyes shut, hearing myself sigh.

'I will,' you said, not understanding what had made me sigh. 'When I'm older, I will take you into the pond,' and you threw yourself at me and for a second I flinched; I didn't want your pity. But then I felt your arms around my shoulders, your heart beating against mine, and when I looked up at Billy I saw he had tears in his eyes.

Suddenly you pulled away. 'I'm sad,' you said.

'Why are you sad?' I smiled.

'Because I love the pond.'

'I know you do. Whatever is wrong?'

Then you balled your hands into fists and began banging them against your sides. 'I'm not allowed to come here any more.'

'Hettie,' I reached out and took you by the shoulders, 'what do you mean? Is it your father, does he know we're here?'

'My Ma told him.' You shifted from foot to foot. 'She went to see him.'

'Where did she go to see him?' I asked.

But you shrugged and I could see you didn't know the answer.

'Does he know it's me who is teaching you?'

You nodded worriedly; perhaps you sensed my fear. 'Ma says I'm not to swim in a pond any more. It's dirty.'

'Nonsense,' I said, 'natural water is the best place for a swimmer to be. And they can't stop you, Hettie, no one can. I won't let them.'

'After tomorrow,' you said, shaking your head in a miserable fashion. 'I'm not allowed to come any more,' and then you started to cry.

'We will find a way,' I promised, glancing up at my brother. 'Somehow, we will find a way.' But in truth I didn't know how.

CHAPTER THIRTY-FOUR

The following morning was strangely chilly; the boatman wore his overcoat while I had a blanket wrapped around my legs for warmth. The air was cooler than the water and steam rose from the pond like a mystical vapour, softening the edges of the trees and silencing the birds. But beautiful as the pond was that day, I was sick with worry. Billy had left on an errand the afternoon before and not come back. It wasn't like him to let me down, when all night long I'd been thinking and worrying. I had only just found my child, and now I could lose you again.

Violet wasn't sure where my brother had gone and I was forced to send word to Miss Hope. She dispatched a man from the Hornsey Baths to take me to the pond and it was an unpleasant journey for both of us. I couldn't think what had happened to my brother, why wasn't he here on this, our last day?

I allowed you to dive higher that morning and you set off, climbing the steps to the first platform, delighted with yourself. I smiled to see you so perfectly poised and to know that you had listened to the lessons I had given you, and after you took the plunge and came to the surface I heard the sound of clapping from the causeway. When I looked across the pond I saw a group of people waving hats and handkerchiefs, and then my eyes fell on a figure standing alone, impatiently tapping an umbrella on the ground. I thought I heard the faint tune of a mouth organ being played and then the sounds of the fairground starting up with a terrible clang of bells and whistles, as I sat there, clutching my stick, watching.

I realised you had got out of the water and were shouting from the jetty. 'You're not looking!' you cried.

'Yes I am,' I replied, 'that was very good, only this time hold your arms higher.'

So you started to climb the steps again but as much as I wanted to watch you, I couldn't tear myself away from the figure on the causeway. Did I know him or not? Then I saw him walk on and become lost in the crowd.

'Are you unwell?' asked Miss Hope. 'You look like you've seen a ghost. Shall I fetch you a drink?' She went to the boatman's hut and returned with a cup of tepid water and I tried to sip slowly, to calm myself.

'I'm fine,' I told her, 'I just had a fright.'

But then I heard the gate to the pond squeak open and the boatman cry, 'Hey! What d'you think you're doing? No gentlemen when the girls are swimming!' And as I listened to the sound of boots crunching on the gravel outside his hut I knew that my worst fears had come true.

I glanced down to the pond, saw you climb out of the water, shaking your head like a puppy. 'Watch me!' you cried as you headed up to the platform and again you steadied yourself, took a deep breath and as swift as anything, in you dived. Then I heard a man whistling and I braced myself for what was to come, because whatever Dob said, I would fight for you.

'Oh Moses,' came a voice from behind, 'will you look at that!'

I felt my heart unclench, my body flooding with giddy relief as slowly I turned my head. I knew that voice; I had heard it so many times in my dreams. Yet how could it be true? There he stood, wearing a heavy English overcoat, but looking much as he had done all those years ago at Rockaway except for a scattering of grey in his fine brown hair. He hadn't noticed me, he was watching as you set off swimming across the pond, using what had become your favourite stroke, arms stretched out as if pulling yourself over an invisible fence. 'What a kiddo,' he said; shaking his head in wonder, and that was when he saw me. The air around us seemed to darken; the leaves on the trees fell still, as he tipped his hat with a polite 'Ma'am'. Then he took a step forward, his eyebrows raised in surprise. 'Daisy?' he asked, his hat clutched in his hand.

I looked at him in silence, not wanting to break the spell. How fine he looked and how much I had missed him. But how could Johnnie Heaven be here at this London pond? Any moment now I would wake and he'd be gone.

'What are you doing here?' I whispered.

'Why, I've come to find you.' Johnnie Heaven walked closer and fell to his knees on the grass. 'What happened?' he asked. He moved to take my hand but I brushed him off, uncomfortable at how he must see me, sitting here gripping my stick. I wanted to stand and take him in my arms, and yet I could not. But then I thought, why should I not be seen? I was still me. Whatever had happened, I was still me.

'I had an accident,' I told him, 'during a dive.'

'But you told me...' Johnnie Heaven paused, 'that you had recovered.'

'Well, I didn't.'

'I didn't know you were hurt. That's why I waited for you, on that Dover beach of yours like a lonesome fool...'

'I told you not to wait for me.'

'But I *did*. I did wait because I never believed you wouldn't come. I never believed you would stay with your husband. I didn't know this,' he gestured at my chair. 'Why didn't you tell me?'

I sighed, picturing myself in the hospital, remembering how desperate I had been. 'I just wanted you to be free.'

'Free!' Johnnie Heaven stood up, brushing the grass from his trousers. 'How could I be free without you? Who do you think I've thought of all these years? Daisy, you are the one who spurred me on. You gave me encouragement. We understand each other, you and I.'

I smiled then and allowed him to take my hands, saw how translucent his nails were, the fingers of a swimmer. 'However did you know I was here?'

'Your brother sent word to me at Dover yesterday. I'm in training again. I didn't manage the Channel that summer I waited for you. Failed for the third time,' he laughed, 'but now here I am back to try once more. Oh Daisy, I wish you had told me. I would have come at once; I would have looked for you everywhere. I thought you had changed your mind. That you had stayed with your husband after all.' Johnnie Heaven let go of my hands and looked at me, waiting for an answer.

I shook my head. 'I didn't stay with him. I haven't seen him for years.'

We heard splashing from the pond then; you had swum to the jetty and were turning somersaults and showing off, desperate to be seen.

'She's quite a swimmer,' said Johnnie Heaven.

I nodded. 'Indeed she is.'

'Hey kiddo,' he called out, cupping his hands to his mouth. 'Swim some more!' He stared at you for quite some time as you made your way across the pond to the other girls. 'Well what d'you know? She has a stroke just like mine. Did you train her?' Then he paused and looked from me to you. 'Is she your child?'

'Yes,' I said and I took a deep breath, steadied myself for what I had to say. 'She is yours and mine.'

'Yours and mine?' I saw the shock on Johnnie Heaven's face and for a dreadful moment I thought he might ask if I were sure. But then I saw his expression of surprise turn into one of pleasure and I knew he was thinking of our night at Rockaway.

'But she doesn't know,' I told him. 'That is the terrible thing. My husband stole her when she was born. I have only just found her. She doesn't know I'm her mother.'

I heard a cough from behind and turned to see Billy standing by the boatman's hut. 'You can tell her,' he said, 'because I've found Dob.'

I stared at my brother, unable to understand why he was smiling.

'He's in Newgate.'

'Dob is in prison?'

'Fraud,' said Billy. 'And this is his second time. That's why I couldn't ever find him.'

'So he can't harm us?' I asked. 'He can't stop Hettie and me?'

'No.'

I looked up then, just as the sun broke through the gloom, the clouds slid away and the tops of the trees blazed with light.

'Watch me!' you cried from down in the pond and Johnnie Heaven laughed. 'Do you swim together, Daisy?'

'No,' I shook my head. 'I haven't swum since the dive.' And then, as suddenly as if I'd been lifted up by a powerful wave, I knew that this was the time. If ever I was going to swim then it was now. 'I can still use my arms,' I told him, 'and walk with my stick. It's getting in that is the difficulty. I would need two people to lift this chair...'

Johnnie Heaven looked at my brother and Billy nodded. So I pushed off my blanket, eased myself as far back into the chair as I could, and together they lifted me down the grassy bank. How still and sharp the water was, how graceful were the cygnets at the far end of the pond, nearly fully-grown and ready to fly. I stood up between the two of them, making my way slowly to the jetty, then Billy helped me to sit and took off my boots.

I was fully clothed, it was a foolish thing to do, but I closed my eyes and waited for the glorious moment when I would go, when my mind would tell my body to take the plunge. I held out my arms and pushed myself forward, and then with all the force I could muster I threw myself off the jetty. A second later, I was under the water gasping from the cold. Would I sink? Of course I would not sink, I was my father's child. If one limb didn't work then I knew to use the others. But I had no momentum without both of my legs and as the left one dragged beneath me I knew I had to try to find a new balance in the water. I thought of the day Father had first taught me to swim at the second-class pool at the Lambeth Baths, the way he'd patted my chest. 'Here,' he had said, 'this is where the floating power is, here in your lungs. Trust the water, Daisy.' And I knew I had to confide in the power of water again. I must find my own buoyancy. So I struck out with my arms, turning myself this way and that until I was steady.

It was then that you came swimming towards me, moving so close that your face almost touched mine and without saying a word you clambered gently onto my back. You were holding yourself so lightly that I could barely feel you were there, but for your plump little feet dangling on either side of my arms and your hands resting around my neck. Then I ducked under and you squealed with delight, thrown with a splash into the water.

When you came up we began to slowly make our way across the pond, and as we did I was certain that I could hear the sound of cheers and applause as if thousands had come to watch us. Halfway across I stopped and turned my head, saw Johnnie Heaven standing on the jetty smiling and waving his hat. Then I cast my eyes higher, up to the diving platform. I had thought my life had ended the day I stood up there, but here I was starting again. And as I looked at the diving platform I had a sudden thought; if I could swim then could I possibly dive? And if I could, then what if you and I were to swim and dive together? I heard a chuckle in my head and my father's voice: 'Just think, Daisy. It will be a sensation. Mother and daughter, never been done in England before!'

At once I caught myself. Whatever was I doing, thinking a thing like that? You weren't here to perform, that wasn't why I was teaching you, it was the joy of swimming for its own sake that I wanted you to learn. I would never treat you as my father had treated me. I would not repeat his mistakes, whatever your ambitions or mine, your happiness would come first. But oh, how I had missed being in the water, and how I had loved to show the world what I could do.

I felt you come close and your hand pat the side of my face. 'I want to dive,' you said, turning to stare at the platform.

I smiled. 'I know you do.'

'I want to dive with you.'

'One day,' I said, 'perhaps we will.' Then I felt so tired that I knew it was time to get out.

That afternoon I took you home to my room above the Essex Road Baths and I sat you down and held you close and told you who you were. I could not explain the full story, not then, for you were far too young to understand, but the joy on your face when I told you the truth was enough for me. The woman you had called mother left London with her children the following week, and she seemed not at all upset to go without you. We were safe from Dob, he could do nothing to us from prison, and we were a family now. At night I would wake and feel Johnnie Heaven next to me, know that you were sleeping in your bed, and in the mornings I watched you swimming on your father's back like a porpoise. Of course there were disagreements sometimes, for you were an obstinate child just as I had been. 'When will we dive together?' you asked every day, 'you promised we would dive together.' And I said soon, when I felt stronger then we would dive at the baths. I would ask if we could have the pool to ourselves for an hour. But this wasn't good enough for you, you wanted us to dive so everyone could see us, and you wanted it to be at the pond.

You remember that day, don't you Hettie? It was Easter Monday of 1888, a mild day with clear skies. The Heath was busy with boisterous crowds; the air full of dust and the scent of oranges. It was the sort of morning when beauty seems to return to the fields and woods. There were no wagers to be had that day, no bets or entrance fees. It was a free event and our only purpose was to inspire.

We had practised for months at the Hornsey Road Baths and then when spring had arrived we'd returned to the pond. It was all a matter of timing, you knew that, we had trained ourselves to work together and now we had to see if we could make it.

'Ladies and gentlemen!' called the announcer as we took our places on the diving platform, you standing on the top and I sitting beneath. I looked to my left and saw Miss Hope next to your father, Billy and Violet standing arm in arm by the boatman, little Percy between them. Then I took a quiet breath and steadied my beating heart.

'Ladies and gentlemen!' the announcer cried again, silencing the murmuring hum of the thousands who lined the banks of the pond. 'Introducing the world-famous Miss Daisy Belle and her very clever pupil... Miss Hettie Belle!'

I looked up and saw your eyes full of delight, your arms held aloft, an expression of utter concentration on your face. You were clearing your mind of trivial things, just as I used to do. Then the gun fired and off you flew and a split second later I joined you. There we were, mother and daughter in a faultless double dive, touching the water together and setting off swimming across the pond, back where we both belonged.

Afterword

Daisy Belle is based on the lives of several Victorian swimmers and divers whose daring deeds were once well-known, but who have now been largely forgotten. Agnes Beckwith was the primary inspiration for the novel. I first came across her in 2010 while researching *Taking the Waters: A Swim Around Hampstead Heath.* I saw a poster advertising one of her performances at the Royal Aquarium in London in 1885 in which she stands dead centre, resplendent in a white satin costume, stockings and boots, one arm resting casually on a rock. Just behind her in the water a man has both arms raised in the air, his mouth open in alarm, presumably in the process of drowning. Then I read a brief reference to a swim Agnes had completed in September 1875, when at the tender age of 14 she had plunged into the Thames at London Bridge and swum all the way to Greenwich. When I came to write *Downstream: A History and Celebration of Swimming the River Thames* I had the chance to further explore her career, and realised just what a trailblazer she had been.

Agnes Beckwith was born in Lambeth, south London, in 1861. Her father Frederick is believed to have come from Ramsgate and was a leading swimming professor, as well as an English professional champion. By the time of Agnes' birth he was swimming master at the Lambeth Baths and his 'Family of Frogs' started giving public displays in the early 1860s. At the age of nine Agnes was performing with her brother Willie, himself a champion swimmer, as 'Les Enfants Poissons' in a plate-glass aquarium at the Porcherons Music Hall in Paris. All seven of Frederick's children were involved in his aquatic galas; his second wife Elizabeth (whom he married in 1876 after Agnes' mother died) played the piano during shows, while his daughter Lizzie went on to became a renowned swimmer and performer.

Agnes Beckwith completed several record-breaking swims in the Thames, including 20 miles in 1878. She then formed her own 'talented troupe of lady swimmers' and travelled the country giving exhibitions. In September 1880 she spent 100 hours submerged in a whale tank at the Royal Aquarium in Westminster, eating her meals in the water and reading daily accounts of her swim in the press. Two years later she was being billed as 'the premier lady swimmer of the world' before setting off on a tour of the United States. In June 1883 she attempted to swim from Sandy Hook, New Jersey, to Rockaway Pier, New York. But a mistake in the calculation of the tides, along with bad weather, meant she was forced to give up.

Back in the UK, Agnes continued to take part in shows with her family and was still holding exhibition swims in the early 1900s, now married to theatrical agent William Taylor. Their son William performed alongside his mother as 'the youngest swimmer in the world'. Agnes later accompanied her son to South Africa, where she died in a care home in Port Elizabeth in 1951.

While my novel draws on much of her long and successful career, Agnes Beckwith's relationship with her parents is entirely fictionalised. I have also taken liberties with some of the dates of her swims, and with various aquatic events and venues. The Hornsey Road Baths, for example, didn't open until the early 1890s.

Other real historical characters who appear in the novel include Emily Parker, a swimmer from Clerkenwell, London, whom Agnes was initially meant to race against in the Thames and who later became a swimming instructor. Captain Matthew Webb was the first person to swim the English Channel and was briefly trained by Frederick Beckwith. On 22 September 1874 he went out on a boat from Westminster Bridge with Frederick and journalist Robert Watson, who described the swim in his memoirs *A Journalist's Experience of Mixed Society*. In 1879 Agnes did indeed join Captain Webb in the pool during a six-day swim at the Lambeth Baths. The Channel champion died in the Niagara River in 1883.

The scenes set in Margate are fictitious, but the Beckwith family did have numerous links to the town. In 1884 Agnes performed and taught lessons at the Marine Palace Baths, situated on what is now the site of the Turner Contemporary, and that same year she saved a drowning woman in the sea off Margate sands.

While there are no records of Agnes Beckwith appearing at the Mixed Pond on Hampstead Heath, north London, this was one of the few places in the capital where women could officially swim outdoors. The Mixed Pond had been a bathing place for men since the early 1800s, and towards the end of the nineteenth century women were allowed to swim at the pond on Thursdays. Their elegant costumes and swimming performances were said to have become a local attraction.

Daisy Belle also draws on the career of high diver Annie Luker. She was born in 1870, in the Thames-side market town of Abingdon, Oxfordshire. Like Agnes, she was the daughter of a swimming professor who also trained Captain Webb. Annie started off as a river swimmer and in 1892 she attempted to swim nearly 19 miles from Kew to Greenwich to establish a claim to 'the female championship of the world'. Two years later she was 'World Champion High Diver', performing at the Royal Aquarium where she plunged head first 70 feet into a tank containing just eight feet of water. Annie Luker successfully challenged a male diver, Professor O'Rourke, and remained at the Royal Aquarium for six years, as well as training female divers at the Caledonian Road Baths in north London.

I'm grateful to four modern-day family members for providing me with further details of Annie's life, and particularly Allie Gallop who sent a wonderful bundle of images and archive documents. According to family lore, Annie Luker was later arrested as a suffragette after a protest dive off a bridge in London and imprisoned in Holloway, under the name Annie Parker.

Women like Agnes Beckwith and Annie Luker are yet to be properly recognised; there has been no induction into any swimming hall of fame for them, and yet what they did made it possible for women to swim and dive today.

Daisy Belle also draws on the biographies and autobiographies of later swimmers, such as the Australian Annette Kellerman who pioneered the one-piece swimming costume for women, and the American Esther Williams, popularly known as the Million Dollar Mermaid. In 1952, while filming a stunt, Esther 'swan dived' from 50 feet wearing an aluminium gold crown, breaking three vertebrae in her neck. She made a full recovery.

Acknowledgements

Thank you to the following people: Dr Dave Day, Professor of Sports History at Manchester Metropolitan University, who is the leading expert on Agnes Beckwith and the first person to rescue her from obscurity. Along with his partner Margaret Roberts, Dave answered numerous questions and generously shared his own research. Dr Ian Gordon, medic to the British Olympic Swimming Team, provided invaluable help on the running of Victorian swimming baths and was always willing to dig into his own extensive archives. Patricia Sener, who in 2015 swam 17 miles from Sandy Hook to Atlantic Beach to raise awareness for local charities working to keep the ocean clean, kindly answered my questions about what it was like to swim the New York Bight. She became the first person to succeed in the crossing, taking a route very similar to that of Agnes Beckwith in 1883, although Patricia had never heard of her Victorian predecessor. Helen Wright from the Cally Masters club in north London re-created a Victorian swimming gala at the Parliament Hill Lido on Hampstead Heath and told me what it was like to swim in full Victorian clothing including pantaloons, a corseted dress, hat and boots.

Thanks also to Keith Myerscough, Paul Hitchings, Ern Dick for his research on Clara Beckwith, Frank Chalmers, Lee Jackson whose Dictionary of Victorian London http://www.victorianlondon.org/ is an excellent resource, Ian Dickie, chair of the friends of Margate Museum for educating me on the history of Margate, the swimmers and lifeguards on Hampstead Heath, and members of the Mixed Pond Association http://mixedpondassociation.weebly.com/. Last but not least, thank you to my editor Claire Baldwin and to everyone who pledged for the novel on Unbound, and made it possible for *Daisy Belle* to see the light of day.

Patrons

Allison Allan
Barbara Allan
Clare Allan
Jamie Andrews
Wendy Arnot
Peter Barratt
Becky Barrow
Charlotte Benson
Isabel Berwick
Etta Bingham
Daphne Bonanos
Nechamah Bonanos
Ronell Boshoff
Sita Brahmachari
Alice Briggs
Angela Buckley
Margaret Cain
Lucy Caithness
Remembering Calum Downes
Janet Campbell
Rosie Canning
Claudia Christie
Ruth Clarke
Philippa Coates
Ruth Corney
Brian Francis Cox
Molly Cutpurse
Dan Dalton
Anne Darlington
Johnny Davies
Jill Dawson
Geraldine Deas

Brian Docherty
Henrietta Dombey
Kerrin Dooley
Rachel Douglas
Deborah Dudgeon
Len Dunne
Kathryn Eastman
Travis Elborough
Adrian Evans
David & Sheila Fathers
Peter Faulkner
Dan Fawkes
Licia Fields
Ange Fox
Maggie French
Alison Gabrielides
Ruth Galloway
Lesley Garner
Maureen Gill
Sophie Goldsworthy
Ann Mary Gollifer
Christine Goodair
Penninah Graham
Sue Grimsdell
Ann Hair
Michele Hanson
Ali Harbour
Amy Harbour
Emma Hardy
Tirril Harris
Ruth Hind
Shawn Hirabayashi
Liz Hogarth
Catherine Horwood Barwise
Marion Hume
Jane Huntley

Sarah Hurcum
Lyn Iglinsky
Kendra Illingworth
Christopher Impey
Ian Jack
Emma Jolly
Alan Jones
Adrian Jowett
Rachna Kanwar
Jackie Kennedy
Imran Khan
Mary Knowles
Anna Kusner
Shannon Kyle
Mary Lederer
Patrick Lefevre
Katy Limmer
Aviva Luria
Jo Macey
Kee Macmillan
Louise Maggiora
Yvonne Mapstone
Lorelei Mathias
Anita Matthews
Vincent McBride
Rebecca McCormick
Seán McPartlin
Sumi Mendis
Andrew Merriman
Bruno Milin
Melanie Mitchell
Karin Moggridge
Anna Morell
Andrea Morreau
Julian Murray
Doug Mussell

John Neal
Ann Nicholls
Natasha Nuttall
John Parker
Simon Parkin
Graham Partridge
Howard Pedro
Doloranda Pember
Jean Perraton
Gemma Pettman
Julie Pickard
Janet Porter
Suzy Price
Annabelle Priestley
Lindsey Priestley
Julie Procter
Vicky Pryce
Alice-May Purkiss
Emma Pusill (Plum Duff)
Arthur Ramdial
Jane Rawle
Clare Reynolds
Sarah Rhodes
Ruby Ridge
Susanna Riviere
Monica Roberts
Darrin Roles
Catherine Rooney
Stefania Rossetti
Rebecca Rouillard
Alison Samuel
Ian Shacklock
Dani Sinclair
Janet Smith
Pat Solomon
Tim Sowula

Foster Spragge
Clive Stewart
Terry Stiastny
Nicola Stow
Catherine Stroud
Geoff Swallow
Carrie Sykes
Julia Taylor
Claire Taylor
Phil Tibenham
Penny Tompkins
Karina Townsend
Alwyn W Turner
Isobel Wade
Wendy Wallace
Nicky Warden
Louise Warner
London Waterkeeper
Nicola Waters
Daisy Waugh
John Weller
Julie Wheeler
Peter Wheeler
Jill Wheeler-Bowden
Patrick Whelan
Margaret White-Wrixon
William Wintercross
Helen Wright